MAKING WAVES AT RIVER VIEW COTTAGE

JENNIFER BOHNET

Boldwood

First published in 2003. This edition first published in Great Britain in 2022 by Boldwood Books Ltd.

Copyright © Jennifer Bohnet, 2003

Cover Design by Debbie Clement Design

Cover Photography: Shutterstock

Every effort has been made to obtain the necessary permissions with reference to copyright material, both illustrative and quoted. We apologise for any omissions in this respect and will be pleased to make the appropriate acknowledgements in any future edition.

A CIP catalogue record for this book is available from the British Library.

Paperback ISBN 978-1-80483-501-2

Large Print ISBN 978-1-80483-497-8

Hardback ISBN 978-1-80483-496-1

Ebook ISBN 978-1-80483-494-7

Kindle ISBN 978-1-80483-495-4

Audio CD ISBN 978-1-80483-502-9

MP3 CD ISBN 978-1-80483-499-2

Digital audio download ISBN 978-1-80483-493-0

Boldwood Books Ltd
23 Bowerdean Street
London SW6 3TN
www.boldwoodbooks.com

To all my Dartmouth friends with love. xxx

1

It was rare for Cassie Lewis to get more than four or five hours' sleep of a night. In fact, she considered herself lucky if she managed to get that much. For over twenty years now, she'd tried everything to get nearer to that elusive seven hours but rarely succeeded, so she'd learned to accept with relief the good nights when they did arrive. Last night, though, had not been a good night and now, at 5.15 a.m., she was lying in bed, listening to the wind and rain hammering against the window and waiting for the bedside radio alarm to switch itself on. After which she would give herself permission to get up.

'And now here is the shipping forecast for sea areas...' Cassie felt herself stiffen in anticipation as she listened to the measured tones of the announcer. She held her breath, waiting for the forecast for the area where Tom, her son, was currently undergoing sea trials with his boat, ready for a new round-the-world race.

'... Biscay. Gale force seven rising to eight or nine.'

Cassie instantly shrugged off her lack of sleep as worry overtook her thoughts. Gales were not good. Tom needed some wind and rough seas on these trials to test the boat, but too much could be dangerous.

Dressing quickly in jeans and a sweater, Cassie made her way quietly downstairs. Polly's bedroom door was slightly ajar and she could just glimpse the hump that represented her sleeping nineteen-year-old daughter, snuggled under the duvet.

From habit, Cassie glanced out of the kitchen window as she filled the kettle, but it was still too dark to see much.

A few lights were showing in the cottages on the hillside on the opposite side of the estuary and the occasional masthead light was visible on boats at anchor in the middle of the river. Through her kitchen window with its small open vent light at the top, Cassie could hear the wind whistling through the rigging and the halyards slapping against masts as yachts moored in the small marina that belonged to her family moved with the incoming tide and the rising wind. The rain, though, appeared to have stopped.

Standing there, sipping her tea, Cassie saw a light go on in the boatyard workshop and she guessed her father was making his customary early start to the day. She finished her tea and reached for a clean mug. Perhaps now would be a good time to talk to Bill before everyone was up and about and the day got too busy. She'd take him a cup of tea and see if the moment was right. Cassie grabbed a coat from the peg by the door and made her way across the yard towards the boatyard on the quay.

'Morning, Dad.'

Bill Holdsworth looked up from the piece of wood he was planing. 'Well, you're the early bird and no mistake. Couldn't you sleep – again?'

Cassie shook her head. 'No. And that was before I heard the forecast for Biscay.'

'I heard it too,' Bill said. 'Reckon we'll get the tail end of it in about forty-eight hours. Still, Tom should make good time coming home.'

Taking the mug of tea, Bill glanced at his only daughter. She clearly had something on her mind.

'You all right?' he asked. When Cassie didn't answer immediately, he went on quietly, 'Not a good year for our Tom to be doing this race, is it?'

Cassie shoulders slumped. 'No, it's not. I always worry when he's away sailing, but doing a round-the-world race when it's the twentieth anniversary of Miles's death...' She shook her head. 'Let's just say the level of my worry is going to be off the scale.'

Bill looked at his daughter, a gentle compassion filling his eyes. He and his late wife, Liz, had been so proud of the way she'd coped with being widowed so young. Both Tom and Polly were a real credit to her. And encouraging them to both take up sailing when they'd shown an interest couldn't have been easy.

'It's different these days,' Bill said, finally breaking the silence. 'It's still a dangerous business – I'm not saying otherwise. But what with hi-tech navigation and satellite phones, it's safer than it's ever been. The boats are built differently too. They're a lot stronger. I reckon if Miles had been sailing today, he'd have been okay. Just like Tom will be,' he said confidently.

'Oh, Dad, I couldn't bear it if anything happens to Tom.'

'Nothing's going to happen to him, lass. He's a good sailor. He's going to bring credit to us all by taking *Holdsworth Clotted Cream* around the world and bringing her home safely.'

Cassie smiled weakly at her father. She should have known she could rely on him to put things into perspective. Perhaps now was the moment to talk to him about the way she was feeling, but Bill was already speaking again and the opportunity was lost.

'Mind you, we could do with a few more sponsors. Any news on that front?' Bill asked.

'Hoping to hear from a couple of firms today.'

'Good. And don't forget Dexter Munro is waiting for Tom's final confirmation as soon as he gets back from these trials.'

'I won't. I'm off into Dartmouth later. I've got a couple of things I need to do and I thought I'd do a bit of shopping afterwards. Anything I can pick up for you?'

Bill shook his head. 'Don't think so, but thanks.'

'Right, I'd better get back,' Cassie said. 'There's a lot to do. I'll email Tom before I go out. You'll be here to take his midday call?'

Bill nodded. 'Of course. Wouldn't miss it.'

Making her way across the yard back to Boatyard House, which had been converted out of what had previously been a large warehouse, Cassie found herself wondering, not for the first time, what her life would have been like if Miles had lived.

He'd been in the lead en route to Cape Town in a single-handed race that he'd been so confident of winning when he'd been lost overboard.

'I'm on a roll,' he'd said. 'I've just won the Round Britain. This is my year.'

But it had all ended in tragedy when Miles and his boat had disappeared somewhere off the Azores during a storm. If Miles had survived the race, they'd planned to base themselves in France, down on the Côte d'Azur near Antibes, and establish a boat business including a sailing school. Instead, Cassie had found herself heading home to Dartmouth, Devon, with two small children in tow, a widow at twenty-nine.

Naturally, all those years ago, Bill and Liz, her mum, had been supportive, and slowly Cassie and the children had recovered from the trauma of Miles's death. Within six months of returning home, Cassie was once again working in the family business, helping her parents to expand it and slowly rebuilding her own life.

It wasn't how she'd envisaged her life turning out, but she'd been happy enough with her children, living back in the security of her own family. Just recently, though, she'd found herself feeling that she'd never left home. If it weren't for Tom and Polly, who were the living proof of her marriage to Miles, she might sometimes have found it hard to believe her seven years with Miles had ever been. Over time, the memories of that short period in her life had taken on the sepia-like quality of a much-loved photograph.

Tom, just five when his father died, said he'd only one real memory of him – not sailing, but playing football with him in the small garden of their house. Polly, a mere two months old at the time, had no memory of him at all, a fact which Cassie knew upset her daughter.

Memories or no, both children had Miles's physical features and Tom, at six foot three, had also inherited his height. And there was no doubt whom they both took after when it came to sailing. For six years now, Tom, as well as being involved in the family business, had been pursuing a career as a professional yachtsman. Eighteen months ago, he had married Mai, and the two of them had settled in River View Cottage with Tom doing less long-distance ocean sailing, preferring shorter races like the Fastnet. Cassie, although incredibly proud of his achievements, had secretly breathed a sigh of when Tom had made this decision. Privately he had told her that he didn't want to risk leaving Mai in the same position as his father had left them.

And the icing on the cake had been only last week, returning after a shopping trip to find Tom and Mai waiting for her in the kitchen when she got home. Cassie had been filled with apprehension when they said they needed to talk to her.

'What's wrong?' she asked.

'Absolutely nothing,' Tom replied. 'Just some unexpected news that we're thrilled about.' He was holding Mai's hand, with a big smile spread over his face. 'We wanted you to be the first to know.'

'I'm pregnant,' Mai said.

'You're going to be a granny,' Tom exclaimed at the same time.

'Oh, congratulations!' Cassie kissed Mai and hugged Tom. 'That's wonderful news. When is the baby due?'

'September – haven't got a definite date yet,' Mai said.

'We must celebrate this evening and...' Cassie stopped. 'The race. We'll have to cancel our entry, hopefully we'll get our registration fee back.'

Tom shook his head. 'Mai and I have talked it through, and we've agreed – I'm still going to do this one last long race.'

'But you said you didn't want to risk putting Mai in the same position as your dad left us in,' Cassie said. 'It also means that you will be away for all of Mai's pregnancy. And for when the baby is born.'

'We've discussed that, and Mai is okay with it, so long as it is my last round-the-world race.' Tom gave Cassie a sad look. 'I know what I said, and I meant every word, but Mai's pregnancy is unexpected and we've been working and planning on the race for almost a year now. There's already a lot of money invested. It was always going to be my last round-the-world race. I know it is still dangerous but it's a new race and I really want to do it and end my career on a high if I can, rather than just having to withdraw. Boats are safer now and satellite navigation tracks everything. The three legs and the enforced stops at the end of each one make it easier in so many ways, for both the skipper and the families on shore.'

Cassie had sighed, knowing she had no real option but to accept Tom and Mai's decision, but she also knew the fear that had resettled in her tummy when he'd told her his decision would be there until Tom sailed over the finishing line at the end of the race.

* * *

As she let herself back into the house, she realised that once again, she hadn't spoken to her father about the things that were adding to her sleepless nights. The moment hadn't been right after all.

Polly was in the kitchen, leaning sleepily against the Aga rail, her hands clasped around a mug of coffee.

'Morning, Mum. Coffee's in the pot if you want one.'

'What are you up today?' Cassie asked as she poured herself a mug.

'Mai and I are still trying to get the main cabin on the barge finished. We're almost there. Just got to paint around the portholes now and the curtains to hang. Then we can start on the galley.'

Over the years, Holdsworth Boatyard had expanded from a small family business into a well-respected company dealing with all things nautical but at its heart, it was still a real family concern.

Cassie had taken over the day-to-day running of the yacht chandlery where they sold everything from inflatables to shackles, life jackets, ropes, paint, varnish and wet weather gear as well as taking over the book-keeping side of the business when Liz, her mother, had died four years ago.

The marina side of the business was run by Cassie's brother, Joshua, and his wife, Bridget. Recently, too, Bridget had been roped in to help out in the chandlery on a regular basis whilst Cassie was busy organising everything for Tom.

The latest Holdsworth Boatyard project was the renovation of a Dutch barge as a base for sailing lessons and to offer holiday accommodation on board. Tom and Mai were in charge of this enterprise and they were all set to open the barge to students this summer. Polly, a qualified sailing instructor, was giving them a helping hand for a year until she decided what she was going to do in the future.

'The business needs to expand, Gramps, if it's to survive and support us all,' Tom had said. 'We can use the barge as a base for a sailing school and offer holiday accommodation as well.'

The hundred foot barge, abandoned in the Isle of Wight, had been bought for a song and towed slowly down channel to the boat-yard. It had been lifted out, its hull checked, some essential mainte-nance done and finally repainted. For the last couple of months while it had been tied up alongside the Holdsworths' pontoon waiting to be allocated a permanent mooring further out in the river by the Harbour Commission, Mai and Polly had spent hours decorating and generally sprucing up the inside in readiness for its first season.

'If you're going into town today, Mum, could you pop into the printers and pick up the barge leaflets? We're going to have to get them out to the various Tourist Offices soon,' Polly said. 'We need to get the word out to holidaymakers who want to spend a day or more of their holiday learning to sail.'

'Yes, okay. Anything else you want whilst I'm there? Will you be home for dinner this evening?'

Polly shook her head. 'No, thanks. Sebastian's booked a table at Le Bistro for tonight. He wants us to have a special evening together before he reports for duty tomorrow.'

'Le Bistro really is special,' Cassie said. 'Very swish.'

'Hmm. I think he plans on proposing to me tonight,' Polly said quietly. 'Recently he's been dropping hints about how life would change if we were married, without actually asking me.'

Cassie felt her heart skip a beat in trepidation but before she could say anything, Polly was on her way out.

'Right, I'm off to the barge,' her daughter said. 'See you later.' And she was gone, the kitchen door closing quickly behind her.

Cassie sighed. She'd wanted to ask Polly what she planned to say if Lieutenant Sebastian Grove did indeed propose this evening. It would be something else to worry about if she accepted his proposal because Cassie wasn't at all sure that marriage to a naval officer was the right step for her daughter. She glanced at the kitchen clock – time to get to work.

2

As Cassie unlocked the chandlery store door and turned the sign to 'open', her phone rang with a video call. Veronica, her best friend.

'Hi. How are you?' Cassie asked, as she switched on the office computer.

'Have you got a moment? Or are you busy with customers?'

'No customers yet. What's up?'

'Can I come and stay for a bit?'

'Of course. You know you don't have to ask.'

'Wednesday?'

'Fine.'

'Great,' Veronica said.

'You going to tell me what's up?' Cassie said. Veronica definitely didn't sound or look like her usual upbeat self and her usual emphatic 'great' had been decidedly downbeat, which was worrying, to say the least.

'When I see you,' Veronica said.

They chatted on for a few moments before Cassie said goodbye, already looking forward to catching up with her best friend.

The two of them had been best friends since primary school

days. Veronica had moved away when she got married and had spent the last twenty-five years living and farming in Wales.

When Veronica's husband had died five years ago, Cassie had tried to persuade her to come home, but Veronica had refused. She was going to stay and help her son, David, to run the farm. Since then, the two of them had stayed in touch with the usual emails, lots of telephone calls and a couple of visits a year. The last time she'd stayed had been about six months ago. Briefly, Cassie wondered how long Veronica intended to stay this visit.

The computer had booted up whilst she was on the phone and quickly entering her password, Cassie checked her emails and gave a sigh of relief. There was finally one from Rule of Thumb Technology confirming their offer of sponsorship, including an official team member to be part of the land-based crew in the three ports at the end of each leg where competitors would rest for a short time and attend to any repairs needed before setting off again. The sum of money they were providing too would certainly help to ease Tom's current cashflow problems. She quickly sent a reply email, thanking them for their support.

No news from the other major sponsor she was waiting to hear from, though. Time was running out on that one.

Emailing Tom, she told him the good news regarding Rule of Thumb, said how much she was looking forward to seeing him in three or four days' time, and wished him continued safe sailing.

The next couple of hours flew by as Cassie made phone calls and sent emails on Tom's behalf in between serving customers. This finding sponsorship and organising things for Tom was rapidly becoming a full-time job on top of all the day-to-day tasks she needed to do for the chandlery and the accounts for the whole business.

It was II.30 when her sister-in-law, Bridget came to work her usual four-hour midday shift and Cassie could leave for Dartmouth.

Holdsworth Boatyard and Marina, although based in a creek only a mile or so upriver from Dartmouth by boat, was a three-mile drive by car, so most journeys into town were made in the boatyard launch and today was no exception. Cassie, at the tiller of the four-teen-foot clinker-built launch with its inboard engine, concentrated on guiding the boat through the choppy water. The wind had dropped to a stiff breeze and she was glad of her warm waterproof jacket as she motored down river towards the town.

Passing Sandquay and Dart Marina, she glanced up at the Britannia Royal Naval College, standing proud on its hill over-looking the river. The river was busy these days, with hundreds of boats moored in marinas on both the Dartmouth and the Kingswear side of the river, as well as on buoys and pontoons placed either side of the main river channel. Cassie smiled happily to herself as she tied up on the public quay and stepped ashore. Springtime was her favourite season and today was a lovely late March day – blue sky, the sun shining and the pink blossom of the cherry trees beginning to show.

Cassie made her way to the printers and collected the barge leaflets before she did the shopping and made her way back to the embankment. As she passed the Harbour Commission offices, Captain James White came striding out and relieved her of the brochures and the tote bag with the shopping. James had become a good friend since arriving in Dartmouth two years ago. Tall, in his early fifties, he'd retained his boyish good looks and since leaving the Navy, his dark hair had been allowed to grow and now skimmed the top of his collar. Today, with a slight stubble of facial hair and a delighted smile on his face when he saw her, Cassie thought, not for the first time either, that he bore a definite resemblance to the actor, Matthew McConaughey.

'Cassie, how lovely to see you. Let me carry that. Have you time to have lunch with me?'

The moment she agreed, Cassie found herself being steered in the direction of the restaurant in the old station situated on the quay and famous for being the only station never to have either a railway track or trains. Train passengers disembarked at Kingswear on the opposite bank and crossed the river by ferry to arrive in Dartmouth. These days it was a restaurant, with the best views of all the activity on the river.

Once seated at a window table with panoramic views of the harbour and the river mouth, she smiled at James. 'This is an unexpected treat.'

'We should do it more often,' James said. 'Make it a regular date.'

Cassie smiled back but said nothing. It was a long time since she'd had a regular date.

James smothered a sigh and looked at the menu. 'What would you like? I'm going to have the mussels with fries.'

'Cod in the herb batter, please.'

James looked at Cassie, wondering if she realised what an attractive woman she was. Ever since he'd arrived in town as the newly appointed Harbour Master, he'd been fascinated by her.

Although she'd accepted his invitation to the cinema once or twice and they'd had supper together on a few occasions, he was still no closer to revealing his true feelings for her. She'd told him on their first evening together that she was happy to be friends but that was all she wanted – friendship. At the time, he'd resolved to be patient and hope their friendship would evolve naturally into something more. But all this time later, while their friendship was firm and enduring, it didn't appear that his feelings were any nearer to being reciprocated by Cassie than they had been in the beginning.

Recently he'd begun to suspect that, despite being surrounded by family, she was as lonely as he'd been since his divorce eight years ago. But getting past the barrier she'd erected around herself was proving far more difficult than he'd ever envisaged.

Now, sitting opposite her, he entertained her with humorous tales of his life among the men who formed the Harbour Committee and were, in effect, his bosses.

'Honestly, Cassie, I don't think there's a man amongst them who remembers the freedom a boat gives you. Come sailing with me on Saturday?' he asked suddenly.

The pain that surged through Cassie's body at his question was as unexpected as it was hurtful.

'I can't,' she answered, frantically trying to think of an excuse. 'Tom is due home at the end of the week. I must be there for him,' she said finally, not meeting his eyes.

Like Tom and Polly, Cassie had loved sailing in her youth. She'd lived for the exhilaration of skimming over the waves, the mainsail billowing in the wind, the freedom James had referred to earlier of being out on the water.

Sailing had given her Miles. Growing up surrounded by boats, Cassie had learnt to sail at a young age and by the time she was in her teens, she was sought after as crew. She'd been just nineteen when Miles, skipper of one of the larger yachts in town for the annual Dartmouth Regatta, needed a replacement crew and had been given her name. The first time they met, there had been an undeniable spark between them and they'd quickly become an item. Sailing might have given her Miles, but sailing had also taken him away from her. After he'd been lost at sea, the sport had lost its personal magic for her.

When Tom and Polly started to sail, she'd forced herself go with them for safety reasons. She'd even sailed with them upriver to

Miles's favourite picnic spot in an effort to keep his memory alive for them, and herself.

But for years now, ever since they'd been old enough to sail on their own, she hadn't set foot in a sailing boat or yacht. She didn't have a problem using the motor launch on the river. It was just a mode of transport that helped her do her job. But sailing was something that belonged most definitely to Miles and her past.

James, watching her intently, was about to say something, but changed his mind when he saw her expression.

'Okay, no sailing,' he said instead. 'How about dinner and the theatre on Saturday evening? Even if Tom is home, won't he and Mai want to be together? They haven't been married that long, have they?' he asked innocently.

'You're right. They will need some time together. Dinner and theatre it is, then. Thank you.'

As she accepted James's invitation, Cassie inwardly chided herself for not remembering that now Tom had Mai, she no longer came first in his life and she had to give them their space, especially now Mai was pregnant and they were starting their own family. It was turning out to be harder standing back now that Tom was married than she'd ever anticipated. She was mindful of all the mother-in-law jokes that regularly populated social media and was determined that Mai should never have any cause to liken her to them.

3

Polly dressed with extra care for her date with Sebastian that evening. The proposal of marriage from the man you love is a moment that is supposed to stay with you forever. If she did accept his proposal tonight, she wanted to be able to look back and remember it as a perfect evening.

Mai had gently teased her that afternoon, when Polly had mentioned her suspicions about Sebastian's plans.

'It doesn't matter where the proposal is made or how you look. It's the fact that you love the man who is proposing.'

'Where did Tom propose to you?'

Mai laughed. 'Oh, it was totally unromantic! I was hanging upside down cleaning the bilge of an old boat. I was filthy, wet and smelled terrible. Tom said he had this sudden urge to take me away from it all.'

She glanced around the barge and laughed. 'Didn't take me far, though, did he?'

'How did you know you wanted to marry him? How could you be sure that he really was *the* one?' Polly asked seriously.

'I just knew. I love him and couldn't bear the thought of him not being in my life,' Mai said simply. 'When he's away, I worry constantly and I miss him terribly.'

She hesitated, looking at Polly thoughtfully, before saying, 'If you have any doubts, say no. And remember, it's not just Sebastian you'd be marrying but, in his case, the Navy as well. A different way of life. Anyway, I thought you had plans of your own to do some more professional sailing?' she said.

There was a short silence before Polly answered. 'I did. I do.'

'Well, how will that fit in with Sebastian and the Navy?'

'He loves sailing too,' Polly said quickly. 'Wants his own boat,' she paused, 'but he seems to think it's just a hobby for me – not a career option.'

Mai looked at her. 'Surely that's for you to decide, not him?'

Polly shrugged her shoulders. 'Lack of sponsorship will probably do the deciding for me. Ocean racing is *so* expensive and even in the twenty-first century, sponsors are attuned to it being mainly a male sport.'

Now, as she put on her favourite earrings, she thought about their conversation. Mai, questioning who would make the decision about her following a career in sailing, her or Sebastian, had voiced the secret fear that had already found a place in her mind.

She loved Sebastian, at least she thought she did. He was so handsome and charming, and her heart quickened at the sight of him. But now, after talking to Mai, the little niggle that had lodged itself in her brain was growing. Did she truly want to spend the rest of her life with him? How did she feel about him not being in her life?

She clearly didn't feel the same way as Mai did about Tom. She was looking forward to some time on her own whilst Sebastian was away on the exercise that began tomorrow.

It was ages since she'd had a proper sail in *It's Mine!*, her battered twenty-five foot sailing yacht. She always seemed to be too busy these days. Her time was taken up with work or with Sebastian and the various functions he wanted her to attend with him – functions that she knew would only increase once she was an official naval wife.

Mai had clearly been happy to give up the lifestyle she'd carved out for herself and throw her lot in with Tom and his ambitions.

Polly sighed. Would Sebastian expect her to do the same once she was Mrs Grove? Would her own desires have to be sacrificed for his? More importantly, was she prepared to make the sacrifices? She and Tom were planning to compete together in next year's 'Round the Islands' race and if she could raise the money, she dreamt of being the next Ellen MacArthur and sailing around the world single-handed. She might be a mere five foot two inches, but she knew she was as good a sailor as Tom.

But with the next Vendée Globe just two years away, so far nobody she'd approached had shown a flicker of interest in sponsoring her and time was running out. It took so long to find and prepare for an event like the Vendée.

Picking up her bag, she went downstairs to wait for Sebastian. Hopefully she was reading too much into this evening's date and she wouldn't have to deal with a proposal.

Cassie and Mai were in the kitchen, poring over a large naval sea chart which Polly recognised instantly as a chart of the Southern Ocean – an ocean that would play a large part in Tom's life in the coming months.

'We're trying to work out some alternatives for Tom,' Mai said. 'But in the end, it will clearly depend on the prevailing conditions when he gets there.'

Just as Polly leaned over to take a closer look, a car tooted outside.

'That'll be Sebastian,' she observed. 'I'm off. Don't wait up, Mum.' And Polly was gone.

Mai and Cassie looked at each other.

'D'you think she will...?' They both asked the question together before laughing wryly.

'Oh, Mai, I do hope not,' Cassie admitted. 'I quite like Sebastian, but I'm not sure he's the right man for Polly.' She sighed. 'I wish Tom was home. She listens to him more than me. He'd stop her doing anything foolish.'

'A few more days and he will be. And if she does get engaged tonight... well, a woman can change her mind and engagements can always be broken, can't they?'

Cassie smiled affectionately at her daughter-in-law, feeling comforted. Tom had certainly made a wise choice when he'd married Mai.

'Have you thought any more about staying on here when Tom gets home rather than moving back to River View?' Cassie asked.

The small cottage Tom and Mai had been living in since their marriage was just fifty metres along the riverbank from the boatyard.

Mai shook her head. 'When Tom is away, I'm glad of the company down here, but when he's home, well...' She smiled shyly at Cassie. 'It will be nice to be on our own – especially as Tom is going to be away for a few months soon. I'll certainly be back then if I may.'

4

Cassie took one look at Veronica, when she arrived mid-afternoon on Wednesday, and sensed there was something major behind her friend's unexpected visit. She'd never seen her friend looking so pale and drawn and when they greeted each other with a hug, Cassie could feel Veronica's bones.

'Are you okay? You've lost weight,' Cassie said, holding her at arm's length.

Veronica nodded. 'I'm fine. Just tired and needed to get away. Can we eat out this evening? My treat for letting me come at such short notice. Don't want to dress up, so nowhere posh. Just somewhere we can sit and catch up on the news and gossip without interruptions. Oh, and please may we go by launch? It's ages since I've been out on the river. I want to take deep gulps of sea air and blow all the cobwebs away.'

Cassie laughed at that, remembering how much Veronica had hated being out on the river when they were growing up.

Now, as they sat sipping a glass of wine, waiting for their lasagne in one of Cassie's favourite gastropubs a short distance from Bayards Cove, Veronica asked, 'What's the news from Tom?'

'He expects to be off Land's End sometime late tomorrow. So, fingers crossed, he should be home Friday afternoon,' Cassie said.

'When does the race itself start?'

'Six weeks on Sunday. How long are you staying? I warn you, though, the preparations for the race are starting to go up a gear, not to mention finishing the barge ready for the summer season. You're likely to get roped into helping even if you're only here for a few days.'

'It'll do me good to be busy,' Veronica said, staring into her glass for several seconds before looking up at Cassie. 'I'm not planning on going back to the farm to live.'

Cassie frowned at her friend. She'd realised there was a reason behind Veronica's unexpected visit but not that.

'What, never?'

'I'll have to collect my things, of course, and tie up some loose ends, but otherwise, no.' She shook her head. 'Except for visits, of course, to see David and Sarah. I'm going to find somewhere down here to buy and try to live a different, independent life.'

'I can understand that,' Cassie said quietly. 'I've been wondering about doing something different with my own life.'

Veronica gave her a curious glance and opened her mouth to speak, but Cassie waved her away. 'We can talk about me later, but you, you loved the farm life, why the sudden decision to leave it?'

Veronica nodded. 'You are right, I did love it, but I've been thinking about moving away for ages. I've signed the farm over to David officially, which leaves me finally free to do my own thing. And I want to come back here.'

'Are you sure? When Harry died, I asked if you were going to come home and you were emphatic your place was with David helping with the farm. What's really changed?'

'A few things, but basically I feel in the way now that he's married. Oh, Sarah and I get on, she's a lovely girl and they're very happy, but they don't need me hanging around, they need to be able to sort things out in their own way.'

'Are they pushing you to move out?'

Veronica shook her head. 'No. It's just something I feel I need and want to do.' She glanced at Cassie.

'So I'm coming back to my roots.'

Cassie was silent for a moment. 'It's going to be fun having you around, so I, for one, am pleased to have you back,' she said. 'And until you find somewhere you like, you can stay with me. There's plenty of room, so no argument.'

'Thanks, Cassie,' Veronica said gratefully. 'So why are you looking for a change?'

Cassie shrugged. 'I feel like I'm stuck in this deep rut. And having the big five-O birthday this year is sobering too.' She took a sip of her drink and paused thoughtfully. 'Miles and I had such plans for our life together but when he disappeared, I gave up not only on those dreams, but also forgot about my personal dreams I'd put aside when I met and married him. Coming home and keeping Tom and Polly safe was all I could focus on. And here we are, twenty years later, they're grown up, doing their own thing and I'm involved in the family business. It's like I never left home.'

Veronica nodded. 'I understand that feeling. Do you have any idea what you'd like to do from here on?'

Cassie gave a small laugh. 'Yes and no. I'd just like to take, say, six months off and drift, really. Do some travelling, meet new people. The no is because I immediately feel guilty about wanting to leave. That I'd be leaving Dad in the lurch.'

'I don't think Bill would react like that,' Veronica said. 'Have you talked to him about how you feel?'

Cassie shook her head. 'I keep thinking I'll talk to him but either the timing isn't right or I get cold feet about telling him how I feel. Besides, until Tom is back from this new round-the-world race,

I can't possibly leave. I'm too involved in the organising. A few more months won't make much difference in the scheme of things anyway, I suppose.'

'Well, while I'm here we can put our heads together and see if we can come up with a plan. Now, you haven't mentioned my god daughter yet. What's Polly up to these days?'

'Can you believe she's considering a proposal of marriage?' Cassie said. 'And also getting extremely frustrated at not being taken seriously by race organisers and sponsors.'

'Who's the boyfriend? The one I met last time I was here? Sebastian something? Very good-looking naval officer?'

Cassie nodded. 'That's the one. He asked her on Monday, and apparently she's agreed to think about it whilst he's away on an exercise for several weeks.'

'Hmm. He's quite a catch – though I can't see Polly as a Navy wife, somehow,' Veronica said. 'She does like doing her own things, doesn't she? Besides, what about her sailing?'

Cassie sighed. 'Can't find enough sponsorship to do much racing at the moment. She's helping with the barge and when Tom gets back, she'll help him with the final preparations on *Holdsworth Clotted Cream* for this new single-handed round-the-world race. I think she's entered in a couple of races later in the season, but I also know Sebastian is putting pressure on her to give it all up.'

Veronica pulled a face. 'That's a bit old-fashioned, isn't it?'

Cassie nodded in agreement.

'If Polly finds some sponsorship and can prove herself as a yachtswoman, I reckon she'll carry on racing whatever Sebastian says. Which is another worry altogether. But,' and she shook her head, 'if not, I'm afraid she'll end up just getting married and becoming a Navy wife, and I worry about that too.'

'Polly's got too much spirit simply to give in,' Veronica said confidently. 'Besides, the fact that she didn't say yes to him immediately and she's thinking about it makes me pretty sure she'll turn him down. I didn't have to think twice when Harry proposed. Did you when Miles...?'

'No. If he hadn't, I was going to propose to him the next February 29th.' Cassie smiled, remembering how much she'd wanted to marry Miles. 'Perhaps you're right. Having to think about it must mean she's not sure. What a dilemma – settling down or sailing the high seas. I'll worry whatever she decides.'

Cassie smiled ruefully before finishing her wine. 'Part of me wants her to follow her dream but because of the dangers involved, I also dread her going ahead with that kind of life. On the other hand, I don't feel marrying Sebastian is right for her.' Cassie stood up. 'I just hope whatever Polly decides turns out to be the right decision for her. Come on. Let's settle up and go for a stroll.'

Wandering through town later, Veronica stopped outside the estate agency and took one of the free advertising magazines out of a rack.

'Bedtime reading,' she said, stuffing it into her bag.

'I think we'd better be heading back,' Cassie said. 'The wind's gusting and the tide will be on the turn soon.'

In fact, they were lucky to make it home before thirty-six hours of bad weather set in. As Bill had predicted, the tail end of the storm from Biscay was making its way up to Land's End and the Channel.

5

The next day, as the gale raged outside, Cassie worked in the office, clearing paperwork so that she could devote as much time as possible to Tom's preparations over the following few weeks.

Polly and Mai roped Veronica in to help with finishing the barge. In the evening, the four of them sat around the large wooden table in Cassie's kitchen drinking wine and stuffing the barge brochures into the addressed envelopes ready for posting out to the various local Tourist Offices.

Although nobody said anything, everybody was anxious to keep their minds off the bad weather Tom would be experiencing on his way home. Both he and the yacht would be battling the elements.

Late on Thursday evening, Mai got an email from him saying he was in the Channel and hoped to be home within twelve hours. Everybody breathed a collective sigh of relief and took themselves off to bed, happy in the knowledge that Tom and *Cream*, as the yacht was affectionately known between them, were now on the local coastguard's radar and almost home.

It was midday on Friday before *Cream* sailed into her home port. James rang Cassie to give her the welcome news.

'I've just been out and given Tom my official routine check, and he's now on his way upriver to you. He's only managed to grab several ten-minute catnaps in forty-one hours because of the weather. He looks all in, but everything else is fine.'

'Thanks, James. I'll see you tomorrow night.' Cassie replaced the phone and went down to the barge to find Mai and Polly. Together they waited on the landing slip and watched as Tom negotiated his way to the yacht's mooring.

Bill went over in the launch and helped Tom secure the yacht before they both jumped into the launch and headed to shore.

Over sandwiches and coffee, Tom told them a little about the sea trials.

'It's all in the log, but basically we're going to have to do some work on the hydraulics. And the self-steering gear wants some fine-tuning. Other than that, it's a question of checking her over, preparing the hull, provisioning her for the first leg and getting her round to Plymouth for the start.'

Cassie looked at Tom. A week's growth of stubble covered his chin; his favourite Guernsey sweater showed signs of having been lived in for several days and his calloused hands looked sore and weather-beaten from over exposure to seawater. But despite his obvious tiredness, his enthusiasm still shone through.

Not for the first time, she was reminded of Miles. Single-minded determination definitely ran in the Lewis family.

'By the way, I had an email from Dexter,' said Tom. 'He's coming to pick up my entry forms himself. We haven't got room in River View, Mum, so is it all right if he stays here for the night?'

'When's he coming?'

'Sometime tomorrow.'

Cassie nodded. She'd always had an open house policy as far as Tom and Polly's friends were concerned. 'He hasn't been here before, has he?'

'No. It must be three years since I last saw him. We crewed together in the Fastnet and then he went off to America and became more involved in the business side of things. Pity, really. He's a good sailor and a nice bloke.'

Tom stifled a yawn. 'I'm absolutely pooped, but before I give in and go to bed, I want to have a look at the barge. And before I forget, we'll need a family conference over the weekend to try and sort out the final preparations for the race. Okay?'

Cassie nodded. 'Fine.'

She stood by the kitchen door, watching as Tom and Mai walked hand in hand down towards the barge, Polly striding out ahead of them.

'I like Mai,' Veronica said unexpectedly at her side. 'She and Tom are good together. But it is hard standing back, isn't it?' and she gave Cassie an understanding look.

'Come on,' she continued, 'I'll give you a hand clearing up and then I'll show you the details of a house I've found.'

Twenty minutes later, Veronica handed Cassie an estate agent's blurb on the house. 'What d'you think?'

Before Cassie could say anything, the kitchen door flew open and both women turned in surprise as Polly ran in.

'Mum. Tom's had an accident on the barge. I've phoned 999. We need an ambulance quickly.'

In fact, it was the air ambulance that landed in the field at the river's edge half an hour later and took Tom off to hospital, leaving Cassie shaking and not believing what had happened.

More familiar with the narrow steep steps leading down into *Cream*'s hull, and tired from the sea trials, he'd misjudged his footing as he'd turned to descend the barge's wider companionway. He'd made a grab for the handrail, which had disastrously given way.

He'd fallen backwards down the flight of steps, his legs slipping through the rungs before ending in an unconscious crumpled heap at the bottom.

James drove down into the boatyard just as they were lifting Tom into the helicopter and had a quick word with the crew before running across to Cassie.

'How did you know about the accident?' Cassie asked, surprised, but pleased to see him.

'Routine call to the office from the air ambulance to say where they were heading on the Dart.'

'Did they tell you anything?' Cassie asked him fearfully.

James shook his head. 'Only that Tom is conscious now. They want to get him to Torbay as quickly as possible. The hospital is already on standby to receive them.'

James had no intention of telling either of the women what the paramedic on board had actually said about Tom's condition.

'Mai and I had better get to the hospital,' Cassie said.

'Is Bill coming with you?' James asked.

'No. He's going to stay with Polly. She's in a bit of a state.'

'I can drive you and bring you both back,' James said. 'Come on. We'll take my car.'

The forty-minute drive to the hospital seemed to take forever. After an initial unsuccessful attempt to break the silence, James switched on the car radio, leaving Cassie and Mai to their own thoughts, and concentrated on his driving.

Accident and Emergency at Torbay hospital was crowded, but the senior nurse led them to an anteroom and said the doctor would be with them shortly.

'I'll go and find a coffee machine, shall I?' asked James.

'That would be nice. Black, no sugar for both of us,' Cassie said, glancing at Mai, who sat on the edge of her seat, nervously twisting her wedding ring round and round.

The doctor arrived just as James was passing round the thin paper cups.

'Mrs Lewis?' Both Cassie and Mai turned at the name, coffee forgotten.

'I'm Dr Webster,' he said talking to Mai. 'We are about to take Tom up to theatre. As far as we can tell at the moment, he is suffering from some internal bruising and both his legs are broken. Once he's been operated on, we'll move him into Intensive Care overnight.'

He glanced at Cassie and then at Mai again. 'I'm afraid only one of you can see him for five minutes before he goes to theatre.'

Mai was on her way out of the room instantly.

Cassie stopped the doctor as he went to follow her.

'He will be all right, won't he?'

'A lot depends on his internal bruising and, of course, it will be a few months before he's walking again, but yes, given time, he will make a full recovery.'

6

The storm finally blew itself out during Friday night and Saturday dawned calm and bright.

Cassie spent the night tossing and turning and was the first one in the kitchen where, on autopilot, she made a jug of coffee. As she poured herself a mug, she heard Polly clattering down the stairs, Polly briefly poked her head into the kitchen. 'I'm going down to *It's Mine!*' And the door banged behind her.

Veronica was the first to join her in the kitchen and gratefully accepted the mug of coffee Cassie poured her.

'Shall I make some toast?' Veronica asked, looking at the loaf on the table.

'If you like,' Cassie said, shrugging.

Veronica placed a couple of slices of bread in the wire toaster and placed it on the Aga hot plate and closed the lid.

'Any sign of Mai or Polly?' she asked, leaning against the Aga rail, waiting for the toast.

Cassie inclined her head in the direction of the boatyard.

'Polly's wandering around out there somewhere. She said something about going down *to It's Mine!* She looks shattered. No sign of Mai yet. D'you think it's too early to phone the hospital?' she asked.

'I'd give it another hour,' Veronica said.

The two of them were silent for a moment or two. Cassie drank her coffee and Veronica checked the toast before removing it from the Aga, buttering a couple of slices and pushing one across the table to Cassie.

'I can't wait an hour,' Cassie said suddenly. 'I'm going to phone now.' She'd always been terrified at the thought of something happening to Tom at sea but had never dreamed an accident would happen on home territory.

Veronica watched her anxiously as she waited to be put through to Tom's ward and asked to speak to the sister in charge.

'I'm Mrs Lewis, Tom's mother. Could you tell me how he is, please? And when I can see him?' She listened attentively.

'I see. Thank you.'

Putting the phone down, she turned to Veronica.

'He's as comfortable as can be expected. He's still quite heavily sedated.'

She turned as Polly walked into the kitchen. 'Veronica's made toast if you want some.'

Polly nodded as she helped herself to a mug of coffee. 'Please. D'you think they'll let me see Tom today?'

Cassie shook her head.

'Sorry, love. I've just phoned the hospital. Mai can go anytime and I'm allowed five minutes this afternoon, but nobody else.'

The morning passed quicker than Cassie had expected. Both she and Mai were kept busy answering phone calls from people anxious to know how Tom was. News of the accident had certainly spread fast.

It was after one o'clock when Cassie, Mai and Veronica finally set off for the hospital, Veronica going along just to keep Cassie company on the drive back. Bill had volunteered to collect Mai when she was ready to come home.

Tom was awake when Cassie walked into the small ward and smiled weakly at her in greeting.

'Hi, Mum.'

Carefully she leant over and gave him a gentle kiss on his bruised face.

'Oh, Tom. It's good to see you. Mai's waiting outside but they said I could have five minutes first.'

'I feel such a bloody idiot, Mum. Falling down the companionway on the barge at my age is stupid.' Tom shook his head in despair. 'And now the race is in jeopardy because of it.'

Cassie tried to reassure him the race didn't matter, getting better did. Not wanting to tire Tom out before Mai got to his bedside, Cassie left before her time was up. To have seen her son and reassured herself that he would be all right was enough.

An hour later, as Cassie and Veronica got out of the car in the boatyard, they saw Polly walking slowly towards the house, accompanied by a tall man whom Cassie didn't recognise. A reporter, perhaps, checking the story of Tom's accident?

'I'll make myself scarce, while you deal with whoever he is,' Veronica said. 'I'll be in the kitchen.'

'Mum, this is Dexter Munro. Tom's friend. And race organiser,' Polly added as Cassie looked at her blankly.

The events of the last twenty-four hours had pushed everything out of her mind.

'I've told him about the accident.'

'Nice to meet you, Mrs Lewis. I can't tell you how sorry I am about Tom. Please give him my best wishes and let him know I'll be in touch. Do you have any idea yet how long he'll be out of action?'

'The doctor said several months.'

'So my visit today to collect the entry forms for the race is rather irrelevant, isn't it?' Dexter said slowly.

Cassie nodded sadly. 'There's no way Tom is going to be able to compete in the race now.'

There was a short silence as they all looked at each other, realising the major consequence of Tom's accident.

'I've been thinking about that,' Polly said quietly, breaking the silence. 'It's down to me, isn't it?'

Cassie and Dexter both turned to look at her.

'What d'you mean?' Cassie said, knowing, even as she asked the question, exactly what Polly meant.

'I can do it instead of Tom,' Polly said determinedly.

Cassie started to protest.

'No, Polly, I don't think that's the answer.'

But Polly interrupted her.

'Why not? Just give me one good reason why I shouldn't skipper *Holdsworth Clotted Cream* in the race instead of Tom?'

Polly's words were met by a stunned silence.

Cassie, struggling to keep her emotions under control, looked at her daughter before turning to look at Dexter, hoping against hope that he would squash the ridiculous idea straight away.

'I'm not sure you're experienced enough, if I'm honest,' Dexter said.

Polly looked at him coldly.

'I am experienced. I've done lots of sailing. Both as crew and as skipper. And I've done a single-handed. Tom and I have also competed with the yacht in a couple of Open 60s classes. The only thing that has held me back from competing more is lack of sponsorship.'

Dexter cleared his throat and his expression was serious as he answered Polly but his voice was gentle.

'I know how hard it is to get sponsorship, I also know you've crewed in the Fastnet, and I know that you've done some single-handed sailing, Polly. Tom's always talking about his gutsy kid sister,' and Dexter gave her a brief smile. 'But two or three weeks crossing the Atlantic alone is nothing compared to the dangers you'd face sailing in the Southern Ocean and the weeks you'd be away on this race. This new race, the Eco Global Challenge, is in a different league to the races you've sailed alone before. The only thing in its favour right now for you is that it's raced in legs, it's not non-stop. So at the end of each leg, there would be help if you needed it.'

'I know I can do it,' Polly said with determination. 'And this may be the only chance I get to prove myself. Besides, there's so much at stake. Gramps has invested a lot of money helping Tom buy the boat. Most of the sponsor's money has already been spent on preparing the boat. If she doesn't compete, will we have to give it back?'

'If it's just a question of the boat being seen to compete, we can find a professional racing skipper to take her round, can't we?' Cassie said, turning to look at Dexter, who nodded. 'You don't have to do it,' she said turning back to face Polly.

'The point is, Mum, I want to do it. I want to do it *so* much. I want the names *Holdsworth Clotted Cream* and Polly Lewis to be up there with the winners. And, in case you've forgotten, competitive sailing is as much in my blood as it is in Tom's.'

'No, I haven't forgotten,' Cassie said quietly. 'But it doesn't mean that I have to stand by and say nothing while you over-stretch your-self doing something that could prove to be beyond your capabili-ties and is dangerous.'

'Perhaps I could take a look at what you've already done? See how much more needs to be organised. How much more sponsor-ship you need,' Dexter asked unexpectedly.

'Can I trust you to be impartial?' Polly stared at him.

Dexter sighed. 'I'm just trying to help here as a friend of Tom, Polly. It makes very little difference to me whether your yacht takes part in the race or not – or who is her skipper. I'm simply the man in charge of organising this inaugural round-the-world sailing race. But at the same time, it would be wrong of me not to take a skipper's competence into account. We're not talking about an afternoon's sail out in Start Bay.' Dexter gave Polly a hard stare. 'I cannot allow the reputation of this new race to be damaged by allowing any skipper who is not competent – and fully aware of the risks involved – to take part.'

A chastened Polly broke the silence that followed his words with a muttered, 'I'm sorry if I was rude.'

Cassie took a deep breath. 'Everything is in my office,' she said. 'Why don't you take Dexter and go through all the paperwork with him, Polly? I'll see you both later.' And she turned away from them and walked down towards the boatyard, not caring where she went, just knowing that she had to get away from them both and try to pull herself together.

Accepting Tom doing a round-the-world race this year of all years had been difficult enough, but Cassie knew how experienced and competent a sailor he was. Polly, on the other hand, was a competent sailor but her experience was nowhere near as vast as her brother's. And at nineteen, her age was against her too. Cassie took comfort in the fact that Dexter had spoken to Polly quite harshly about the realities of the situation. He was unlikely to agree that she should replace Tom on *Holdsworth Clotted Cream*. Wasn't he?

* * *

In the office, as she went through the paperwork with Dexter, Polly tried to keep her thoughts centred on the race and not think about Tom lying in a hospital bed.

Dexter was certainly very efficient going through files and grasping their contents quickly. He soon had several sheets of paper filled with figures.

'Everything is exceptionally businesslike,' he observed. 'Is that your doing?'

Polly shook her head.

'No, I can't take the credit for that,' she admitted. 'It's Mum's department. She's extremely organised. I do more on the practical side. Most of my time's been spent working on the boat with Tom. I really do know her inside out. How are the finances looking?' she went on, indicating his sheaf of papers.

Dexter shrugged noncommittally.

'I'll have to run the figures through the computer before I can tell for sure. Incidentally, d'you know where the logbook is?'

'I haven't seen it, so Tom probably left it on the yacht. Do you want it?'

Dexter nodded. 'I need to see what happened on the sea trials to get the full picture of what still has to be done. I can work out a rough estimate then of how much more money you're likely to need for running repairs and adjustments to equipment.'

'I'll go and collect it. Do you want to come with me?' Polly offered, glad of an opportunity to escape from the office and get out on the river. 'Or wait here?'

'I'll come with you,' Dexter said.

Whilst Polly started the launch inboard motor, Dexter untied the boat from the quay before joining her and they quickly chugged across the river. Once on board the yacht, Polly opened the companionway door and they both went down into *Cream's* hull.

Built for speed rather than comfort, the main cabin of the yacht, built to the IMOCA 60 class specifications, was a mass of navigational aids and electrical equipment. A small galley and a bunk made up the spartan living area and the rest was storage space.

The logbook was in the drawer of the chart table and while Dexter began his study, Polly lifted the inspection hatch in the bow to check that all the water-tight compartments were still dry.

'Everything all right down there?' Dexter called out after a few moments. 'Tom certainly had a rough passage home, with winds gusting at force 10 most of the time. There were a few problems with the self-steering overreacting too. That'll need sorting before you or anybody else take her out.'

Polly looked at him as she came back up into the main cabin. Was he coming round to the idea of her doing the race?

'Everything seems nice and dry down there. I'll take the logbook ashore. Gramps is sure to want to read it. Are you ready to go?'

Dexter nodded. Once on deck, he stood in the cockpit, looking over the stern of the yacht towards the river mouth.

'There's something about these boats that makes you yearn for the open sea, isn't there?' he said quietly.

'D'you do much sailing these days?' Polly asked. 'Tom said you were good. He enjoyed the races he did with you.'

'Not a lot,' Dexter shrugged. 'I had to sell my boat when I went to the States. I'm lucky that I've got friends who invite me to crew for them, but these days I'm rarely in the country.'

'We could go for a sail early tomorrow morning if you like,' Polly offered. 'That's my boat over there.' She pointed to *It's Mine!* on her mooring, thirty metres upriver.

'I'd enjoy that,' Dexter said.

'Six o'clock too early for you?'

'No, that's fine. I'm an early-morning man.'

Polly smiled. For some reason, she'd expected Dexter to quibble about the early hour she'd deliberately suggested and was glad he'd agreed so readily. She should have remembered as a sailor he was used to being on watch during the night, early mornings wouldn't be a problem.

'Come on. We'd better get back. I want you to go through those figures and tell me how much more money we need to keep *Cream* on course for the race. And how I convince everyone that I can do it.'

7

_____

Mai was in the kitchen, giving Cassie the latest news from the hospital about Tom, when Polly and Dexter walked in.

'His right leg is broken in two places and his left in one. The left one is in plaster but the right one, because of the multiple fractures, has had to have a frame attached through the tissue into the bone. He's going to be out of action for weeks, months. Even when the plaster and the brace are off, he faces weeks of physical therapy and exercise before the break will be completely healed.'

There was silence, while they all took in the enormity of Tom's injuries.

'What about his other injuries?' Cassie asked.

'The doctors are confident that his internal bruising is just that – bruising – but they are obviously keeping an eye on him. He'll be in a wheelchair for some time, but the good news is he should be home by the end of next week.'

'So I can definitely see him tomorrow?' Polly asked eagerly.

'Yes. He's looking forward to your visit.' Mai smiled.

'We'll have to sort out where he's going to stay once he's discharged,' Cassie said thoughtfully. 'River View Cottage is obviously out of the question. All those steps leading up to it and the spiral staircase inside.'

'Could we put a bed in your sitting room?' Mai asked, indicating the room that led off the kitchen. 'It's all on one level and Tom would be able to be a part of things.'

'He could direct operations from there too,' Polly said.

Mai looked at her, puzzled, but it was Cassie who answered, realising that Mai hadn't been home when Polly had dropped her bombshell.

'Polly wants to compete in the race instead of Tom. She says there's too much at stake to simply withdraw *Cream*. But nothing has been decided yet.' Cassie cast an anxious glance at her daughter. 'We need to have a family conference. Tom will have the final say.'

It was around six o'clock that same evening when the telephone rang. Cassie and Veronica were in the kitchen, looking through the house details Veronica had found.

'I can't face another sympathetic enquiry about Tom,' Cassie said. 'Would you answer it, please?' She carried on studying the estate agent's handouts.

'Seven o'clock? Fine. See you then.' Veronica put the phone down.

'That was James, phoning to remind you about the theatre. He's collecting you in an hour.'

Cassie sighed.

'I'd forgotten all about it. I'll ring back and cancel. I can't possibly go out tonight. I'm too tired.'

'Of course you can go. It'll take your mind off things.'

'What about supper? And there's Dexter. I can't just go out and leave him to his own devices.'

'I'll cook supper for everyone. And I'm sure between Polly, Mai and myself, we'll manage to entertain Dexter for a couple of hours.'

'But...'

'Not another word. Go and get ready,' Veronica ordered.

Up in her bedroom, Cassie stood staring out of the window for a few moments. All she wanted to do was curl up in bed and sleep.

But Veronica was right. It was ages since she'd been to the theatre. A good play would take her mind off things for an hour or two and help her feel better.

By the time she headed downstairs, James was already waiting, so they set off straight away.

'I thought a pre-theatre drink and then supper afterwards?' James said on the way to town. 'I've booked a table at the Stage Door. If that's okay with you?'

'The pre-theatre drink sounds good. Not too sure I'll be awake for supper afterwards. I didn't get much sleep last night.'

'How is Tom?'

By the time Cassie had filled him in with all the details, they were parking in town.

Whether it was the effect of the glass of wine James bought her or simply his pleasant company, Cassie began to relax. When, as they crossed the street to the theatre, James took her arm, she didn't protest but rather found comfort in his action.

The play, a well-known farce, certainly cheered Cassie up and she had to wipe tears of laughter from her face as the curtain came down on the last act. As well as banishing her exhaustion, the laughter seemed to have triggered her appetite and to James's delight, she agreed to supper after all.

Sometime later, they drove back into the boatyard.

'Thank you for a lovely evening, James. I really enjoyed it. Would you like to come in for a coffee?' Cassie invited.

James shook his head. 'I'd love to, but I'd better get back. I enjoyed this evening too. Perhaps we can have dinner one day next week? I'll give you a ring. And don't forget, if I can help in any way with regards to Tom, you just have to ask. Take care.' And he leant in and gave her a kiss on the cheek.

* * *

The next morning, Cassie was up early enough to see Polly and Dexter sailing *It's Mine!* downriver to the open sea. Polly was at the helm and Dexter was out on deck tightening the main sail. Cassie smiled. Polly would be enjoying herself with Dexter on board to do some of the hard work. Cassie remembered how cross Polly had been with Sebastian the one and only time she'd taken him out on *It's Mine!* He'd apparently taken on the mantle of captain together with control of the tiller, even though it was Polly's boat, and he stayed in the cockpit issuing instructions. Sebastian might be in the Navy, but Cassie would lay money on Polly having more fun this morning with Dexter, a real sailor, on board than she did that day with Sebastian.

Cassie turned as Veronica came into the kitchen.

'Morning. I was going to bring you breakfast in bed as a thank you for everything you did yesterday,' Cassie said.

'Let's have it together instead,' Veronica smiled. 'And you can finish looking at the house details and help me decide which ones to check out today. That's after you've told me about last evening with James, of course.'

'I had a lovely time. The play was funny and supper afterwards was delicious.'

'And?' Veronica looked at her quizzically.

'And nothing,' Cassie said. 'Show me the house details.'

Out of the dozen or so house detail leaflets Veronica had collected, they narrowed it down to four.

'I really like the sound of this one,' Veronica said. 'But it's right in the middle of town and I don't know whether I can cope with life as a townie. I've lived in the sticks for so long.'

'It would be a complete change. You'd certainly have everything on your doorstep.'

'I don't suppose there's any chance of you doing a recce with me today? Just looking at locations and the outsides of places?'

Cassie shook her head. 'Sorry. Polly and I are visiting Tom after lunch, then we've got to have this family meeting to decide what is the best thing to do about the race. I don't need to tell you how torn I am about it. My initial reaction that of course we'd have to withdraw is fighting with agreeing to let Polly take Tom's place – which goes against all my maternal instincts. She knows it's the last thing I want her doing but it's not because I don't believe she's a good sailor – it's my selfish desire to keep her out of danger. And how can that be a fair reason to stop her doing it?'

Veronica shook her head and gave Cassie a sympathetic look. 'Think you'll have to hang back and go with the general consensus in the end. Give Tom my love and tell him I'll be in to see him as soon as he's allowed extra visitors. I think I'll drive into town and have a mooch around anyway. I'll be back early enough to organise something for lunch and dinner, so don't worry about feeding people.'

'Thanks, you're a star. I think I'll try and catch up with some paperwork in the office for an hour or so. Catch up with you later.'

8

Tom was awake when Cassie and Polly arrived and was pleased to see them when they walked into his small side ward that afternoon. Looking tired and drawn, he was still clearly in some pain from his injuries and the ward sister suggested that perhaps they could keep their visit short, particularly as Mai would be in soon.

'We come bearing gifts,' Cassie said, putting a bottle of apple juice, grapes and a packet of Tom's favourite custard cream biscuits by the water jug on the bedside table.

'Thanks. As a prize idiot for ending up here, not sure I deserve anything,' Tom answered. 'I've really cocked things up, haven't I?'

'Nothing that can't be sorted. The main thing is getting you well,' Cassie said. 'I'm going to have a word with the ward sister,' and she left the ward. Seeing Tom lying there with a horrible contraption on his right leg and plaster below the knee on his left one had upset her and she didn't want him to see how emotional she was.

Polly placed two large bars of his favourite milk chocolate and the latest Lee Child paperback alongside everything on the bedside table. 'There you go, bro.' Knowing that he wasn't really well enough to talk about the race, she deliberately tried to keep her voice light with her next words.

'How would you feel about me skippering *Cream* in your place?'

'Shattered,' was his instant, uncompromising reply. 'And I honestly don't want to think about it, but I suppose I might have to – after I've talked to Dexter about other, probably more sensible, options. Mai's bringing my mobile in this morning – I'll ring Dexter and talk it through with him.'

Cassie returned then and Polly had to be content with the thought that at least Tom hadn't instantly vetoed the idea. She could only hope that she'd managed to get Dexter on her side. She'd enjoyed their early morning sail and hoped she'd proved to him that she was a competent sailor – even if the conditions out in the bay had been ideal sailing weather rather than blowing a gale.

Both Cassie and Polly were quiet on the drive home, Cassie concentrating on her driving and trying to stop her thoughts returning to the possibility of Polly skippering the yacht instead of Tom. Polly, next to her, was trying to work out what would happen at the family conference later that afternoon. She had a feeling that a lot would depend on what Dexter said to Tom.

Deep in her thoughts, Polly jumped when her mobile phone rang. Sebastian. Apparently he'd just heard about Tom's accident.

'Why didn't you let me know?' he complained to Polly. 'He is almost my brother-in-law.'

No way was Polly going to admit that it hadn't even crossed her mind to ring Sebastian to tell him about the accident.

'It's been a bit full on here since it happened. I was going to email you this evening with all the news,' Polly said instead.

'I imagine there will be a lot to deal with, cancelling *Holdsworth Clotted Cream*'s entry for that race you were all preparing for. Give him my regards when you see him. It sounds as if it'll be a while before he's up and about again.'

'Of course. How are things with you?' And Polly deftly changed the subject back to Sebastian.

'Okay. Should be in Gib tomorrow. After that, who knows? Very hush-hush, this exercise. I'd better go. I'm on duty in fifteen minutes. Love you. Email me. Bye.'

As Polly put her phone back in her bag, the uneasy silence that hung in the air was broken by Cassie.

'I take it you haven't discussed your plan about the race with Sebastian, then?' she said quietly.

Polly looked at her mum. 'Sebastian' was all she'd mouthed by way of explanation at the beginning of the call. 'How do you work that out?'

'Sorry, I couldn't help overhearing, Sebastian has a loud voice even when the phone isn't on speaker, and I imagine if you had told him, he would have been very vocal and against the idea.'

Polly sighed. 'No, I haven't mentioned it to him yet. I'd rather wait until it's a fait accompli. He'll only try and talk me out of it.'

'I'm not the only one, then,' Cassie said grimly. The two of them spent the rest of the journey deep in their separate thoughts once again.

Once home, Polly went in search of Dexter to tell him that Tom was going to ring him for a chat about whether she should be the replacement skipper or not, while Cassie went to the kitchen to make a reviving cup of tea. She'd barely poured it when Joshua, her brother, arrived.

'This family get-together later?' he said. 'It will be just Bridget, I can't make it. I've got a meeting with the owner of a large motor-yacht who is looking for a permanent berth.'

'Can't you rearrange the meeting?' Cassie said. 'Everyone should have their say really.'

Joshua shook his head. 'He's just the sort of customer we are hoping to attract. Money no object. And probably the sort who would take offence at being rescheduled,' Joshua said. 'So I don't want to cancel. Obviously, I'm not keen on either the yard losing money by withdrawing or Polly putting herself into danger but if she really wants to do it...' He shrugged. 'If it's between a replacement skipper or letting Polly take part, I'm happy to let you and Dad decide.'

Cassie sighed. She'd been hoping to do as Veronica had suggested, hold back and let the family decide without her having to vote.

Dexter walked into the kitchen just before four o'clock, a sheaf of papers in his hand.

'I'll leave these with you for everyone to look at. These are the costing figures you'll all need to discuss before you reach a decision. Everything's quite easy to follow. I'm sure you will all reach the same conclusion as me when you go through them.'

'Which is?' Cassie asked.

Dexter shook his head. 'I'll tell you afterwards. I wouldn't want to influence your decision one way or the other. Now, what time would you like me back?'

Cassie looked at him in surprise. 'But you're staying for the meeting, aren't you?'

Dexter shook his head. 'It's a family thing. I'd be intruding.'

'Nonsense. We need your expert input. Besides, I was hoping you'd be the calm, impartial voice of reason this afternoon,' Cassie said. 'Stop any family quarrels.' She smiled at him.

Dexter was silent for a few moments.

'Okay. But I warn you, you mightn't like everything I have to say.'

The figures, as Dexter went on to explain once everybody was settled around the kitchen table, indicated that, with Tom at the helm of *Holdsworth Clotted Cream*, there was enough money and sponsorship for a successful entry.

'Whether all the sponsors would remain committed if a substitute skipper was to take his place is open to question,' he continued. 'As is the possibility of Polly becoming the skipper being accepted by the committee.' He shuffled a couple of the papers.

'As for the financial side of actually participating in the race. If you withdraw, the deposit Tom paid as his initial registration fee is non-refundable. If you resubmit with Polly, or somebody else as replacement skipper, you'll need to pay the remaining outstanding balance, which as you know is a substantial sum. The good news is that if the race committee reject the replacement application, you will get that money back.'

Dexter paused.

'The biggest problem could be if the race committee accept the new skipper but the sponsors don't and withdraw their support, which would leave you short of necessary funds.'

'What do you think we should do, Dexter?' Bridget asked. 'Forgo the deposit and withdraw or go for a replacement skipper? And hope the sponsors will stay on board.'

'What are the chances of both the race committee and the sponsors accepting Polly?' Bill asked before Dexter could answer Bridget.

'It's difficult to say. I know the race committee would prefer someone older and with more experience. But, on the plus side, she's done lots of sailing and competed in a single-handed race already. Also, there are other sponsors who would be keen on supporting a woman in the sport.'

There was a short silence and then Bill spoke up bluntly. 'D'you think Polly's up to it?'

Dexter hesitated, looking at Cassie and Polly before he answered. 'Yes,' he said finally.

Cassie sighed and slumped back into her chair. Polly would be even more determined now.

'Has anybody spoken to Tom about all this?' Bridget asked. '*Holdsworth Clotted Cream* is his boat.'

'I mentioned it this morning,' Polly admitted. 'He promised he'd think about it.' She glanced across at Dexter. 'Did the two of you talk? What did he say?' she added as Dexter nodded.

'He's angry with himself for causing the situation and he has reservations about giving Polly the go-ahead but admits there is very little choice.'

A tense silence filled the kitchen for thirty seconds or so before Dexter spoke again.

'I'm sorry to put the pressure on, but I really need to take the balance of the entrance fee and the replacement skipper details with me when I leave tomorrow – if you decide to keep *Holdsworth Clotted Cream* in the race – otherwise there is a danger you'll miss the deadline.'

Bill took a deep breath.

'So we have to make a decision today. Find a substitute professional skipper in the next few hours or appoint Polly in Tom's place.' He paused, looking first at Cassie and then at Polly.

'Like Dexter and Tom, I have reservations, but I think Polly should be given the chance if the race committee will accept her application.'

Cassie closed her eyes and took a deep breath before she looked at her father and Polly. 'Okay.' Her voice was barely audible as she agreed to give her beloved daughter the opportunity to prove herself as a sailor by taking part in this race that would take her into one of the world's most inhospitable oceans.

'Thank you.' A delighted Polly leapt to her feet and hugged her mother and then her grandfather. 'I won't let you or Tom down, I promise.'

* * *

As Dexter was leaving early the next morning, taking Polly's application form and a cheque for the outstanding entry fee with him, Cassie asked, 'When d'you think we'll hear from the race committee?'

'Well, it's under five weeks to the race, so they'll have to respond quickly. I've already emailed them all the details, told them about Tom's accident and...' He hesitated. 'I've also told them I have every confidence in Polly. You need the time to fine-tune things and to get the boat to Plymouth a fortnight before the start date. I think you should hear by the weekend.'

He turned to Polly. 'You've got my mobile number. If you need any advice, give me a ring. If I can help, I will. Otherwise, I'll see you in Plymouth in three weeks. Good luck.'

He kissed Cassie on the cheek. 'Thanks for letting me stay. Tell Tom I'll see him soon. Bye.'

As they turned to go back into the house, Polly looked at her mother. 'Are you still angry with me?'

'I was never angry with you, just afraid. I've always known you'd want to follow in your dad's footsteps and be a sailor. I understand you see this as your chance to prove yourself, but I can't stop worrying about you – the same as I worry about Tom when he's away. And you must remember, I've already lost someone who meant the world to me.'

Polly didn't say anything. The unexpected bear hug in which she enveloped her mother was more expressive than any words.

Cassie knew deep down that however much courage Polly might need to find in the coming weeks, she too would have to find her own inner courage to cope with the journey her daughter was embarking on.

9

The next few days passed in a blur for Cassie. There was so much to do. All negative, worrying thoughts had to be pushed aside as she gave all her attention to organising the logistics of a round-the-world sail for Polly. Normal office work for the boatyard too, had to take a back seat and Cassie was immensely grateful when Bridget appeared in the office earlier than usual on Tuesday morning, saying she'd work longer hours to give Cassie more time to concentrate on organising Polly for the race.

'Just until things get back to normal,' Bridget said. 'Or at least until the race has started.'

Cassie emailed all the sponsors, officially informing them of Tom's accident and telling them about Polly. She hoped they'd continue to offer Polly the same level of support as they had her brother.

There was good news from Daedalion Technological Sails. They'd finally agreed to supply *Holdsworth Clotted Cream* with the new sails she desperately needed. And they weren't worried about the change of skipper.

But then Bridget took a phone call from Mr Hollis at the bank. He wanted Cassie to make an appointment to see him.

'She's very busy. Can she telephone you?'

'She can, but really I'd prefer to explain the position face to face,' Mr Hollis said.

Cassie groaned when Bridget reported the conversation.

'It doesn't sound too good. I was positive the bank was going to sponsor us. We really do need their money. I'll phone him back. I haven't got time to go over to Torquay for an appointment.' Minutes later, she put the phone down with a sigh.

'The bank are going ahead with their sponsorship but not for the full amount. They're halving it because Tom is no longer the skipper.'

'At least they're still onboard with some,' Bridget said. 'Maybe when they see how good Polly is, they'll come back with more.'

Cassie gave Bridget a sceptical look. 'Rather than wait for that to happen, I'll need to try and find another sponsor.'

Bookings were also starting to arrive for the newly advertised sailing lessons as well as enquiries about accommodation on the barge. Cassie simply put those letters on one side. Mai and Tom would have to deal with them once Tom was home.

Veronica put her house hunting on hold and took over the remaining work on the barge. Mai helped her for a couple of hours every morning, but her days were mainly taken up visiting Tom.

James rang, asking Cassie to have dinner with him on Friday evening.

'I'm sorry but I can't this week. I'm so busy. Veronica and I are working until eight or nine every evening and then we all just collapse with supper on a tray. And I'd earmarked Friday evening to convert the sitting room into a bedroom, ready for Tom coming home.'

'How about I bring a takeaway and a bottle of wine for you all?

I'll come up by boat so everything should stay warm. And then I'll give you a hand moving furniture.'

'What a lovely idea. Although, I warn you, changing the sitting room around is going to be hard work. Thanks, James. See you Friday.'

Every day saw an improvement in Tom's general condition, but his spirits were low. He was finding it difficult to come to terms with the fact that his dream of competing in this new round-the-world race had been snatched away from him. The dream of going out on a high before settling down to family life with its responsibilities was over. The depressing thought that it would be months before he was properly on his feet again was also on his mind.

For a few days, he couldn't even face Polly, which upset her greatly. Eventually, though, he pulled himself together enough to ring her to apologise, promising to give her all the help he could.

'Not that I'll be much use, stuck in a wheelchair,' he added bitterly.

'Once you're home, I thought you could become my Operations Director,' Polly suggested tentatively. 'I really do need your expert knowledge. That way, too, you'd still be involved.'

'It's hardly the same, sis, you know that. But I'll do it for you. Just make sure you look after my boat.'

As promised, James arrived on Friday evening, bearing wine and fish and chips for everyone.

Supper was almost finished when the telephone rang.

'I'll get it,' Polly offered, jumping to her feet.

'Cassie, I need to talk to you,' James said quietly, choosing his moment.

'Why? What's wrong?'

'It's about the barge. Since Tom's accident, the Harbour Commission have become concerned about your proposed sailing school.' He paused. 'They're going to refuse you an operator's licence until the Health and Safety have inspected it and passed the barge as safe to have the public on board.'

'But it's already got a Health and Safety Certificate,' Cassie protested. 'Tom's accident was just that – a stupid accident because he was so tired. The barge itself is perfectly safe.'

'The fact that a companionway handrail came away is what worries them. They want reassurance that everything is as it should be before they grant the licence. They've asked for another inspection.'

He placed an envelope on the table. 'I've had to write you an official letter to that effect.'

He looked at Cassie. 'I didn't want to post it. Please believe me, Cassie, when I say I tried to stop them taking this action. I know the barge is as safe as anything else on this river, but they refused to listen.'

'When will the Health and Safety visit?'

James shook his head. 'I don't know. They may write to inform you, but the chances are they will just turn up.'

He glanced across the room as Polly put the telephone down and came back to them, her face serious.

'That was Dexter.'

Cassie waited. What now?

'He's just posted the letter informing me that my entry has been accepted by the race committee.' She let out a whoop of joy. 'I'm now the official skipper of *Holdsworth Clotted Cream*,' she added excitedly.

'Oh, well done, Polly,' James and Veronica said in unison.

Cassie got up and put her arms around her. 'Yes. Congratulations, Polly.'

'What were you and James looking so serious about?'

'We have a problem with the barge.' Cassie filled Polly in on the latest developments.

'That's the official letter,' she said, indicating to the unopened envelope on the table. Cassie looked at everyone, suddenly feeling very tired.

'I wish to goodness we'd never bought that blasted barge. Tom wouldn't be in hospital with both legs broken and we wouldn't be in this mess. And you,' she looked at Polly, 'wouldn't be thinking about sailing alone around the world.'

10

The day before Tom came home from hospital was the day that the media woke up to the fact that his young sister was to take his place in the round-the-world race.

The phone rang constantly, and one or two reporters even turned up at the boatyard. With Polly out on the river, it was Cassie who had to deal with it all – on top of everything else.

When the telephone rang for the sixth time in as many minutes, she sighed as she picked it up. Thankfully, however, it was Dexter.

'Hi! How's Tom?'

'He's coming home tomorrow,' Cassie replied.

'That's great news.' Dexter sounded pleased. 'And how's the work progressing on the boat?'

'I think it's all going to plan,' Cassie said. 'But you'd really need to talk to Polly or Bill about that. My main problem at the moment is trying to find more sponsorship and dealing with journalists.'

'From their point of view, it's a good story,' Dexter pointed out. 'And your sponsors will be pleased with all the publicity.'

'Yes, of course. It's just the time it's taking up.' Cassie sounded exhausted. 'And there are still so many other things that have to be done.'

'I can probably help out with the press, but I need to talk to Polly first. Is she around?' Dexter asked.

'She's out working on the yacht, but she's got her mobile with her.'

'Great! I'll give her a buzz right now. Talk to you later.'

Half an hour later when Cassie had begun to tackle the mountain of paperwork on her desk, Polly walked into the office.

'Don't talk to any more journalists, Mum.'

'Why not?'

'Dexter has just suggested that I sell my story to one paper. Not only will it bring in some more money, it'll make things easier for you, too. He's got a contact in London. Hopefully they'll be in touch today.'

As if on cue, her mobile rang.

'Great. Thanks, Dexter. I know Mum will be pleased. Talk to you soon.'

Polly turned to Cassie. 'Sorted. Somebody will arrive tomorrow to interview me and take some photos with Tom too, if possible. They've also suggested I do a regular report from the boat. For another fee, of course.'

'Oh, before I forget,' said Cassie, 'Gramps wants to know if there is any news on when we can expect the self-steering gear back?'

'Not yet. Tell him not to be so impatient. It's only been gone five days and they did say it would take about eight. I'll start to chase tomorrow.'

'Have you told Sebastian you're doing the race yet?' Cassie asked, as Polly was about to head off.

'No. I was going to email him last night but I was too tired,' Polly said.

'If you don't tell him soon, he'll read it in the newspaper and that won't go down very well.'

'You're right, Mum.' Polly sighed. 'I'll do it this evening.'

As Polly closed the door behind her, the phone rang again and Cassie picked it up, hoping it wasn't a journalist, but happily it was Rule of Thumb Technology, confirming their sponsorship for the change of skipper and, as arranged, one of their technicians would be available to be part of the shore crew that would meet Polly in all the mandatory ports of call.

The first of these would be Cape Town, a mere thirty days or so after the start if all went well. In the meantime, the technician was on his way to Devon to help prepare the boat for the race.

Cassie felt relieved. The more experienced hands there were to ensure the safety of Polly and *Holdsworth Clotted Cream*, the happier she felt.

* * *

Later that morning, Cassie made her way down to the barge to find Veronica carefully touching up and painting the repaired and reinforced companionway rail broken in Tom's accident.

'It's looking good,' Veronica said. 'I'm sure the Health and Safety visit won't be a problem.'

She glanced at her friend, remembering how Cassie had reacted the night James had told her about the Harbour Commission calling in the Health and Safety, how tired and depressed she'd looked.

'I hope not,' Cassie said now. 'There were more enquiries in today's post about booking lessons and accommodation. Once Tom's home, he and Mai will be able to start organising that side of things at least.' She sighed.

'The trouble is, I keep feeling that we've taken on too much with the barge. Teaching people to sail is fine, but doing the catering for them as well means a lot more work.'

'Everything will settle down into a routine once Tom's home and Polly is away racing. You'll be able to concentrate on things here then,' Veronica said. 'And I'll help whenever I can. Do you know what time Tom will be home tomorrow?' she asked.

'Around midday,' Cassie replied. 'At least the sitting room is ready for him.'

James had been as good as his word, helping them to rearrange sofas and beds. He'd even dragged a large desk in from the store-room to take all the equipment Tom would need in his role of Polly's Operations Director for the race.

Cassie had already put some of the files on the table, along with the new scanner and printer, leaving plenty of space for one of the brand-new laptops the technician from Rule of Thumb would be bringing. The other new laptop would be taken out to the boat and then everything would be synced together and Tom would be able to track the boat in the race.

She wanted Tom to know that his new role of Operations Director was crucial, that he was still important to the success of *Cream* even if he wasn't at the tiller. Polly needed his experienced input.

It was unfortunate that Tom arrived within minutes of the journalist and cameraman the next morning, and what should have been a happy homecoming turned into a confrontation.

Nobody had remembered to tell Tom about the deal Polly had made with the newspaper and he objected to being photographed as he was lifted out of the ambulance by what he thought was an opportunist reporter.

Sharply telling the photographer to 'Put that camera away,' he totally refused to even think about having his picture taken. And rudely told everyone to 'Go away.'

In the end, Cassie suggested Polly take the reporter out to the yacht.

'They'll want some photographs of you on the boat so you might as well do the interview out there. When you get back, hopefully I will have convinced Tom to have found his manners again,' Cassie said grimly.

Tom had the decency to look ashamed when Cassie tackled him about his rudeness and muttered something that Cassie took to be an apology.

'Right,' she said, 'let's get you indoors and settled.'

Between them, Cassie and Mai rearranged pillows, made Tom some lunch and generally tried to make him comfortable.

'The journalist will want to talk to you as well as Polly – and take your photograph with her. That was part of the deal,' Mai said eventually. 'Do you feel up to it this afternoon? Or shall I ask him to come back tomorrow?'

Tom sighed.

'Quite honestly, I feel exhausted. If I could have a bit of a sleep before I see him, that would help. I promise to be good.' He glanced at Cassie as he said this.

'I'm sorry I was rude earlier. I know it's no excuse, but I'm finding it hard to accept the fact I'm going to be out of action for so long. And Polly taking my place just seems to be rubbing it in.'

'I'm sorry you feel like that,' Cassie said. 'But it's the way it is. And remember, it's stopping the yacht from being a drain on the boatyard finances whilst you're laid up.'

The fact that even thinking about Polly doing the race caused her anxiety levels to hit an all-time high was an unwelcome side effect of stopping that drain on their finances, and something she had no intention of telling Tom.

11

Tom was still asleep when Polly brought the reporter back to the house, so it was mid-afternoon before he got the photograph he wanted of Tom and Polly together.

Tom chatted politely for a few minutes, but it soon clear that he was still exhausted and needed to rest more.

Once the reporter had left, an excited Polly told Cassie and Veronica about the interview. 'Apparently he's going to write a couple of features, which hopefully will go in the national papers as well as the *Western Morning News*. One feature will be from the angle that I'm not only the youngest participant but also female – this generation's Ellen McCarthy type of thing. And another one showcasing me as part of Dartmouth's female maritime history. I told him about how you remembered Dame Naomi James setting off from and returning to Dartmouth on her solo round-the-world sail back in the late 1970s. Can you believe he'd not heard of her?'

'Well, it was forty years ago,' Cassie said.

'He knew all the names of the male sailors around that time, though, Chay Blyth, Robin Knox Johnson, to name but two.'

'Anyway, it sounds as though you'll get some good publicity thanks to Dexter's contact,' Cassie said.

'Yes, I must phone and thank him,' and phone in hand, Polly went back to finish some work on the boat.

'Fancy a walk?' Veronica said. 'Mai's here for Tom. Some exercise and fresh air will perk us both up.'

'Good idea,' Cassie agreed and the two of them set out companionably along the riverbank path.

'Have you made an appointment to see any houses yet?' Cassie asked.

'I've viewed a couple of totally unsuitable ones, but I've two more promising places lined up for next week. One's in Castle Gardens and the other is the one in town I showed you the details of, I've got an early evening viewing for that one. The owners work and they like to be there for viewings.' Veronica paused before continuing.

'James has asked me to stay in town and have dinner with him afterwards.' She glanced apprehensively at Cassie, as if unsure of her reaction to this news.

'That's nice for you. He's good company and you'll enjoy the Royal Castle Hotel,' Cassie said, assuming that James would take Veronica to his favourite local restaurant for dinner. 'The food's really good there.'

'You don't mind?' Veronica asked.

'No. Why on earth should I?' Cassie said. 'James is a free agent. Come on, let's make for that willow and then turn back. I'm glad you talked me into this walk. I'm really enjoying it.'

Increasing her pace to keep up with her friend, Veronica didn't have the breath to enlighten her that James had suggested the Seafarers Restaurant at the country club for dinner – a far more expensive restaurant than the hotel in the centre of town.

* * *

At nine o'clock that evening, Polly sat in her room staring at her computer screen, trying to compose an email to Sebastian.

Dear Sebastian, she typed. That was the easy bit. She knew he was going to be furious about her taking Tom's place in the race, no matter how she broke the news.

She glanced across at the red velvet ring box sitting on her dressing table. Sebastian had been upset when she hadn't immediately accepted his proposal, simply promising to think about it whilst he was away. Even so, he'd insisted on giving her his ring.

'Next time we see each other, I hope you'll be wearing it,' he'd said, sounding confident that this indeed would be the case.

It was a beautiful ring – a large ruby surrounded by diamonds – the sort of ring anybody would be proud to wear. As yet, though, she hadn't even tried it on.

Polly sighed. What on earth was her problem? She was supposedly in love with Sebastian. So why was she so afraid of committing herself to marrying him?

She took a deep breath and started to type again.

I hope the exercise is going well. Tom's home, but he's finding it difficult to cope with the thought of being out of action for so long.

Sebastian didn't like receiving long emails. He said the whole point of emails was that they were short and to the point. Perhaps she should come straight out with it.

Also, he's a bit jealous that I've got the go-ahead to skipper the boat in his place. But he has agreed to be my Operations Director. I'm so sorry for Tom but pleased I've got the chance to prove myself.
The bad news is that it means I'll still be at sea when you get back, so it

will be nearly six months before we see each other again. I'll miss you so much, but at least we can still email whilst I'm away. Love, Polly. xxx

She hesitated a fraction of a second before hitting the send button and watched as the message disappeared from the screen. It was done.

At least there wouldn't be a face-to-face confrontation.

The email she sent to Dexter was much easier to compose. In fact, it turned out to be quite lengthy, telling him how the preparations for the race were progressing and how she hoped to be doing her sea trials soon.

Hopefully he liked receiving long, rambling emails as opposed to short pithy ones.

Finally, Polly shut down her computer and walked across to the dressing table. Picking up the ring box, she opened a drawer and buried it in amongst her jumpers.

She'd forget about it until after the race. She had too much to do right now to make such an important decision. Maybe by the time she came back, her feelings would be a whole lot clearer.

Heading downstairs, she found Cassie, Mai and Veronica all in the sitting room talking to Tom. After few hours' sleep, he seemed to have cheered up immensely. He was certainly looking less tired.

'Hi, sis,' he greeted her. 'You're just in time to join us for a glass of wine, although sadly I'm on the orange juice with Mai because of the painkillers.'

'I thought we were going to check through the medical supplies tonight?' Polly said, glancing at Cassie.

'There's still time. We're just celebrating Tom's first night home,' Cassie said.

Taking her glass, Polly perched on the edge of Tom's bed and clinked her glass with his.

'Welcome home. You know, you didn't have to break both your legs,' she said cheekily, 'one would have done. But thanks anyway.'

'Here's to you, Polly,' Tom said. 'But be warned, little sister, if you don't bring *Cream* back home in one piece, I'll break *your* legs!'

Cassie listened to the pair of them sparring, relieved that things seemed to be back to normal between them.

The next few weeks would be as tough on Tom as they would be on Polly. He'd have his own battles to fight, both physically as his legs mended and mentally as he helped Polly achieve what he longed to be doing himself.

'As enjoyable as this is,' Polly announced, finishing her glass and standing up, 'some of us still have work to do before bedtime. I'm off to the office. I'll see you tomorrow, brother dear.' She patted Tom lightly on the head.

Cassie joined her in the office five minutes later, just as Polly was lifting a large cardboard box filled with medical supplies onto the table.

'No sign of the freeze-dried foodstuffs?' Polly asked. Cassie shook her head.

'Not yet. They've promised delivery within the next few days.'

Polly put some sealed syringes on the table.

'If you call out the items, I'll tick them off the check list,' Cassie said. 'There's an awful lot here. Heaven forbid you ever have to use any of it.'

She looked at the DIY kit for setting broken bones and the ready-threaded needles for sewing up deep cuts and shivered apprehensively.

'These days, it's a case of being prepared for any eventuality. Like rescuing somebody who's injured,' Polly added quickly. 'The painkillers might get taken if I have one of my migraines but otherwise this lot will hopefully all come back unused.'

'I remember the medical box your dad took on his trips,' Cassie said slowly. 'It had a large packet of plasters, an antiseptic spray, a pair of scissors, bandages and a small tub of painkillers. How times have changed. Oh, and Dad always put a small bottle of brandy in. Purely medicinal, he always said.'

She smiled at Polly. 'The brandy was always gone when he got home. Funny, that.'

Polly laughed as she put her hand into the box and pulled out a bottle of brandy. 'I didn't realise it was a family tradition.'

There was a short silence while Cassie looked at Polly.

'You will take...'

Polly interrupted her before she could finish the sentence.

'Mum, I know what you're going to say and it's as pointless as me telling you not to worry. I know nothing will stop you worrying about me until the race is over and I'm home again. And you know deep down that, yes, I will take care, but you also know that I will take calculated risks if I have to.'

'You wouldn't be your dad's girl if you didn't,' Cassie said shakily.

12

Over the next few days, things settled down into something of a routine.

Now that Tom was home, Mai was able to divide her time between looking after him and working on the barge. Thankfully Mai's mild morning sickness had decided to abate totally, and she was feeling more like herself, with more energy. With Bridget in charge of the routine office work and Veronica helping out wherever needed, Cassie and Polly were able to throw themselves into the preparations for the race.

Within a few days of being home, Tom had taken up his role as Operations Director and by ten o'clock most mornings, he was in his wheelchair in front of the computer.

A day after the self-steering was back and refitted, Polly took off on her much-needed sea trial. The plan was for her to go down channel, get clear of the shipping lanes and spend some time sailing the Atlantic before turning and making for home. There wasn't time for anything longer, and everything Tom had noted in his log on his original sea trial as needing attention had been done.

This sea trial was Polly's chance to really get to know how *Cream* handled and responded in certain conditions.

Standing in the cockpit, Polly kept a firm hand on the boat's wheel, concentrating hard on maintaining a steady course and trying to keep her excitement under control.

Once out in the river mouth, she moved forward to hoist the jib sail and felt a tremor of excitement flood her body as the yacht responded to the pull of the small sail by leaping forward into the waves. Already the spray on her face and the feel of the boat moving beneath her feet was filling her with happy excitement.

Ahead of her lay the Channel, with its busy shipping lanes, and then the relatively open space of the North Atlantic Ocean, space in which she would begin to get to know the yacht's idiosyncrasies before they started on her dream voyage together. It was a voyage on which she was determined to show everybody just what she was capable of.

Cassie and Bill had followed in the launch as Polly guided the yacht down river and into the mouth of the Dart. As Polly cut the engine and hoisted the main sail, she turned and waved goodbye.

'See you in a few days,' she shouted as the yacht heeled to the wind and began to speed through the water. Soon she was out in the Channel, a mere speck in the distance.

Bill turned the launch and they slowly pushed their way back against an outgoing tide into the river mouth and towards the harbour. Bill needed to collect some spare parts from the garage and Mai had asked Cassie to pick up a prescription for Tom, so Bill tied the launch up alongside the public quay.

'See you back here in what? Fifteen minutes?' Bill said as they went off in opposite directions.

Errands completed, Cassie popped into the newsagent's on her way back to the launch. She wanted a copy of the local paper.

Standing by the till waiting to pay, she glanced at the front page of the paper and felt her body stiffen.

Under the headline 'Local Girl Keeps Family Name to the Foresail' was a colour picture of a smiling Polly on board *Holdsworth Clotted Cream*. Halfway down the page was another picture – an old black and white one of a beaming Miles that Cassie recognised instantly as having been taken after his Round Britain win. His penultimate race.

Bill was deep in conversation with James when Cassie got back to the quay.

'Anything interesting in that rag this week?' Bill asked.

'Oh, yes,' Cassie nodded, holding the front page up for them both to see.

'It's a good picture of Polly,' Bill said. 'What do they say about her?'

'I haven't read it yet,' Cassie answered. 'The other picture rather took me aback. I wasn't expecting it.'

'I read the article earlier,' James said. 'Apart from the terrible headline, it's a good report. Wishing her bon voyage and all that. The picture of Miles was just to make the family tradition link – how she's following in her dad's footsteps.'

'That's the last thing anybody wants to happen in this race!' Cassie snapped at him, bursting into tears.

'Can we go, please, Dad,' she begged as she scrambled into the launch.

Bill started the engine as a stricken James untied the ropes and cast them off.

'Cassie, I'm so sorry,' he said. 'I didn't think before I spoke. I wouldn't upset you for the world, you know that.'

Cassie shook her head and tried to smile.

'I know, James. It's just that what happened to Miles is always at the back of my mind.'

There was no time for anyone to say any more as the launch moved further away from the quay. James stood watching for several moments before sighing and heading back to his office.

They chugged their way upriver with Bill at the tiller.

'He's a nice man, James,' Bill said casually after a few minutes.

Cassie sniffed, her tears starting to dry up.

'Yes. I know. I'll ring him later to apologise for shouting at him.'

Bill looked intently at Cassie. 'You know, love, you've got to start living again. Tom and Mai are happily married and expecting. Polly is doing her own thing. They're not children any longer. You can't go on living your life through them and constantly worrying about whether they're going to suffer the same fate as Miles.'

'Is that what you think I've done all these years?' Cassie asked, feeling the tears pricking the back of her eyes again.

'We all knew you'd take a long time getting over losing Miles,' Bill told his daughter quietly. 'But when he died, it was as if you stopped living too. I know how much you loved him, Cassie, but twenty years is a long time to grieve. And I'm sure he would want you to move on with your life.'

He manoeuvred the launch around some flotsam before speaking again.

'Your mum always hoped that you'd meet someone, and so do I. Someone new, someone who'll love you and bring you back to the real world. I'm sorry it hasn't happened yet, but I don't want to see you wasting any more of your life. Tom and Polly are a credit to you. Stop worrying about them and concentrate on getting your own life sorted.'

Listening to her dad, Cassie realised that Veronica had been right – there was no way Bill would have thought she was rejecting them if she'd told him about wanting to do something different. After all these years, he still wanted what was best for her, and she knew her mum would have been the same if she'd still been alive.

She should have talked to Bill. Instead, she was guilty of letting her life – and her chances of happiness – slip by.

Unconsciously Cassie straightened her shoulders. Once this round-the-world race was over and Polly was safely home, she'd definitely find a way of somehow moving on her with life.

When Cassie and Bill got back to the boatyard, they noticed Mai saying goodbye to a small blonde woman. Father and daughter exchanged a glance. Her businesslike dark suit wasn't exactly the normal gear for climbing around on boats.

Mai spotted them and she and Cassie walked back to the house together.

'That was Mrs Catchpole, Health and Safety Inspector,' Mai said.

Cassie glanced at her quickly. 'And?'

'I think everything's going to be okay. She looked at all the handrails, not just the one broken in Tom's accident. She wants them all adapted to the same standard as the replacement, and some more safety catches on the two forward hatches. Basically that's it. She's going to put it all in writing, but she doesn't see a problem with issuing a licence in time for the season.'

'Thank goodness for that.'

'Oh, I nearly forgot,' Mai said. 'The supplies you and Polly were waiting for arrived today. They're in the office. All twelve boxes.'

Cassie groaned. 'Didn't Veronica ask the driver to take them straight down to the yard ready for loading on *Cream* when Polly gets back?'

Mai shook her head. 'Veronica isn't here. She's gone to look at houses, remember? And then she's having dinner with James.'

Cassie had forgotten about Veronica's date with James. To her surprise, her heart constricted at the thought of the two of them together and she felt a pang of... jealousy?

But that was ridiculous. As she'd said to Veronica, she and James were just friends. He was free to see anyone he chose.

All thoughts of James were banished to the back of her mind, however, as soon as she and Mai walked into the house. To her relief, Tom greeted them cheerfully.

'How did the Health and Safety go?' he asked Mai. 'Will we get our certificate?'

Mai nodded. 'Cassie can tell you whilst I get some supper organised. You need to talk about the other problem we have with the barge too.' Mai disappeared into the kitchen.

'What other problem?' Cassie asked bluntly.

'We've been going through the paperwork and checking how the bookings are coming in,' Tom said. He pulled a file towards him.

'The response to the marketing has been good, I thought,' Cassie said. 'You and Mai should have a flourishing business there in a couple of seasons.'

'In theory, you're right, Mum, but...' Tom paused. 'Our first booking is for a family of four with the two lads wanting to learn to sail, the following week it's a party of five teenagers. They all want to book cabins on the barge, which isn't a problem, and they all want sailing lessons, which is.'

Cassie looked at him, puzzled. 'Why? The barge was bought as a base for your sailing school.' Her voice trailed away as she began to realise what the problem was. Polly had agreed to be their sailing instructor for the season while Tom was away.

'I won't be able teach until this season is virtually over,' Tom said. 'Mai can sail, but she's never taught anyone. Besides, she's pregnant and she'll be too busy to do anything other than organise the catering side. The problem is—'

'We don't have a sailing instructor,' they both spoke at the same time and looked at each other.

There was a short silence before Cassie spoke. 'We'll just have to hire someone for a few weeks until you're back on your feet again. I'll ask James next time I see him if he knows anyone who is available.'

'There's not enough money in the kitty to do that for very long,' Tom pointed out. 'The renovation and fitting out has taken more than we expected, and now there's the extra work the Health and Safety want for the new licence.'

Cassie was silent, waiting for him to continue, hoping against hope that he wasn't about to say the words she dreaded hearing.

'There is another solution,' Tom said slowly. 'You taught Polly and me to sail. You could do it until I'm out of this thing.' He thumped the arms of his wheelchair.

'That was different,' Cassie protested. 'I haven't sailed a dinghy for years.'

'You still have an RYA teaching qualification. You can do it, Mum. You know you can.'

He was looking directly at her, and Cassie had to take a deep breath. This was the very last thing she wanted to do.

13

Cassie went up to her room after supper, Tom's words ringing in her ears.

'You can do it, Mum. You know you can.'

But she had no intention of teaching sailing – even for a couple of weeks. They'd just have to sort something else out.

Upstairs, Cassie switched on the radio and lay down on the bed, hands behind her head. She needed some time on her own, to think more about what her father had said in the launch on the way home and what she could do about it.

It was true. Twenty years of her life had gone by – not without her noticing, but certainly without her playing a leading part in it.

To the outside world, she assumed she'd appeared whole. Tom and Polly's mum, indistinguishable from their friends' mothers, getting on with her life. But inwardly she knew she'd never emerged from the lethargy she'd allowed to creep over her the day Miles was reported missing.

At first, it had been easier to live in the past with her memories and exist through the children, rather than get out and create a new life for herself. After a few years, it had become an ingrained habit she seemed incapable of changing and even stopped wanting to change, until now.

She reached over and picked up the silver-framed photograph from her bedside table and studied the young couple who smiled out at her.

The colours of this last photograph of herself and Miles were fading. Like her, the image was beginning to show its age.

Miles, though, had never grown old.

Just then, there was a knock on the door. Cassie replaced the photograph on the bedside table before calling out.

'Yes?'

'It's Veronica. May I come in?'

'Of course.'

'Are you all right?' Veronica asked. 'It's not like you to hide away in your room.'

Cassie sat up. 'I needed some time to think. Sort things out in my mind. It was something Dad said, actually. He reckons it's about time I started to get a life of my own.' She looked at her friend. 'You think the same, don't you?'

Veronica nodded.

'I think you've missed out on a lot of things you could have done – would have done if things had been different. I've been a widow for five years, but I've realised how hard it is to come to terms with being alone without that special person at your side.'

'Do you still miss Harry?'

Veronica smiled ruefully.

'Yes, of course. It's no easier being on your own after twenty-five years of marriage than it is after seven. But life goes on and I think moving away from the farm will be good for me. Have you ever thought about moving away?'

Cassie shook her head. 'Not moving away permanently. Where on earth would I go? All my family and friends are here.' She sighed. 'I'll have to try and make my new start on home ground. But I do fancy taking a sabbatical of, say, four or five months.'

'I hope you mean it, Cassie. You've hidden away from the world for far too long.'

Cassie stood up and straightened the bedspread.

'So, how was your day?' she asked Veronica. 'Did you like either of the houses? And how did your meal with James go?'

'The one in Castle Gardens is nice but too small. As for the house in town, I'm really tempted. Will you come and see it with me and give me your honest opinion?'

'Of course. How about tomorrow?'

'Great. We'll take my car and I'll treat us to lunch,' Veronica said.

'So how was the Royal Castle tonight? Did you enjoy your meal?' Cassie asked again.

'James took me to the Seafarers,' Veronica said quietly.

'Gosh, that was pushing the boat out a bit!' Cassie looked surprised.

'I wasn't the one he really wanted to be with. He spent most of the evening talking about you, how nice you are and how he regrets upsetting you.' Veronica gave Cassie a serious look.

'He treated me to a lovely dinner simply because he wanted to talk to me about you. Among other things, he wanted to know if you'd ever said anything to me about your feelings for him. He looked so dejected when I had to say no, you've never talked about him other than as a friend.' Veronica paused. 'He's very fond of you, Cassie,' she said. 'He was so cross with himself for upsetting you earlier.'

Cassie nodded. 'I meant to phone him and apologise for my outburst earlier today. It wasn't his fault at all. It was me overreacting. I know he likes me, but I haven't encouraged him because...

actually, I don't have a reason. But I'm probably guilty of taking him for granted.'

'Well, he should be home by now. Why don't you phone him? I'm sure he'd be only too pleased to be a part of your new start here in Dartmouth.' Veronica laughed as she said it, but her eyes were serious as she looked at Cassie.

After Veronica had left, Cassie let her thoughts drift guiltily to James. Deep down, she knew the only reason she hadn't given their friendship the opportunity to develop into something more was because she had clung on to the memory of her love for Miles for far too long. Plus she was too scared to take a chance on loving someone new and it not working out. James was a lovely man who deserved to be happy.

James was home when she phoned him a few minutes later and was pleased to hear from her, as Veronica had predicted.

'I'm sorry I was so rude, James.' Cassie got straight to the point. 'I don't normally snap at people. Please forgive me.'

'Consider yourself forgiven. I realise you're under a lot of strain right now.' There was a short pause before he went on. 'Would you like to have dinner with me on Saturday evening?'

'I would like that very much, thank you.' Cassie hesitated. Could she talk to James about the problem with the barge? 'There's a couple of things I'd like to ask you then as well.'

'Ask me now.'

'No. They'll keep. I'll see you on Saturday.'

As Cassie replaced the receiver, she wondered whether one of her questions for James would in fact keep. Or whether she would have changed her mind by Saturday and lost her nerve.

* * *

It was raining again the next morning as Cassie and Veronica prepared to leave for town. Cassie nearly suggested putting their outing off, but Veronica was so keen to show her the house that she didn't have the heart to even suggest postponing their visit.

Polly sent an email just before they left which they read over Tom's shoulder.

My first night on 'Cream' was wonderful. The self-steering is working a dream. Weather so far good, but there is a depression forecast. Hopefully I'll be able to skirt around the edge of it. Turning for home about midday. See you all sometime tomorrow morning. Love Polly. P.S. Any chance of a curry for dinner tomorrow, Mum?

'If you are emailing or speaking to her, tell her yes,' Cassie said, mentally adding the curry ingredients to her shopping list.

'Right, we'll drop the last of the barge leaflets down to Joshua in the marina office and then we're off to brave the rain in Dartmouth. See you later.'

When Cassie and Veronica ran into the reception office of the marina, Joshua was talking to a large man dressed in expensive wet weather gear.

'Cassie, Veronica, meet Doug Hampshire. He's berthing his yacht down on Pontoon E for the next year.'

As Pontoon E was reserved for the largest, most expensive boats, Cassie reckoned Doug must be the wealthy client Joshua had been so keen to sign up.

She smiled at Doug as he took her hand in a firm grip.

'Pleased to meet you,' he said. 'I'm having an Open Boat Happy Hour for a couple of hours on Sunday, for friends and fellow yacht owners and as an opportunity to meet some locals. I hope you'll both come? About 6.30. You'll pass the word around, Joshua?'

Cassie and Veronica thanked Doug before saying goodbye and making a dash for the car.

'Nice man,' Veronica said. 'Wonder what his wife's like?'

Cassie shrugged, but there was a warmth in his eyes that made her think she must be a lucky woman.

Once in town, Veronica collected the key from the estate agent and took Cassie to see Glebe House.

Situated down a lane off one of the main streets, Cassie saw immediately why it appealed to Veronica. Built at the turn of the nineteenth century, it stood squarely in what had once clearly been an orchard, and through the rain, Cassie could see several gnarled apple trees dotted around the large garden.

A high red-brick wall around the entire perimeter of the property encased it in perfect solitude from its neighbours, creating a little bit of countryside in the heart of town.

Once they were inside, Cassie turned to Veronica.

'I can see you living here. It's got such a wonderful feel about it – even on a day like today.'

The next hour flew by as they wandered from room to room, discussing the best way to redesign and decorate the house.

They finished the tour of inspection in the kitchen. 'The only thing I must have in here apart from an Aga is a dresser,' Veronica declared.

'The only thing I must have right now is lunch!' Cassie said. 'I'm starving.'

'Come on, then. Let's take the key back. Shall I make an offer, d'you think?' Veronica asked seriously.

'You'd be mad not to,' Cassie said.

Veronica, as promised, treated them to lunch in the bar of the Royal Castle Hotel. Before leaving town, they did some shopping and then drove slowly home in the rain that was still pouring down.

As they drove into the yard, Cassie was surprised to see Dexter's sports car parked in front of the house.

'Lovely to see you, Dexter,' she said. 'Tom didn't say you were coming. Are you staying?'

'It was a spur of the moment thing. I'm on my way down to Plymouth but I don't have to be there until the end of the week. So if you can put up with me for a couple of days, I'd like to stay.'

Supper that evening was a jolly affair. Tom was pleased to see his old friend and as they all gathered around the table, he and Dexter were soon deep in reminisces about the times they'd sailed together, the races they'd taken part in and their mutual friends.

Because Tom was hemmed in and unable to move quickly, it was Dexter who got up to answer the satellite phone when Polly called.

'No problems to report? Good. So we'll see you tomorrow, about midday? D'you want to talk to Cassie? Tom? Okay, I'll give everyone your love. Take care out there,' he said.

'Everything is fine.' He turned to Cassie. 'She's planning on having something to eat then grabbing a catnap, so she'll be awake and ready to tackle the busiest part of the Channel tomorrow. Sends her love to everyone.'

14

Mid-morning the next day, Cassie and Dexter were down on the landing pontoon as Polly motored upriver. They both gave her a hand securing *Cream* alongside.

Within minutes, the shore crew from Rule of Thumb Technology were on board, checking out all the electronics. Cassie took comfort in the fact that they would be in each of the required stop over ports to check *Cream* over for every stage of the voyage. As the technicians worked, plans were made to begin loading provisions that afternoon.

'Did you have much trouble trimming the boat?' Dexter asked, looking at Polly's slight frame and remembering how difficult it had been for him to balance the last boat he'd raced properly.

Polly shook her head.

'Not really. The only problem is, with the wind continually changing direction, you know that you'll be shifting it all back again within a few hours. Hopefully during the race itself, the wind will be more consistent.'

'Probably be much stronger too,' was Dexter's only comment as he picked up Polly's sail-bag, ready to go ashore.

That afternoon, Polly and Dexter loaded and packed provisions into the hold of the yacht with an easy familiarity. As they walked tiredly back to the house, Polly turned to Dexter.

'Thanks a lot for your help. I really appreciate it.'

Dexter glanced at her before replying.

'I gather from Tom that your boyfriend is worried about you doing this trip?'

'Mum's worried too. But she hasn't said I shouldn't.'

'And he has?'

Polly shrugged and pulled a face but didn't answer.

'Are you and he engaged?' Dexter asked quietly.

'No.' Polly shook her head. The exercise Sebastian was on was clearly keeping him busy, as he hadn't replied to her email yet. She didn't feel the need to tell Dexter about the ring box hidden in her drawer – or about the doubts she was having over her feelings for Sebastian. She'd pushed all those thoughts out of her mind, the race was enough to think about right now.

The next twenty-four hours were busy ones. Everybody in the boatyard and marina was roped in to help with all the preparations necessary to get Polly and *Cream* down to Plymouth in two days' time, ready for an intense time of preparation for their big adventure.

As Cassie told James over dinner at the Seafarers on Saturday evening, she found it hard to believe how quickly the race date was approaching – and how much work was involved.

'Honestly, James, there are far more regulations these days compared with twenty years ago. And the amount of paperwork is unbelievable.'

'A lot more people are involved, I suppose,' James said. 'Like everything else, it's big business these days too.' He glanced at her. 'How did Polly cope with her sea trials? *Cream* is a big boat to manage single-handed.'

'Fine. Polly is very determined. She feels that if Ellen MacArthur could race Open 60s, so can she!'

They were eating dessert when James turned the conversation. 'Well, Cassie, what was it you wanted to ask me?'

'The first question is, do you know of any qualified sailing instructors looking for a job? There are bookings for the barge already and...' She shrugged. 'Now, because of Tom's accident and Polly, who was our designated instructor, taking his place, we have no one to teach them.'

'Can't say I know anyone off hand, but I'll ask around. Second question?'

Cassie put her spoon down and took a deep breath. 'You once asked me to go sailing with you.'

James smiled at her. 'Yes, I remember. The invitation still stands.'

'In that case, will you please take me sailing as soon as possible?' There, the words were spoken.

'Of course. Monday is my day off, so how about in the afternoon?'

'That would be great, thank you.' Cassie smiled.

'Can I ask what brought on the change of mind?'

'Tom seems to think that I could be the answer to our lack of sailing instructor, if we fail to find one,' Cassie said. 'I tried to point out that I haven't sailed a dinghy for years and that he and Polly were the last people I taught and...' She hesitated. 'I haven't set foot in a dinghy since Polly was old enough to sail alone. So it's at least ten years since I sailed. I've probably forgotten how to do it, let alone teach it.'

'I don't think you ever forget,' James said simply, placing his hand over hers in a comforting gesture that felt too intimate to Cassie. 'It will be like what they say about riding a bike – you never forget,' he added.

To her relief, an attentive waiter appeared with the offer of coffee and she was able to reclaim her hand without undue fuss. Despite her conversation with Veronica about new starts and however much she liked James, right now she simply wasn't ready for any complications in their relationship. Once the race was underway and a more normal routine had been re-established, she'd have time to concentrate on sorting out her life.

'My social life suddenly seems to be taking off,' she said brightly, hoping to change the subject. 'I haven't been so busy in years at work, I'm here tonight with you, we're going sailing next week and tomorrow it's the "Open Boat" party in the marina. Are you going?'

'Yes. Not really my sort of thing, but I have to make an appearance. Doug Hampshire seems nice enough.'

'Joshua says his boat is amazing – the last word in luxury. He reckons it should be moored in Cannes rather than here!'

* * *

The following evening, as the others prepared to leave for the 'Open Boat' party, Tom professed himself to be glad for once that he had an excuse not to go – parties were so not his scene. Dexter was going to keep him company before leaving early the next morning and heading on down to Plymouth. Although Tom did admit to Mai before she left that he would have liked to have seen over this expensive yacht now moored in their marina, if only for a snoop around. 'Still, it's something to look forward to when I'm back on my feet,' he said.

Cassie was inclined to agree with her brother, Joshua, that this yacht should be berthed somewhere down on the French Riviera as she, Polly, Mai and Veronica waited to board.

'Now we know how he made his money,' Polly observed, looking at the yacht's name. 'He is into computers.'

The four women were welcomed on board *Megabyte* by a steward and shown into the saloon, where another steward offered them glasses of champagne.

'Wow!' Veronica exclaimed. 'It's a floating palace. Perhaps you ought to talk to him about some sponsorship for *Cream*.'

'Come on,' Cassie said to Polly, 'I'll introduce you.' The four women moved across the thick cream carpet of the main saloon towards Doug, who was standing by an ornate dining table laden with food and drink, talking to James.

'No sign of a Mrs Hampshire, is there?' Veronica whispered.

Cassie, looking round at the opulent furnishings, the original paintings on the walls, the priceless ornaments placed strategically, had to keep telling herself that she was on board a boat. It felt more like a very expensive and exclusive hotel.

But Veronica was right. With nothing personal or feminine on display, one couldn't help wondering about the existence of a Mrs Hampshire.

'All ready for your big adventure, Polly?' Doug asked, after Cassie had introduced her daughter.

Polly nodded.

'I can't wait. There's the trip to Plymouth tomorrow, a fortnight's final sorting out and then it's all go.'

'Are you going to Plymouth, too?' Doug asked Cassie.

'I'm planning on being there for the start of the race,' Cassie said. 'I'd hate to miss that. Otherwise, work here calls.'

'I've organised a berth down there for *Megabyte* for the weekend of the race start. I hope you'll all join me on board. Then we can go out to sea and give Polly a proper send-off.'

Cassie smiled her thanks at Doug. She had been wondering how she was going to manage to join the flotilla of boats that always followed competitors out to the line at the start of a big race. Going on Doug's boat, she'd certainly be seeing Polly off in some style.

'My daughter, Heidi,' he inclined his head in the direction of a tall dark-haired girl talking to Mai, 'will be there. She's the one you need to talk to, Polly, if you are interested in some additional sponsoring.'

'We could always do with extra support,' Polly said quickly. 'If you'll excuse me, I'll go and have a word.'

Doug turned to Cassie. 'You'll have to excuse me too. I think I'd better circulate. I'll see you later. Help yourself to food.' He waved his hand in the direction of the buffet.

'Not me, thanks,' James said. 'I have to be off. I'll see you tomorrow, Cassie. Two o'clock down on your landing stage, okay?'

'I'll be there,' Cassie promised.

Both Veronica and Mai looked at her as the two men left them, waiting for an explanation.

Cassie sighed.

'I'm going sailing with James tomorrow. And I'd appreciate it, Mai, if you don't mention it to Tom. I don't want him jumping to the wrong conclusions.'

15

Despite getting up at five o'clock the next morning, Cassie still missed saying goodbye to Dexter. According to the thank you note he left, he'd crept out of the house at 4.30 and hoped he hadn't disturbed anybody.

Thanks for having me. Tell Polly to have a good trip and I'll see her in Plymouth later. Dexter.

Drinking her coffee, Cassie thought about the day ahead. Polly was planning to leave at mid-morning, when the tide would help her out of the estuary, for her trip along the Channel down to Plymouth.

Cassie realised Tom was still having a hard time accepting that Polly was taking his place, but he was hiding his feelings well. He'd given his sister all the support and advice he could. And Cassie knew that mentally he'd be with her on every wave of the voyage.

He even managed to make it to the boatyard quay to see her off. Polly came across to kiss him goodbye as the crew for the trip began to untie the moorings.

'Thanks, bruv. I'll see you. Bye,' she said gruffly.

'I'm coming to see you off next week, so no goodbyes,' Tom said. 'I want to make sure you've got *Cream* set up properly before we let you loose on the Atlantic.'

'But...' Polly began, looking at Tom and then the wheelchair.

'But nothing. I'll be there,' Tom said, an edge to his voice.

As Polly motored the yacht down river, Tom sat watching until she was too far away to focus on. Mai came over to move him.

'I'm fine,' he said quietly. 'But please just leave me here for a bit.'

It was another half hour before he asked Mai to help him wheel himself back to the house.

Polly and the crew made good time getting to Plymouth. As they motored the yacht into Sutton harbour and slowly eased their way into a berth between other competitors, Polly could almost taste the excitement in the air.

As chair of the race organising committee, Dexter was on the quay to officially welcome her, and as soon as the yacht was secure, he jumped on board.

'I'll give you five minutes to phone Cassie and tell her you've arrived safely,' he said, 'and then I have a mountain of things to go through with you.'

Polly made them both a cup of coffee and they settled down to making sure everything was in order for *Holdsworth Clotted Cream* to take part in the race. As Dexter stamped the last official piece of paper, he looked at Polly.

'Before I take you to meet people, I have to say something.' He paused before continuing. 'You know you have only to ask for my help and I'll give it, but there may be times when it would be best for us not to appear too friendly. The other competitors...' Dexter hesitated again.

'Might read the wrong thing into one of the organisers being too friendly with a competitor,' Polly finished for him. 'I know the score, Dexter. Don't worry.'

'Thanks for understanding, Polly. I didn't want you to feel that I was suddenly keeping my distance.'

He gave her a helping hand as she jumped onto the quay.

'Right,' he said, 'let's go and introduce you to some of the other competitors.'

Dexter's mobile phone rang as they turned to walk along the quay.

'Sorry. Duty calls. I'm needed back in the office. Just go and introduce yourself.' And he was gone.

Polly stood undecided for a second or two before turning to climb back on board *Cream*. Dexter introducing her to the other skippers was one thing, doing it herself was more than a bit daunting. She'd meet everyone later.

'Hi, you must be Tom's little sister.'

She turned back to see a huge bear-like man standing on the deck of the next yacht. Polly recognised him immediately as the world-famous solo yachtsman she regarded as one of the heroes of the sport.

'Want to join us for coffee?' he asked, indicating a group on a yacht behind him.

Ten minutes later, sitting in the cockpit of the yacht, holding a mug of coffee, Polly wanted to pinch herself.

These fellow competitors of hers were all well-known sailors and they were treating her as one of them, her presence amongst them taken seriously.

They all knew Tom and were pleased to hear that he hoped to be in Plymouth for the start of the race.

As she moved to make room for yet another competitor to join them for coffee, she glanced across the quay and felt the happiness drain from her.

Walking briskly towards the yachts was Dexter – and at his side, a clearly angry naval officer. Polly's heart sank. What on earth was Sebastian doing here? He was supposed to be somewhere in the Med.

Looking at the rigid set of Sebastian's body as he and Dexter marched towards the boats, Polly jumped up nervously. If she wanted to avoid an angry confrontation in front of everyone, she'd have to move quickly.

'Thanks for the coffee, guys,' she said. 'I'll catch you all later.' She leaped onto the quay and hurried to meet the two men.

'Polly, I haven't issued an official pass for your fiancé because he assures me his visit is purely a short personal one. For security reasons, please see that he leaves the competitors' area by ten o'clock tonight.'

Dexter's tone left Polly in no doubt that he was not happy with her 'unofficial' visitor. He turned and walked away, leaving her to face Sebastian.

* * *

Cassie was back down on the landing stage in good time for her two o'clock meeting with James and nervously watched as he began to bring his small sailing yacht alongside to pick her up. Was she ready for this?

'I thought we'd go up to Stoke Gabriel. There's usually a bit of breeze up there. Do you want to steer whilst I get the sails up, or d'you want to do the sails?'

Cassie took the tiller from him and concentrated on steering the boat out through the mooring trots to the main Channel. She was used to this, doing it several times during the course of a working week with the yard's launch. It was easier to do something she was familiar with rather than raising sails, a job she hadn't done for years.

Going upriver to Stoke Gabriel, though, was different. She rarely ventured that far. There were too many sailing memories associated with it. She and Miles had often gone there for an afternoon's sailing. Now she was going with James.

She watched as he pulled up the mainsail and turned the outboard motor off as he hauled the front jib sail up the forestay.

When he joined her in the cockpit, she released the tiller and moved forward on deck, ready to do her bit with the sails when James changed course to take advantage of the fluctuating wind.

Without the noise of the outboard, she could hear the natural noises of the river – seagulls screeching, curlews on the mud banks calling their plaintive cries, the wind rustling through the trees. It was a perfect early May afternoon. Even the noise of sheep bleating in distant fields drifted down on the wind.

As James called, 'Ready to jibe,' Cassie automatically ducked, and the boom swung across, taking the mainsail to catch the wind now blowing from the east. And that was the start of an exhausting hour during which James really put her through her paces and Cassie rediscovered her love of sailing.

'Thank you so much, James,' she said as they motored back down river. 'I've really enjoyed this afternoon.'

'I told you, you never forget the basics. We must do it again. Fancy crewing for me in this year's regatta?'

'We'll see,' was all Cassie said.

Ghosts might have been slain, but it was too soon to commit herself to doing more of something that once before had been her life.

16

Polly, aware that everyone on board the yacht who had greeted her so warmly was watching curiously and could overhear them, began walking along the pontoon away towards the main yard before she greeted Sebastian. She kept her voice low when she did speak.

'What are you doing here, Sebastian?' she asked as calmly as she could. 'I thought you were on a hush-hush exercise?'

'We had to put back into Gibraltar for some essential repairs and I managed to wangle a two-day pass. Can we go somewhere and talk?'

'There's the marina café,' Polly said. 'I'm told they do a mean hot chocolate. While we walk, you can start explaining – beginning with why you told Dexter I was your fiancée.'

'It was the only way I could persuade him to let me through to the competitors' area to see you. He also seemed to think you wouldn't have time for visitors.'

'He was right. There's still loads to do.'

'You didn't seem very busy just now,' Sebastian pointed out peevishly.

'I only got here a couple of hours ago. The guys were just being friendly. So, what are you doing here?'

'I can't talk to you on the telephone. And you know I dislike long emails,' Sebastian said. 'I couldn't bear the thought of not seeing you for six months, Polly. I simply wanted to see and talk to you face to face before it's too late.'

'Too late?' They reached the café before Sebastian answered and he pushed open the door. Together they made their way to an empty table in a far corner.

'Too late?' Polly demanded as she sat down. 'For what?'

A smile fleetingly touched Sebastian's lips as he took her hand in his.

'Polly, I love you. I really don't want to come over all heavy-handed, but professional sailing is no sport for a woman.' He waved his hand in the general direction of the marina.

'I've come to ask you to withdraw from the race.'

Polly stared at him in disbelief, pulling her hand away.

'I'm frightened for you.'

Sebastian barely glanced at the waitress who arrived to take their order. 'Two hot chocolates, please.'

Polly took a deep breath. 'I'm frightened for me, too. But I've told you, Sebastian, I'm doing this race. And there's nothing you can say or do that will stop me.'

'You could at least have discussed it with me. I would have thought you'd care about how I felt.'

Polly sighed. 'I'm sorry. I should have talked to you about it. But everything happened so quickly after Tom's accident there wasn't time. Besides, I guess I knew what your reaction would be.'

She ran her hands through her hair distractedly.

'Anyway, we're having a discussion now. Only it's not a discussion, is it? You want me to do what you want. Not what I want. Can't you understand how important this race is to me?'

'It's too dangerous. Why can't you content yourself with doing smaller races? When we're married, we can go sailing together. I enjoy the sport as much as anyone. It's not as if I'm asking you to give up sailing altogether – just this race. Please, Polly – for my sake.'

'For your sake?' Polly repeated incredulously. 'Sebastian, this is the twenty-first century. Women make their own decisions, live their own lives.'

She took a deep breath.

'Who knows, the whole thing may scare me rigid and when I get back I won't want to go anywhere near another ocean-going yacht. I'll be ready to settle down, we'll get married and have lots of kids.'

Sebastian sighed.

'But what if it has the opposite effect? What if you want to do more and more competitive sailing? To tell you the truth, I'm not sure I want a wife who's prepared to take such risks.'

They both sat silently, each deep in their own thoughts, as the waitress put their hot chocolates on the table.

'Thank you,' Polly murmured. She had to try to make Sebastian back off. Why couldn't he accept that she was doing this race, come what may?

'Sebastian, I won't pull out of the race. There's too much at stake, both for me personally and because of the investment the yard has made in *Cream*.'

'Polly, I love you. Can't you see that I just don't want anything to happen to you? I couldn't bear to lose you.'

'There's more than one way to lose me, and emotional black-mail is a sure fire one,' Polly retorted sharply.

She stabbed her teaspoon into the cream on the top of her drink several times until it was dissolving into a disgusting-looking gooey brown mess and she pushed the mug away, before looking directly at Sebastian.

'I'm really sorry you've had a wasted journey. I can only suggest you return to your ship and concentrate on your own life and career whilst I'm away for the next month or so.' She paused. 'The separation will give us both time to really think about what we want.'

Sebastian shrugged his shoulders. 'So nothing I can say will make any difference?'

'No. It would have been nice to have sailed with your support and good wishes, but I'm going – with or without them.'

Sebastian put his hand lightly on her arm. 'I wish you all the luck in the world, Polly. I think you're going to need it.'

Without another word, he stood up and walked out of the café – and out of her life? Polly watched in silence, her emotions in turmoil.

17

Polly hadn't been exaggerating when she'd told Sebastian there was still a great deal to do before the race.

But it wasn't all work. As Dexter had predicted, there was a lot of partying and comradely banter in the evenings too.

The morning the official race engineer came to seal off *Holdsworth Clotted Cream*'s engine a few days before the race began, Dexter walked down the pontoon towards Polly.

'I wondered if you'd like a quick walk into Plymouth whilst Andrew does his stuff? We could have lunch.'

Polly gave him a brilliant smile. 'Yes, please. There are a few things I need, and I'd been wondering about going into town on my own but I...' Polly stopped. She'd been about to confess that she'd rather go with him but wasn't sure how he would react to that.

'I'll meet you by reception in, what?' Dexter glanced at his watch. 'Ten minutes okay?'

If Polly had expected Dexter to mention Sebastian's visit on the short walk into town, she was disappointed. She briefly contemplated apologising for the incident, then dismissed the idea. Dexter had probably already forgotten about it.

Once in town, the two of them separated, arranging to meet up again in half an hour, and she whizzed around, picking up some essential underwear and a couple of T-shirts. Finally, she treated herself to a lipstick and some perfume, justifying the purchase to herself as morale boosters.

Coming out of the large department store, she spotted Dexter emerging from the toy shop opposite, deep in conversation on his mobile.

He waved and crossed over, slipping his phone into his jacket pocket.

'Finished?'

Polly nodded. 'I've all the essentials for the Southern Ocean now!' She laughed.

'Well, here's another one.' He handed her a package.

'No, don't open it now,' he said quickly, as she was about to pull the wrapping paper off. 'Wait till we get back.'

'Thanks.'

Dexter smiled. 'I was going to treat us to lunch, but something urgent's cropped up at the marina. Will you have supper with me tonight instead?'

'I'd like that.'

Once back at the marina, Dexter made straight for his office and Polly walked along the pontoon towards the yacht, deep in thought. Dexter had been scrupulous in not treating her any different to any of the men competing and she respected that, but today's outing and now supper this evening seemed suddenly much more personal, as if he liked her and wanted to get to know her better. She hugged the present he'd given her and couldn't wait to open it.

Andrew, the engineer, was just about to leave *Cream* when she reached the boat.

'You're now officially engineless,' he said, pointing out the seals he'd placed on the engine and the prop. 'It's wind power only for the next few months.'

Once she was alone on board, Polly opened the present Dexter had given her and laughed before giving the black and white emperor penguin cuddly toy a welcome kiss on his yellow beak before placing him alongside her old Fred Bear. Fred Bear had been her companion from the day she was born. Miles had arrived at the hospital with the soft toy and gently placed it alongside her in the crib. Since then, he'd gone everywhere with her.

'Fred Bear, meet Nero. The three of us are going on an adventure.'

Early that evening, waiting for Dexter under a star-filled sky, Polly began to wonder if he'd forgotten their supper date. She smiled happily as she finally saw him heading towards her.

'Hi. Sorry I'm late. Thought we'd walk through the Barbican,' Dexter said. 'There's a good bistro down there.'

'Sounds great,' Polly said, picking up her fleece. 'Thank you for Nero.'

'Good name,' Dexter said.

As they walked, they saw the American and British flags flying either side of the Doric columns of the commemorative portico. Erected in 1934 to honour the Pilgrim Fathers' departure from England in the seventeenth century, it was close to where the original Mayflower Steps and quay would have been. Polly stopped and looked at the granite block placed in front of the portico with the words 'Mayflower 1620' inscribed on it.

'Dartmouth has a plaque, too, in Bayards Cove, where both the Mayflower and the Speedwell tied up,' she said. 'Shame they had to put into Plymouth later before abandoning the Speedwell as unseaworthy.'

Conversation, as they walked on, was about the race and boats in general. By the time they got to the bistro, Dexter had Polly laughing about an incident involving him and Tom a few years ago.

The laughter set the tone of the evening, which passed all too quickly for Polly. It was gone midnight when they arrived back at the marina. Dexter jumped down into the cockpit, turned to take Polly's hand and helped her back on board *Cream*.

'Would you like a coffee?' Polly asked, suddenly feeling shy at their closeness.

Dexter shook his head. 'No, thanks. But I do want to ask you something.'

Polly waited.

'Sebastian called you his fiancée the other day. Is that true? You told me you weren't, so why does he think you are?' he asked quietly.

'No, I'm not engaged to Sebastian, as much as he wants me to be. It's never going to happen,' Polly said, realising that she'd unconsciously always known that Sebastian wasn't the man for her.

'In that case, I don't have to feel guilty about kissing you goodnight after a lovely evening.' He gathered her into his arms and, feeling her respond, gave her a gentle goodnight kiss, before releasing her.

'I'll see you tomorrow.' Turning, he stepped out of the cockpit and strode away down the pontoon.

18

Back at the yard, life settled down into a new routine now that all the preparation and urgency had dissipated. To her surprise, Cassie found she was missing the excited buzz of the last few weeks, even though she was busy catching up on some of the things that had inevitably been pushed to one side.

All the new strengthened handrails were in situ on the barge and Veronica had helped Mai finish the decorating. There were just two weeks before the first clients for the sailing school were due.

The fact they still didn't have an instructor was a problem that Cassie knew she'd have to tackle once Polly had set sail. Having proved to herself she still had the basic skills, she really had no choice but to agree to do the teaching until Tom was up and about again. Dinghy sailing qualifications never expired apparently, according to what she'd read online, but she'd need to organise a medical.

Tom had completely taken over the organisational side of the round-the-world race for Polly and everything seemed to be running smoothly. Sitting in his wheelchair at the computer, he was totally engrossed now in the background organisation of getting *Cream*, with Polly at the helm instead of him, safely around the world.

Cassie knew he and Mai were desperate to get back to River View, but even when he was out of the wheelchair and on crutches, it would be weeks before he could manage the spiral staircase in the cottage. In the meantime, he and Mai were making the best of living in Cassie's rearranged sitting room.

As the weekend of the race approached, the main discussion at the yard concerned Tom. He was determined to go to Plymouth to see Polly off and badgered the doctor for permission until he finally said yes.

Doug had offered Tom and Mai a berth on *Megabyte* for the weekend, which Mai had regretfully turned down on his behalf but had accepted the offer of a place on board for the beginning of the race. Both she and Tom realised he could cope on board for a few hours, but any longer would pose problems. But at least he'd be there to see *Holdsworth Clotted Cream* sail over the start line. Doug assured both Mai and Cassie there wouldn't be a problem getting Tom and his wheelchair on board when they raised the subject. 'Trust me,' he'd said. 'We'll get him on board.'

Cassie and Veronica had gratefully accepted Doug's offer of a cabin for the night before the race when Doug told them he planned to hold a small good luck party for Polly. After seeing Polly cross the start, they would drive back to the boatyard together on Saturday afternoon or evening. Mingled in with her apprehension about what Polly might face in the coming months, Cassie was looking forward to the weekend, to spending time with Polly before she left on her big adventure.

James rang on Friday afternoon, just before Cassie and Veronica were preparing to leave.

'I was hoping to come up and see you before you left,' he said to Cassie. 'But I've been delayed. So, have a good weekend, give Polly my love and wish her good luck from me. And I'll see you when you get back.'

'Come for supper on Sunday evening,' Cassie said. 'If you're not on duty and are free.'

'I'll be there, thanks, Cassie. Drive carefully.'

* * *

Cassie was quiet as she drove along the A38 dual carriageway down to Plymouth, and Veronica gave her a few anxious glances before she said what was on her mind.

'I know you won't stop worrying about Polly until she's home again but once we've wished her bon voyage and seen her set off, you need to concentrate on you – living the best life you can for you.'

'I know you're right,' Cassie sighed. 'And I will try, but it is hard not to worry.' She concentrated on negotiating the numerous lanes of traffic at the Marsh Mills roundabout before she spoke again. 'I've been thinking, ever since you said you were looking forward to living alone for the first time ever, that maybe it's something I need to do too. I was wondering about suggesting I swap homes with Tom and Mai. Tom is going to be limited in what he can do for a few weeks more, and when the baby arrives, the cottage isn't big enough anyway. D'you think they'd like the idea?'

'I think they'll jump at the suggestion,' Veronica said. 'If you're sure that's what you want.'

Cassie nodded. 'If nothing else, it will give me space and more time away from everyone to work out exactly what I do want. Now, let's talk about Glebe House. Has your offer been accepted yet?'

'No. The agent says the owners are considering it and he'll get back to me when he hears. I think they're just waiting to see if they get a better offer. Fingers crossed gazumping is no longer a thing.' And the subject of the cottage was dropped after Veronica had had a quick moan about the stress of buying a new home.

By the time they reached the marina, Cassie was feeling more settled in herself and happier about suggesting the plan to Tom and Mai.

The part of the marina where all the yachts taking part in the Eco Global Challenge were berthed was heaving with people when Cassie and Veronica arrived. However, with the VIP passes that Dexter had arranged, they had no difficulty parking and then finding their way to *Megabyte*'s mooring in a separate part of the marina. Doug welcomed them on board and his daughter, Heidi, showed them to their cabin.

'As you know, Dad's arranged a small party for tonight,' she told them as she opened the cabin door. 'He is, of course, hoping you're both free to join us.' A remark instantly countered when she continued, looking directly at Cassie as she spoke. 'But if you've made other arrangements, don't worry if you can't make it,' and Heidi gave them both a false smile.

To Cassie, the unspoken words 'you won't be missed' seemed to hang in the air but Veronica seemed unaware of the atmosphere.

'That would be lovely, I'll definitely be there,' Veronica said, but Cassie didn't commit herself. She wanted to find out what Polly was doing first.

As Heidi closed the door behind her, Cassie and Veronica looked around the twin-bed cabin with its luxurious fittings and the marble and gold bathroom. 'How the other half live,' Veronica said. 'So pleased we packed our glad rags for this evening. You did, didn't you?'

Cassie shrugged. 'Posh white jeans and a floaty top will have to do.' She watched as Veronica began to unpack her suitcase. 'Do you mind if I go and find Polly straight away?'

'Of course not,' and Veronica waved her hand. 'Go. I'll catch you later.'

19

As Cassie made her way through the crowded marina, the excitement all around was palpable. People jostled each other on the pontoons, small children sat on shoulders to get a view of the boats, jazzy music drifted on the air. The razzamatazz of a lively international event had taken over.

Polly was saying goodbye to a cameraman and a TV presenter who had been interviewing her for one of the local West Country channels when Cassie reached *Holdsworth Clotted Cream*.

'Hi, Mum,' Polly called out. 'Come on board and I'll make you a coffee. Today has been crazy. So many international reporters wanting to talk to me. I can hardly believe they're interested in me.'

Cassie looked around the sparse cabin that was to be Polly's home for the next six months, trying to imprint every little detail in her memory so she'd be able to picture it all when she thought about Polly in the coming weeks.

By necessity, the cabin was functional and business-like, and Cassie smiled as she saw the pictures and mementoes of home Polly had pinned around the chart table, together with lots of good luck cards and messages.

She couldn't help laughing when she peered at Polly's sleeping bunk and saw Fred Bear's head peeping out of the sleeping bag. Today he had a companion of his own. One Cassie had never seen before. A cuddly black and white emperor penguin was alongside him in the sleeping bag, its yellow beak gently nudging Fred Bear's ragged ear.

Cassie picked up the toy.

'Love the penguin. Where d'you get him?'

'Dexter gave him to me as a good luck token. He's called Nero,' Polly said. 'Isn't he gorgeous?'

'A very handsome fellow,' Cassie agreed. She smiled as she replaced Nero alongside Fred Bear in the sleeping bag. What a lovely gesture from Dexter.

'Have you heard from Sebastian since his visit?' she asked quietly.

'Not a word. Not even one of his reproachful emails.'

'He's just worried about you, Polly.' Cassie looked at her daughter. 'He rang me, you know – after he left you.'

'He shouldn't have done that,' Polly said crossly. 'And?'

'He was very upset. He said you didn't love him enough to do what he asked. I did try to tell him that loving someone doesn't give you control over them.'

'What did he say to that?'

'Muttered something about me sounding like you and hung up.'

There was a short silence.

'Did you ever ask Dad to stop sailing?' Polly asked eventually.

'No. It was his life.'

'Did Dad ever ask you to give up something he didn't approve of?'

Cassie shook her head. 'He never had cause to. I've never been the adventurous type. I just wanted to be with him.'

'Would you if he'd asked?' Polly persisted.

'I don't know, love. It was a long time ago. Things, attitudes were different.' Cassie paused. Now was not the time to tell Polly that she'd loved Miles so much she'd have done anything he asked.

'You're doing what you want to do, Polly. Give it your best and enjoy it. Put all thoughts of Sebastian and marriage out of your mind. There will be plenty of time for that afterwards.'

'Mum, I need to tell you something in case...' She hesitated. 'Sebastian's ring is in the top drawer of the cupboard in my room. Would you make sure he gets it back if...?'

Cassie interrupted quickly. She didn't want that thought put into words. It would be tantamount to sitting the devil on the wall, as her own mother would have said. She pulled Polly quickly to her and gave her a big hug.

'Of course, love. But nothing is going to happen. You're going to sail around the world and come back a heroine.'

Cassie gave Polly another tight squeeze before releasing her. 'Are you going to the party on *Megabyte* this evening?'

'I've promised Doug I will put in an appearance for a short time because of his generous extra sponsorship money, but I'm planning an early night and no hangover.'

'Wise decision,' Cassie said. 'I'll see you there.' As she turned to go, her eyes caught sight of a large white envelope resting against one of the inboard computer screens. 'Does that want posting? I can pop it into the box on the way back to the other side of the marina.'

Polly followed her gaze and picked up the envelope. 'No, you're fine. It's just something for Dexter. I'll give it to him next time I see him.'

* * *

When Cassie and Veronica made their way up to the yacht's saloon an hour or two later, the party was already in full swing. Doug immediately made his way over to them, Heidi at his side, limpet-like, and a steward following with the obligatory tray of champagne – pink, this time. Sipping her drink, Cassie looked around for Polly but there was no sign of her, and she wondered whether her daughter had been and gone already. She'd stay for another ten minutes and then leave to go and find her.

Just as she turned to ask Doug if she'd missed her, Polly arrived and made her way over to them.

'Hi, Doug, Mum. Sorry I'm late. Some last-minute stuff to go through with Dexter.' She shook her head at the offer of a glass of champagne. 'Please may I have a juice? Need to keep a clear head for the morning.'

'Of course,' Doug said. 'I should have thought. Heidi, can you organise that, please? The stewards are all busy circulating.'

Heidi turned away without a word.

'Ready for your big adventure, then, Polly?' Doug asked.

'As ready as I ever will be, I guess,' Polly said, looking at Cassie. 'Thanks to a lot of help from everybody.'

'Weather forecast is good, the wind is set to be a strong five or six, I gather,' Doug said. 'Should be a great start to the race tomorrow.'

Heidi returned with a glass of orange juice. 'Here,' and she thrust it in Polly's direction.

'Thank you,' Polly said, with a puzzled look at her rudeness.

Doug frowned at his daughter's manners but before he could say anything, she'd moved away.

Cassie finished her drink and refused another one while she waited for Polly to drink her juice. She could tell that Polly didn't want to be at this party any more than she did, and she was hoping they could both leave and spend some precious moments alone together. In the end, it was another twenty minutes before Polly was able to say her goodbyes to Doug. Cassie made her excuses too, saying she was going to walk back to the yacht with her and she'd be back in a bit.

As they walked, Cassie put her arm around her daughter's shoulder and Polly responded by putting her own arm around Cassie's waist. Neither of them spoke, the shared contact sent the unspoken message of filial love that united them both. Cassie knew it would be a few months before she would be able to hug Polly again and she bit her lip in an effort to smother a sad sigh.

Once back at *Cream*, they gave each other a tight hug. 'Go and get some sleep,' Cassie said. 'You've got some exciting times ahead of you.' Polly jumped into the cockpit.

'I love you, Mum.'

'I love you too. Take care.' And Cassie turned and walked back along the pontoon, managing to keep the tears of worry at bay until she was far enough away for Polly to be unable to see her shaking shoulders.

20

Saturday morning – race day – dawned grey but dry. A brisk easterly breeze was blowing, which promised good sailing for the yachts as they crossed the start line.

Cassie, standing on *Megabyte*'s deck early that morning, sleepily took in the activity all around her. Having promised Bill a full report of the weekend, she was determined to soak up the atmosphere.

Just then, Veronica appeared at her side.

'Compliments of the chef. Breakfast will be on the upper deck in five minutes, madam,' she said, as she handed Cassie a welcome mug of tea. 'There was a lot of champagne consumed last night. Doug sure knows how to entertain. He's good company too. I'm guessing you haven't got a headache like me, as you left early with Polly. Doug covered his frustration over your absence quite well, considering how disappointed he actually was,' Veronica said, looking at her. 'Mind you, I think Heidi was happy. Need to watch your back with that one. She's a real possessive daddy's girl and woe betide any woman Doug decides he likes.'

Cassie sipped her tea. 'I was a bit emotional after I left Polly and didn't feel up to partying and being sociable with anyone. Certainly not up to facing Heidi, but she needn't worry about me. Doug is way out of my league, even if I was interested, which I'm not.'

'Are you going out with Polly as she's towed out?' Veronica asked.

Cassie shook her head.

'No. Polly did suggest I could if I wanted to go out with the crew to the start, but I'm too much of a coward. Besides, I hate crying in public.' She took a deep breath. 'We said our goodbyes late last night.'

There was a short silence before Cassie pointed along the quay. 'There's Tom and Mai. Doug said they were arriving early and breakfasting on board.' She waved to her son and daughter-in-law.

Getting Tom and his wheelchair on board proved more difficult than Doug had anticipated, but Dexter appeared in the nick of time. His extra strength was enough to propel Tom up the extra-wide steep gangplank Doug had provided.

'Thanks, mate,' Tom said gratefully. 'Have you seen Polly this morning?'

Dexter nodded. 'She's fine and raring to go. The shore crew are all on board, ready for the tow out. It's all systems go.'

Declining the offer to join them for breakfast, Dexter took his leave.

'I've to shepherd some VIPs to the launch in about ten minutes,' he explained.

As he turned to run down the gangway, he smiled at Cassie.

'Don't spend the next weeks worrying. Polly will be okay. She'll be phoning you from Cape Town before you know it.'

While they were having breakfast, the crew slipped *Megabyte* from her moorings and slowly they began to make their way, with the flotilla of boats that was already building up, out into Plymouth Sound.

Inevitably Cassie found her thoughts turning to the past. The times she'd been on board small motorboats following Miles out to start lines for various races. The general atmosphere of heightened excitement swirling around like ozone in the air. The fear in the pit of her own stomach she tried to hide from Miles, not wanting him to know how afraid she was for him. This morning, that fear was back for Polly. She took a deep breath, determined to keep it well hidden and to join in the air of adventure that was almost touchable as the competing boats gathered.

As *Megabyte*'s hull cut her way through the rough water, there was an air of anticipation on board despite the uncomfortable motion of the choppy water. The large crowd of boats, intent on giving the racing fleet a good send-off, were churning the sea into a jumble of criss-crossed swells, wakes and waves. Standing on *Megabyte*'s deck, Cassie saw *Holdsworth Clotted Cream* being towed out to join the other boats and Polly gave them an excited wave.

For Cassie, one of the worst moments came when the support boat drew up alongside *Holdsworth Clotted Cream* and she saw the crew all hugging Polly goodbye, before climbing over the rails and leaving her on board alone to hoist the sails. Surreptitiously, Cassie wiped a tear away with the back of her hand and hoped that nobody had noticed.

As the time drew nearer for the start of the race, everybody watched as the boats did some tactical sailing in a bid to capture a good position in the start zone. Every skipper wanted to be first over the line when the starting gun was fired.

With only ten minutes to go now, Cassie knew that nothing would stop Polly from crossing the start line. Her fear leapt from the pit of her stomach into her throat and she watched with mounting anxiety as Polly manoeuvred the yacht into what she hoped would be a good position for the start.

The split-second silence that followed the firing of the start gun was drowned by the raucous sound of hundreds of foghorns and hooters being blasted simultaneously. Cassie held her breath, watching Polly tack, come round and race over the start line in third position.

'Yes!' Tom shouted, his fist striking the air with delight. 'Good start. Well done, Polly. Proud of you, sis.'

Then his voice broke and a sob almost escaped his lips. He was delighted for his sister. But he couldn't help the bitter disappointment that suddenly welled up inside him. It should have been him sailing out on the adventure of a lifetime.

He turned away, unable to watch as the fleet sailed off, rapidly becoming mere specks in the distance.

'Be careful, Polly, be careful, Polly.' Cassie closed her eyes and muttered the words over and over again to herself.

'Cassie – champagne to celebrate Polly's good start?'

Startled out of her reverie, Cassie turned and accepted the glass Doug was offering her. As she took it from him, a mobile phone began to ring.

Doug gave the toast. 'To Polly and *Holdsworth Clotted Cream*. Safe race,' and everybody raised their glasses.

Cassie had barely taken a sip when Tom said, 'Text message for you, Mum,' and he handed her his mobile phone.

Just to say thanks Mum. Couldn't be doing this without your blessing. Have left u a present with Dexter. Love u lots Polly. xxx

Cassie, despite her promise to herself not to cry in public, promptly burst into tears. Veronica was instantly at her side, a comforting arm around her shoulders.

'Hard not to be afraid for her, but you have to trust in her abilities. She wouldn't have been allowed to take part if those in charge weren't confident that she was capable.' Veronica squeezed her shoulders. 'My goddaughter is made of strong stuff. She'll be fine.'

* * *

Because of the large number of boats making their way back into Plymouth after the start of the race, it was a couple of hours before the *Megabyte* crew were able to tie up the motor-yacht at her mooring.

Tom was clearly tired and Cassie was relieved to see Dexter waiting on the quay, ready to give them a hand getting him ashore, which thankfully was easier than getting him on board had been earlier in the day.

Once Tom and Mai had left, Cassie and Veronica said their thanks and goodbyes to Doug and Heidi and made their way to the car.

'Would you like me to drive?' Veronica asked.

'No. I'm fine, thanks,' Cassie said. 'I'm quite looking forward to the journey back. Thought we might stop for supper – maybe somewhere in Kingsbridge?'

'Good idea.'

It was nearly ten o'clock when Cassie turned onto the lane that ran down to the boatyard. She'd barely gone a couple of metres when her headlights caught something at the side of the road and she slammed the brakes on.

'There's something in the hedge. It looked like a body.'

Frightened, Cassie and Veronica looked at each other. The boatyard was still a mile or so down the track. Should they go for help or investigate it themselves?

Winding the car window down a fraction, Cassie listened to the night sounds, trying to hear if there was anybody about. An owl hooted in the distance. Nothing out of the ordinary.

Cassie slowly backed the car up until the headlights illuminated the hedge at the right place.

She and Veronica got out of the car and cautiously made their way towards the 'body'. Curled up in the hedge, eyes watching them fearfully, was a dog. As they approached, it slowly got to its feet, all the while regarding them uncertainly with soft brown eyes.

Both Cassie and Veronica breathed a sigh of relief. They could cope with this.

'Poor old thing,' Cassie said, stretching out a hand to gently stroke the dog. 'It's a bitch. Do you think she's been hit by a car?'

'I don't think so,' Veronica said, carefully running her hands over the dog's body. 'I think she's either been dumped or she's a stray. She's terribly thin.'

'Come on, let's get her into the car,' Cassie said. 'We can't leave her here. I'll take her home for the night and call the RSPCA tomorrow.'

The dog looked at Cassie and a tongue cautiously licked her hand. It was as if she sensed this human was to be her saviour.

Once back home, Cassie opened a tin of stewing steak, which the dog wolfed down, before having a long drink from the bowl of water Cassie had put down for her.

The dog's eyes followed her every movement and, as Cassie knelt down to make her up a bed out of some old cushions, she felt her ear being gently nuzzled.

'Hey, that tickles,' Cassie laughed.

The dog leaned against her, and Cassie absently stroked the soft head.

'That should do you for the night,' she said finally. 'I'll see you in the morning. Everything is going to be all right. I'll make sure you go to a good home.'

The dog's eyes looked trustingly into Cassie's and she gave a very slight wag of her tail before heaving a deep sigh and settling on the cushions.

Once in bed, Cassie said a prayer for Polly's safety, turned off the light and went to sleep.

In her dreams that night, she was running alongside the river, trying to catch an elusive figure in the distance. A familiar-looking dog bounded happily at her side.

When she woke in the morning, the dog was curled up alongside her feet.

21

'What are you going to call her?' Veronica asked the next morning when she brought Cassie a cup of tea and saw the dog on the bed.

'I'm not keeping her,' Cassie said. 'First thing this morning, I'll ring round and see if anyone's reported her missing. If not, I'll take her to the dog sanctuary across town.'

The dog turned, looking up at the sound of Cassie's voice, before deliberately snuggling in closer and uttering a deep sigh.

'Oh, yes?' Veronica laughed.

'She can't stay here,' Cassie said. 'It's out of the question.'

'Why?' Veronica asked. 'You like dogs – and the feeling is clearly mutual! At least think about it.'

Three hours later, Cassie finally put the phone down, having drawn a blank with all the vets, police and animal sanctuaries in the area. Nobody within a fifty-mile radius had any record of what appeared be a brown lurcher cross bitch being reported missing.

Cassie looked across the room to where the dog was stretched out, sleeping peacefully alongside Tom as he worked on the computer. As Cassie watched her, she opened her eyes, her gaze full of trust.

'Why don't you go and get some fresh air?' Tom suggested. 'Have a think. Take the dog.'

Cassie realised he'd studiously avoided saying the word 'walk', but the dog was on her feet, looking at her expectantly.

'I could do with some fresh air to clear my head,' Cassie said. 'I'll get some rope from the boatyard to use as a lead.'

Once the dog was on the lead and trotting along happily at her side, Cassie took the short cut down from the boatyard to the river path. The dog waited patiently as she unlocked the gate in the perimeter fence, before bounding excitedly down to the river's edge as soon as Cassie took the rope off.

'Come on, girl, this way.' Cassie began to walk upstream.

Walking past River View, Cassie wondered when Tom and Mai would be able to move back in. It would be several weeks yet, she suspected. Veronica would probably have moved on too before Tom and Mai returned to the cottage. When they all moved out, she'd be on her own. She couldn't even count on Polly wanting to live at home again once the race was over.

Cassie sighed. Everybody's lives were changing, and she was determined not to miss the boat this time.

The idea of swapping homes with Tom and Mai was still lurking in the back of her mind. She needed to talk to them at some point soon before dismissing the idea altogether.

A heron, keeping a rock-like solitary vigil at the water's edge, took off over the river with a deceptively graceful slow flapping of its large wings, startling both Cassie and the dog by its previously unseen presence.

There were a few boats on the river, including James at the helm of the Harbour Master's official launch. He waved as he passed and shouted a greeting that was mainly carried away on the wind, but she caught the word 'tonight' and remembered she'd invited him to dinner that evening.

As she waved back, she glanced down at the dog, who was gently nuzzling her hand.

'What is it, girl?' Cassie said, stroking her. 'I like you too. We're going to have to find you a proper name, aren't we? Can't keep calling you "the dog" or "girl", can we?'

Realising what she'd just said, Cassie laughed out loud. Her subconscious had made the decision while she walked. The dog was staying.

'So, how about Willow?' She shook her head. 'No. Tess? Honey?'

Undecided, Cassie studied the dog for several minutes before inspiration struck.

'I know. You were on your own when I found you, and Polly has gone off alone. I'm going to call you Solo.'

Solo looked at her, ears cocked, licked her hand as if in agreement and then bounded off to chase an imaginary rabbit.

'Come on, Solo. Time to go home,' and together they turned and began to make their way back along the river path.

When they finally returned to the boatyard, Doug was coming out of the office.

'Hello,' he greeted Cassie. 'I've been having a word with Bill about doing some maintenance work on *Megabyte* whilst I'm away.' He glanced at her.

'I was hoping you'd have dinner with me one evening, but I'm afraid it will have to wait until I get back from Scotland.'

'I'll look forward to that,' Cassie said. 'When do you leave?'

'First thing in the morning. I'll be away two or three weeks.'

'Why don't you join us for dinner tonight?' Cassie said impulsively. 'It would give me a chance to say thank you for your generous hospitality in Plymouth. Half past seven okay?'

'Perfect. I'll see you then, thank you,' Doug said.

Tom was in the sitting-cum-operations room and Mai was in the kitchen when Cassie got back to the house.

'Something smells good. Is it for dinner this evening?' Cassie said. 'Can I do anything? Will there be enough? I seem to have asked both James and Doug to join us – Doug as a small thank you for yesterday and James has also been terribly kind and helpful with everything.'

'I've made a big saucepan of spaghetti Bolognese,' Mai said. 'If we do extra pasta, there should be enough.'

'It's turning into quite a party,' Tom said. 'Dexter rang to say he'd call in on his way back to Bristol. I invited him for dinner too – and offered him a bed for the night.'

'Any news from Polly?' Cassie asked.

'Here,' Tom said, holding out a piece of paper. 'She sent an email, which I've printed out. I thought you might want to keep them.'

'Good idea,' Cassie said, taking the printout.

First twenty-four hours at sea have been fine. We are well on our way round the Finistere coast. Weather forecast is reasonable, so hopefully it won't be too rough. Love Polly. xxx

'Another day or two and she'll be down around the Azores, won't she?' Cassie said thoughtfully.

Tom glanced at her, his expression one of concern. He knew only too well how his mother felt about that particular stretch of ocean.

When Dexter arrived that afternoon, he was full of the latest news about the race.

'Polly is fine,' he reassured Cassie, before telling them the story of an unfortunate competitor who'd got caught in the edge of a weather system off the coast of France and lost his mast.

'He's had to put into a French port for repairs. Hopefully he'll be able to rejoin the fleet next week and still make it to Cape Town within the time limit,' Dexter said.

'Luckily, another competitor has a similar mast in a yard in Cowes, which he offered as soon as he heard the news. I've been working on the logistics of getting it over to France quickly, that's why I'm so late getting here today.'

James and Doug arrived together and the seven of them settled into a good-humoured evening with much laughter and lively conversation. In a pause between courses, Dexter asked how bookings for the barge were going.

'Trickling in nicely,' Tom said. 'Only problem is we still haven't found an instructor yet.' He glanced at his mother.

'I've put an ad on the Yacht Club notice board and James is asking around,' Cassie said defensively. 'Somebody will turn up. But if they don't...' She paused. 'I'll do it.'

'Thanks, Mum,' Tom said gratefully. 'Problem solved.'

'Um, actually, I don't think it is. Depends when the first booking is,' Dexter said unexpectedly. 'Cassie, I'm sorry, I should have given you this earlier.' He handed her the large white envelope.

'This is the envelope I saw on *Cream*,' Cassie said.

Dexter nodded. 'It's the present Polly asked me to give you.'

'I'd forgotten all about that,' Cassie said, slitting open the envelope. 'D'you know what it is?'

Dexter nodded. 'I helped arrange it.'

Cassie was speechless as she took a hotel brochure and a return ticket to Cape Town out of the envelope.

'Polly would like you to be on the quay when she sails in,' Dexter said. 'She also reckoned you'd quite like it too! The hotel booking is for a week.'

Cassie was stunned.

'But I can't go. I've just agreed to do the dinghy instructing. And what about Solo? And things here?'

'I think I can help with the sailing,' Doug offered. 'One of my crew on *Megabyte* is a qualified dinghy instructor. I'd be more than happy for him to help out whilst you're in South Africa.'

'And I'll still be here,' Veronica said. 'I can keep everyone fed and watered and fill in for you wherever I'm needed.'

'Don't worry about Solo. Tom and I will take care of her until you get back,' Mai put in.

'There you go, Mum. No excuses. In a couple of weeks' time, you can jet off to Cape Town to welcome Polly ashore,' Tom said.

22

'Jibe ho,' Cassie shouted from her position at the tiller. The two teenagers ducked and made for the other side of the dinghy as the boom swung the mainsail across and the small boat changed tack.

'Good. Well done. Now, I think it's Wayne's turn to helm and steer us back to the barge.'

Just three days into their holiday, the boys were getting the hang of sailing. Cassie was pleased with the way they'd responded to her lessons and quietly proud of herself.

The barge had opened for business over the late May Bank Holiday and everything was going well. To Cassie's unspoken relief, the party of five teenagers had cancelled due to family problems and the Rogers family had taken their place at the last minute, with just the two boys needing tuition.

Wayne and Terry's parents loved their accommodation on board and were delighted with the freedom that the boys' sailing lessons gave them.

After Wayne had brought the dinghy gently alongside the barge to the enthusiastic hand-clapping of his proud parents, Cassie had a word with Mai. She was in the small galley, preparing dinner for the guests.

'How are you feeling? Are you coping all right with the cooking?'

'I'm fine. Thank goodness the sickness has gone – unless I try to fry onions! By the way, James called. Something about next week?'

'He's been trying to get tickets for a concert. I'll ring him when I get indoors.'

When Cassie got back to the house, Tom was busy on the computer, Solo lying at his feet, her favourite place when Cassie wasn't around. The moment she spotted her mistress, though, Solo jumped up and gave her an enthusiastic welcome.

'Has James left a message for me, Tom?' Cassie asked.

'He just wanted you to know he's got the tickets for the concert next Thursday.'

'I leave on Friday morning,' Cassie said. 'I was hoping to spend the evening here with you and Mai.'

'Look on it as an early start to your holiday. We'll have a family evening on Wednesday.'

Tom changed the subject.

'Polly's just posted a copy of her first article for the newspaper on the website. It's good.' He sounded surprised.

'You should have more faith in your sister,' Cassie said. 'How close to the Canaries is she now?'

'Almost there. She'll be picking up the Trade Winds any day now on her way down to the Equator.'

Involuntarily, Cassie found herself letting a deep breath go. One that she hadn't been aware she was holding. Polly was safely past the Azores. The dreaded anniversary of Miles's disappearance had come and gone with nothing untoward to mark it. She could relax slightly.

'If there's nothing I can help you with, I think I'll take Solo for a quick walk before dinner. Honestly, it's years since I've had so much exercise. It must be good for me, I suppose.'

'If you're going along the river path, could you pop into River View and pick up a couple of paperbacks for me, please? They're on the table by the settee,' Tom asked. 'I keep forgetting to ask Mai. Here's the key,' and he handed her the key to the cottage front door. 'Thanks. And if you see my AirPods, that would be great too.'

Ten minutes later, Cassie let herself into the cottage and stood for a moment, surveying the sitting room. Tom and Mai hadn't had a chance to do much decorating since they moved in after their wedding and the furniture wasn't anything special. A comfortable settee and a couple of armchairs, a bookcase that also held the TV and a disc player, a small oak gate-leg table and a cream rug on the wooden floor was all there was room for, but the room had a good feel to it. Cassie nodded to herself. She could see herself living here.

'Reckon we'll make enough room for a basket in here, Solo? Although the amount of time you spend on my bed or the settee, I'm not sure you really need one.' The dog looked at her and nuzzled her hand as though saying 'thank you'. Cassie stroked Solo's head and smiled before she crossed over to the table and picked up both the paperbacks and Tom's AirPods. As she left, she double-checked the door was locked and secure.

When she got back to the house, Tom and Mai were deep in conversation with an excited Veronica.

'They've finally accepted my offer for Glebe House. No date for completion yet, but the solicitor reckons about ten weeks, less if I'm lucky.'

'I'm so pleased for you,' Cassie said. 'We'll miss having you here but you'll be a lot closer than you've been for years. Glebe House is going to be a lovely home for you.'

'There are a couple of furniture auctions coming up next

month. Will you come with me when you get back from Cape Town?' Veronica asked.

'Yes, try and stop me. I love auctions. Just let me know the dates.'

'Oh, I'm so looking forward to getting to grips with Glebe House. It's going to be such fun decorating and furnishing.' Veronica smiled happily.

* * *

Extract from Polly's private journal

Wednesday, 1 June

Have decided to try and keep a semi-regular private journal as well as my official log but, five days into the race, this is the first opportunity I've had to write it up, although I have kept the official log up to date.

Sailing with the fleet out of Plymouth Sound was fantastic. So many people had come to see us off. I felt very insignificant but proud to be a part of the whole pageant. Waving goodbye was very emotional, but I managed to keep the tears at bay until nobody could see me.

I felt so sorry for Tom. *Cream* is his boat, after all. It must have been difficult for him, seeing me take off in a race that he should have been doing.

Getting down channel was hair-raising – there was so much traffic in the shipping lanes, but at least we got past The Lizard in daylight.

There were three of us setting much the same course the first afternoon and evening and we all did a lot of tactical sailing. Overnight, though, we all altered our courses slightly and by dawn I was alone.

By the time I got to the west coast of Finistere, the wind had increased as a front came through. It certainly lived up to its forecast reputation – freezing wind and fine driving rain. I know, though, I'll encounter worse conditions down in the Southern Ocean, so I'd better get used to it.

Very excited by the telephone conversation with Race HQ this morning. They told me I'm currently lying in second position. I know, I know, it's early days but I'm pleased that I chose the right overnight course.

I've had several emails since setting sail – one from Mum, thanking me for the ticket and looking forward to seeing me in Cape Town. I'm so happy that she's going to be there.

Dexter sent me an email too, telling me to take care and sail safely. He promised he'd be waiting with Mum in South Africa. Still no word from Sebastian, but I didn't really expect to hear. I will email him in a few days just to see how he and his bruised ego are. Whatever happens, I need to try and keep things on a reasonably friendly footing.

We came through the front overnight and this morning I was rewarded with a group of dolphins leaping and swimming and joyfully escorting us for a few miles.

Oh, I do so love being at sea.

Tonight the weather is much calmer and everything on board is fine. The moon is out and the stars are shining. Ed Sheeran is playing on the iPod and I'm going to have a bowl of pasta and the last of my bananas for supper before having a snooze in the cuddy. I set the timer to wake me every fifteen minutes but usually wake by myself before it goes off.

Tomorrow I'll be that much nearer to the Azores. I'm trying not to think about Dad, but every now and again a shudder goes through me when the waves smack unexpectedly noisily against the hull or some debris brushes past.

I'll be glad when I'm further down off the coast of Africa.
Hopefully I'll have left the ghosts behind by then.

* * *

The next couple of weeks were busy ones for everyone in the
boatyard. Tom, although frustrated with his lack of mobility was
relishing his role liaising with Polly and Race HQ, not that he'd ever
admit it, of course. In between giving sailing lessons and keeping
everything up to date in the chandlery, Cassie had to organise
things for when she was away and – a major problem – find enough
clothes for her holiday.

Veronica was a great help, not only offering to drive her to the
station, but raiding her own wardrobe and lending Cassie a few
choice items. With socialising being low on her list for so many
years, her wardrobe consisted mainly of well-worn jeans and tops,
apart from a dress or two.

Two days before Cassie left, Mai took Tom to the hospital,
where the plaster on his left leg was removed. It would be another
month before the brace on his right leg would be eased off. In the
meantime, he was to try to do some physio with his left.

Finally, everything was done and it was the day before Cassie
flew out to South Africa. Her suitcase was packed, with the exception of her only posh dress, which would go in after tonight's
concert with James.

Gazing critically at her reflection in the wardrobe's full-length
mirror as she got ready that evening, Cassie thought she looked
reasonably presentable, if a trifle boring.

She was about to fix her pearl stud earrings in place, when she
stopped and went through to Polly's bedroom. Polly often borrowed
bits and pieces from her, and Cassie knew she wouldn't mind her
rummaging through her more modern jewellery.

The dangly silver earrings she found were perfect. With the addition of a scarlet pashmina, the whole outfit was transformed, and Cassie no longer felt boring. Finally satisfied with her appearance, Cassie made her way downstairs. She had a proposition to put to Tom and Mai before James arrived.

'You look great, Mum,' Tom said.

'Thanks,' Cassie smiled. 'I want to ask you two to think about something while I'm away, and there won't be time in the morning.'

Tom and Mai looked at her, puzzled.

'How would you feel about swapping houses with me?' She held a hand up to silence them before they could say anything. 'No, hear me out. You're going to be living here for the next couple of months anyway, until Tom is fully mobile again. And when the baby arrives, River View will be too small. It makes much more sense for you to make this place your family home. Polly, of course, would need to keep her room.'

'But why would you want to go and live on your own in River View?' Mai asked.

'Because I'm nearly fifty years old and I've never lived on my own. I just feel it's about time for me to take charge of my life. Living in River View would be the first step. You're going to need more room with the baby, and this place will be Tom's eventually anyway. Besides, I won't be alone, I'll have Solo.'

As Cassie heard James's car drive into the yard, she picked up her bag.

'Promise me you'll think about it while I'm away. We can have a proper discussion when I get back.'

23

The concert James had tickets for was being held in the grounds of a nearby manor house. The advertising posters promised an 'evening of music and romance in the spirit of yesteryear'.

Having parked the car, James and Cassie joined the crowds that were moving towards the wide expanse of lawn where the stage had been set. Huge smoky torch candles lit the way, while smaller candles in glass globes set amongst the trees shimmered in the twilight like fireflies.

'It's as if we are stepping back in time,' Cassie whispered, as they found their seats. 'All these people in period costume – I feel as though I'm an extra in some historical film.'

'Cassie, the way you look tonight, you're the star,' James said, his expression one of genuine admiration.

As the sun finally set behind the manor house, throwing golden streaks across the darkening sky, a solo flautist began to slowly play, gradually teasing the other orchestra instruments into life. Cassie closed her eyes and allowed herself to float with the music.

James held her hand in his, their fingers entwined, letting go only occasionally to applaud the musicians. The concert came to an end far too soon for Cassie. Turning to James, she sighed.

'Thank you so much, James. That was a truly magical experience.'

He leaned forward and kissed her gently on the cheek. 'The evening's not over yet,' he said. 'I've booked a table for supper in the restaurant. So if m'lady will accompany me?' He took hold of her hand again.

Together, they followed a footman down a path that wove its way through gardens before finishing at the foot of the flight of stone steps leading up to the huge oak doors of the house.

Within minutes, they were seated at a table for two under the huge candle-burning chandelier of the Tudor dining room with its minstrel gallery.

'I feel as if I've been transported back to the sixteenth century,' Cassie whispered, looking around her at the tapestries and costumes. 'I can scarcely believe that tomorrow I'm getting on a plane and jetting off to South Africa. This world seems so real.'

High up in the minstrel gallery, a trio were softly playing and already there was a couple swaying gently together on the small area of dancefloor at the far end of the room.

'Shall we join them?' James asked.

As his arms went around her and they began to move in time to the gentle notes of the famous 'Blue Danube', Cassie felt a twinge of misgiving. She hoped that James wasn't going to try this evening to take their relationship beyond friendship. She'd only just come to terms with the fact that she'd been letting life pass her by. She didn't want to hurt him, but she had to find out what she really wanted before becoming involved in a serious relationship with anyone.

James's next words confirmed her fears.

'Cassie, I know you are only going away for a week, and I haven't forgotten that you once told me it was just friendship you were looking for, but I wanted this to be a special evening.' He paused. 'The first of many for us. I want to be more than your friend. Will you think about us whilst you're away?'

James drew her firmly towards him, his lips gently caressing her cheek as he whispered in her ear.

'I've fallen in love with you, Cassie.'

* * *

Extract from Polly's private journal

Monday, 4 July

At 3 a.m. yesterday, *Cream* and I were bathed in moonlight as we crossed the Equator. I am very proud of myself – I managed to set the video and capture my celebrations on tape.

It feels really good to have covered this distance, although it is getting harder with each day.

My hands aren't helping. They're a mass of tiny salt blisters, which are very painful.

The Equator is renowned for being a temperamental place to sail in and I've been trying to keep as far to the west as possible, hoping to pick up a steadier breeze. For the last few days, that ploy has worked, but now the winds are getting stronger and the waves bigger.

The autopilot was struggling as *Cream* hurtled down, riding the waves, so I've spent a lot of time on the helm – wonderfully exhilarating, if tiring!

Unfortunately, one of the results of all these strong winds and fast sailing has been a broken batten in the sail.

When the wind finally abated and the rain came, the only way round it was to lower the mainsail and replace the batten. It took me twenty minutes to re-hoist the sail, but eventually it was up and we were sailing again after a delay of nearly two hours. It could have been worse.

Rewarded myself for all the hard work with the last of my caramel chocolate bars. They're top of my shopping list for Cape Town. The rest of my food supplies seem to be holding out well, though I'm looking forward to some fresh fruit and veggies. As we're in flying fish territory, I could easily have fresh fish every mealtime as they land on the deck frequently, but I feel so sorry for them I can't eat them.

And don't they make a noise when they hit the deck! Most of them land unhurt and the din as they desperately slap their tails and flap their butterfly-shaped wings, trying to find their way back to the ocean, is unbelievable.

I seem to be forever going out on deck and throwing them back into the sea. I'm sure too, I've thrown some of them back two or three times during the course of a day.

After my daily chat with Race HQ this morning, I typed my weekly bulletin for the newspaper and emailed it. With a bit of luck, I'll be doing the next one from a berth in Cape Town.

Can't believe that I'm still in second place. Hopefully I can hang on to it. Don't think there is much chance of me catching up with Colin on *Flight of the Seagull*. He's nearly 200 miles in front of the fleet.

My biggest worry is the third-place boat, *World Wanderer*. She's only about seventy miles behind me. I could easily drop a place in the next week if I don't keep pushing hard – or if I make a bad route choice.

The generator is on, recharging all the electrics. Seems to be extra noisy and hot tonight for some reason (must check that with Tom).

24

Veronica, driving Cassie to the station to catch the train to the airport, glanced at her friend.

'Everything okay? You look a bit strained.'

Cassie nodded. 'I'm fine. Bit nervous. Never did like flying much and this is the first time I've ever flown on my own.'

'You'll have a marvellous time in Cape Town. Don't worry about anything back here. Just concentrate on enjoying the time with Polly.'

Cassie tried to follow Veronica's advice, but by the time the flight to Cape Town was in the air, thoughts of home were still occupying her mind. Telling herself sternly that 'no one is indispensable', she hoped she'd done everything necessary to help keep the place ticking over for the week she was away.

An air hour or so later, when the stewardess arrived with her meal tray, Cassie remembered last night's supper with James – and their conversation after he'd confessed he'd fallen in love with her. James was a lovely man, a very dear friend, but she still felt uncertain about moving their relationship up a gear. What if it all went wrong? Their friendship would be over, and she really enjoyed spending time with him. Once back at their table after their waltz, she'd steeled herself to tell him the truth.

'I've had a wonderful evening, James, and it will always be a special memory for me.' She'd paused before continuing. 'You know I like you a lot. And I look upon you as a good friend – the best. But I'm not sure about love.'

James was silent for some time, then he sighed. 'Cassie, your friendship is very precious to me and I don't want to lose it. I had hoped it might be growing into more on your part, but I've clearly spoken too soon. Let's not spoil what, as you say, has been a special evening, through my foolishness.'

He'd reached across the table and gently stroked her hand. 'I just want you to know I do love you, and if you ever feel you can love me in return, I'll be waiting.'

Now, as she looked out at the floor of clouds beneath the plane as they sped towards the Cape, Cassie's thoughts returned to the present. She was determined to enjoy this holiday. Hopefully, when she returned home, she'd be fighting fit and ready to get her life in order. And nearer to knowing how she truly felt about James.

Twelve hours later, as an exhausted Cassie walked into the arrivals lounge of Cape Town International Airport, she was surprised to see Dexter waiting for her.

'This is a lovely surprise, Dexter. I didn't expect to see you until tomorrow.'

'I thought a friendly face might be appreciated – and a helping hand to get you to your hotel. I'll have to leave you then for a few hours. I've got some organising to do for tomorrow. The first boat is due to cross the line in about twenty-four hours.'

He shook his head in answer to Cassie's unspoken question.

'No, sorry. It's not Polly, but last I heard, she was still in second place. Now, come on, let us find a taxi and get you into Cape Town.'

The hotel Polly had booked her into was in the Victoria and Alfred Waterfront development.

'I've reserved a table for dinner,' Dexter told her. 'I'll leave you to settle in and I'll see you later.' He headed off, leaving the porter to show her to her room.

Situated on the top floor of the spacious and airy hotel, the twin-bedded room had a view out over the harbour. There was a magnificent arrangement of flowers on a low table at the foot of one of the beds.

It wasn't until after she'd had a hot, energy-reviving shower that Cassie noticed the card nestling in between the tight red buds of the roses.

Have a wonderful time. Looking forward to our dinner on your return. Regards, Doug.

Thoughtfully, Cassie put the card in her bag – a reminder to say thank you when she got home.

Refreshed by the shower and a couple of hours' sleep, she made her way down to the foyer to wait for Dexter.

Outside, the quay was preparing for the evening's entertainment. Neon lights were flashing on and off, table candles were lit at various harbourside restaurants, and music was beginning to infiltrate the night air.

A schooner moored at the far end of the harbour was dressed from stem to stern with flags and small lights that added their reflections to others in the rippling water as the boat tugged gently at its anchor.

Above it all, the silhouette of Table Mountain could be seen against the darkening night sky. Wisps of gossamer-thin mist teased Cassie's view of it.

'It's a view you never ever forget,' Dexter said as he appeared at her side. 'Shall we go?'

Companionably, they walked along the waterfront. The restaurant he'd chosen was well placed for watching the comings and goings of both boats and people and Cassie was soon soaking up Cape Town's unique harbourside atmosphere.

* * *

The next day, after a good night's sleep and breakfast at the hotel, Cassie set out for the Yacht Club. Dexter had told her *Flight of the Seagull* should cross the finish line sometime in the afternoon and given her a pass that would get her into the reception area without any problems.

Now, hesitantly, with her pass in her hand, Cassie stood inside the Yacht Club. She could feel the buzz of excitement already in the air. Smart yachty types in navy blazers and white slacks bustled around self-importantly. As she stood there uncertainly, searching for Dexter in the crowd, one of the men came over and glanced at her pass.

'Ah, Mrs Lewis – little Polly's mother.' He smiled at her.

'Welcome. I think your team are out on the terrace.' He turned, clearly expecting her to follow him through the club house.

Team? In the midst of all the excitement, Cassie had forgotten that the shore crew would be in Cape Town waiting for Polly. In fact, they'd be following her all around the world. At the finish of every leg and during the compulsory stopover between the stages, they'd go over the yacht and get her ready for the next part of the voyage.

'What's the latest news of Polly?' she asked.

It was one of the Rule of Thumb technicians who answered her.

'She's still in second place, about twelve hours behind Colin on

Flight of the Seagull, but she's got a problem with her generator which may have slowed her down. Still, with luck she should be here in the early hours.'

'There's nothing seriously wrong, is there? You would tell me, wouldn't you?' Cassie asked anxiously.

The man shook his head. 'The generator is the only problem. I've spoken to her and so has Tom. She's fine. Looking forward to this leg of the race being over.'

Cassie accepted the offer of a cup of coffee from a passing waiter. A few more hours and she could breathe a sigh of relief – Polly would be here.

'Cassie? Cassie Lewis?'

Hearing her name, Cassie turned, her eyes widening in disbelief.

'Becky?'

When the two women finally disentangled themselves from their spontaneous hug, they stood back and looked at each in amazement.

For Cassie, it was like turning the clock back twenty years. Becky, wife of Miles's best friend and rival, Trevor Thomas, was as tall and glamorous as ever.

Once upon time, she and Becky had been great friends and had spent a lot of time together in various harbours whilst their husbands were off sailing. After Miles's death, however, Cassie had deliberately lost touch with all her friends in that world, it was just too hard. Particularly seeing Becky and Trevor still together as a couple was too painful, a reminder of what she'd lost. Becky had tried for months to keep their friendship going, but in the end, even she had given up in the face of Cassie's refusal to respond.

Now, as Cassie looked at her old friend with affection, she regretted those lost years.

'What are you doing here?' Cassie asked.

'We live here. It's been about seven years now – ever since Trev gave up racing professionally. He runs his own charter business but still gets involved with yacht racing whenever he can. He's skippering the official boat out to meet all the competitors as they arrive.'

Becky looked across at the growing crowd of spectators lining the quay, the small boats setting off to escort a triumphant *Flight of the Seagull* to her temporary berth.

'I can't believe Polly is grown up enough to be taking part,' she went on. 'When I saw Tom's name on the initial competitors' list, I promised myself that I was going to make myself known to him as the woman who had frequently looked after him. His accident was spectacularly bad timing, wasn't it? As for Polly, the moment her name came up, I was determined to meet her. I didn't dare to even think about you being here to welcome her ashore.' Becky sighed contentedly. 'Oh, it's good to see you again.'

Cassie, her emotions at meeting her old friend again all over the place, could only nod in agreement.

'Promise me we won't lose touch again?' Becky said. 'Oh, Cassie, we've got so much to catch up on. Come on, let's find a seat and talk about the old days, before the place is swimming in champagne for the winner.'

25

'Veronica and I are going to walk Solo. Will you be okay for a while?' Mai asked.

Tom nodded, concentrating on the computer screen.

'I'm trying to find some more info for Polly. She's still having problems with the generator. Apparently it's down in power and is getting very hot.'

'Okay. We'll leave you to it,' and Mai took Solo's lead off its peg.

As she and Veronica made their way down through the yard, Mai glanced across at the barge, secure on its permanent mooring in the river.

Nearly school holiday time and so far, everything was going well with this new venture, despite the initial problems. Justin, the *Megabyte* crew member Doug had lent them, had turned out to be an excellent and enthusiastic instructor.

'How are you feeling now this far into your pregnancy? Not that long to go now, is it?' Veronica said as Mai let Solo off her lead. The dog bounded away, sniffing her way along the path.

'I seem to get bigger every day,' Mai said. 'Must admit, I'm looking forward to being able to move easier when the baby arrives.'

'Do you know the sex of the baby?' Veronica asked.

Mai shook her head. 'No. We decided we didn't want to know. Just need it to be born healthy. Have you had any more news on your house?'

'The survey was done yesterday. A couple more weeks to completion, after which the builders can go in and sort the bathroom and install the Aga. And then I can move and get out of everyone's hair.'

'I don't think anyone thinks you're in the way. I know Cassie likes having you around,' Mai said. She gave Veronica a quick glance. 'Has Cassie mentioned her idea of swapping houses with Tom and me?' Mai asked casually.

Veronica nodded. 'Yes. She's very keen on the idea.'

'She hasn't just suggested it because she knows it will be easier for us?'

'Definitely not,' Veronica said firmly. 'Cassie wants to do something she has never done before – live alone, with no responsibility for anyone but herself. And Solo, of course.' She laughed as the dog came racing back to them with a large stick for them to throw.

'How do you feel about the idea anyway?' She looked at Mai.

'It would be great. Tom's brace will be removed soon and the stairs there are a lot easier for him to manage. We could have a proper nursery for the baby.'

Sudden frenzied barking from Solo brought the conversation to an end as Mai and Veronica began to run towards her.

A man was trying to free a small wooden boat from the mud flat on the river's edge. An outboard motor fixed lopsidedly to the boat's stern looked in danger of falling off. As Solo continued to bark at the man, he kicked out at her.

'Hey, stop that,' Veronica and Mai both yelled together.

'The dog attacked me. Dangerous dogs are supposed to be muzzled.'

'She's not dangerous. You must have done something to her,' Veronica snapped.

'Solo, come here.'

With a last loud warning bark at the man, Solo reluctantly did as she was told and Mai quickly clipped her lead on. Solo continued to utter low-throated growls as they walked away, leaving the man struggling to get the boat into the water.

Back at the yard, they told Tom about the incident.

'He was probably doing some illicit fishing.' Tom shrugged.

'I don't know, Tom,' Veronica said. 'He looked pretty shifty to me. And Solo definitely didn't like him.'

'Well, if you're worried, mention it to James. He usually knows which rogues are out and about on the river. Right now, though, I've got enough to worry about.'

He looked at them steadfastly.

'I've lost contact with Polly. And so has Race HQ.'

* * *

Flight of the Seagull had sailed into Cape Town to a rapturous welcome before the news filtered through that contact had been lost with Polly and *Holdsworth Clotted Cream.*

Around her, the noise of the celebrations faded into the background as a shocked Cassie tried to take in what Dexter was telling her.

'Cassie, please don't worry. We know her position as of twelve hours ago when she was fine and making good time. We also know she's been having problems with her generator. More than likely, that's what has caused the communication problem.'

Cassie looked at him numbly. Willing him to be speaking the truth.

'Right now, Race HQ is contacting the boat in third position to see if he has seen her. As soon as we have any news, you'll be told.'

'It could be some time before we hear anything, though,' Dexter continued. 'Why don't you go back to the hotel and get some rest?'

'I'd rather wait here,' Cassie began to protest, when Becky interrupted.

'I'll drive you. We've both got mobiles, and as soon as there is any news, Trev or Dexter will phone. We can be back here in minutes.'

Dexter looked at her gratefully.

'Honestly, Cassie, nothing is going to happen for a few hours.'

Once back at the hotel, Becky insisted on ordering some sandwiches and a pot of coffee from room service.

'Come on, Cassie, you need to eat something. It's going to be a long night.'

But Cassie was too wound up to eat or drink a thing.

Becky's prophecy of a long night ahead of them proved to be true. It was gone two o'clock when Becky's mobile phone rang.

Cassie, lying on the bed with her eyes closed, feigning sleep, was immediately on her feet, staring fearfully at her friend.

'Thanks, Trev. I'll tell her.' Becky looked at Cassie.

'They've had a sighting of Polly. There's still been no contact, but she appears to be sailing hard and, on her current course, is about three hours away from Cape Town.'

'What else?'

'The sighting was made by the yacht in third position, *World Wanderer*. He's a few miles upwind of her and there is a chance that Polly will lose her second position.'

'So long as she's safe.' Cassie's reaction was instinctive.

'Dexter has arranged for you to go out in the launch with Trev when we get back to the Yacht Club and escort *Holdsworth Clotted Cream* into her berth,' Becky told her.

Cassie immediately picked up her yellow waterproofs. 'Let's go,' she said.

As they drove back towards the Yacht Club, Cassie was amazed at the number of people making their way along the waterfront.

'They'll have heard of Polly's problems and be determined to give her a proper welcome to Cape Town, even if it is the middle of the night,' Becky said.

Dexter was waiting for them, Trev and Colin, the winning skipper, with him.

'Cassie, we've got an estimated time of five o'clock for Polly crossing the finish, so we plan to leave here in about an hour.'

Now she knew Polly was within sight of the coastline, Cassie felt the nervous tension of the past few hours slipping away.

She struggled into her waterproofs and headed off with the others down to the boat. On the way, Cassie asked Dexter about the yacht which had reported sighting Polly.

'Is he still gaining on her?'

Dexter shook his head. 'No, she's managing to hold onto her lead, but the wind a couple of miles offshore is very fickle. She's going to lose speed the closer she gets to the finish line. But then, so is *World Wanderer*.'

There was a discernible hum of excitement aboard the flotilla of boats going out to the finish line.

As Trev said to Cassie as they took off into the night, 'To have two yachts still racing in such close quarters for second place after nearly 7,000 miles is almost unheard of.'

It was Colin, the skipper of *Flight of the Seagull*, who spotted the first sails.

'There's one of them,' he shouted, his binoculars with their night sight trained on the distant sea. 'It's *World Wanderer*,' and he began to scan the sea again while Cassie's heart began to pound. Where was Polly?

Half a minute passed before Colin handed Cassie the binoculars and pointed out the direction she should look. Polly was coming in on a different course and *Holdsworth Clotted Cream* would cross the finish line at a different place to *World Wanderer*.

Everyone held their breath, wondering which skipper had chosen the best option.

As the sky began to lighten and dawn approached, *Holdsworth Clotted Cream* drew closer, its mainsail taking full advantage of the available wind. Finally, she was close enough for Cassie to see the small figure of her daughter standing in the cockpit.

Cassie felt the telltale pinprick of tears starting in her eyes and a sense of overwhelming pride for her daughter. She knew Polly would be desperate to finish before *World Wanderer*, whereas she was just pleased to have her daughter complete this first leg safely.

'Wind's died,' Trev observed.

Polly's sail began to flap and she quickly tacked in an effort to find some air movement. The next few minutes were nerve-racking as *Holdsworth Clotted Cream* wallowed in the sea, tantalisingly close to the finish line, and her rival sailed closer.

Then, at the moment the sky turned pale pink with the dawn and a wispy tablecloth tumbled over the edge of Table Mountain, *Holdsworth Clotted Cream* found an elusive breeze. Two minutes later, the gun rang out as she crossed the line to a tumultuous welcome. Polly had done it. She was second. Nigel, skipper of *World Wanderer*, followed her in six minutes later to an equally enthusiastic reception.

Flares were set off, boat hooters sounded, cameras flashed and champagne corks popped. The shore crew boarded *Holdsworth Clotted Cream* and took control of her as she was towed into port.

Polly, punching the air with delight, was overjoyed to see Cassie in the launch.

'Come on board, Mum!' she cried.

By the time Cassie had clambered onto the deck of the yacht, the tears were flowing freely from both mother and daughter.

As they made the short trip into the harbour, Cassie struggled to control her tears and asked Polly why she'd lost contact in the last twenty-four hours.

'Unfortunately the batteries hadn't charged fully the night before the generator packed up completely. The only thing I could do was to switch everything off so there would be enough battery power to work the autopilot every hour whilst I had a catnap. Thank goodness it happened at the end of the leg. No autopilot means no sleep.'

Once the yacht was tied up in her allocated berth, Dexter came on board to congratulate Polly.

'Well done, Polly,' he said, giving her a warm hug, holding her tight for several seconds.

Cassie was amused to see that Polly wasn't averse to staying in his arms for as long as he held her.

'Ready for the crowds?' he asked. 'The reception committee and the press are waiting for you in the club house.'

'All I really want is a hot shower and a comfortable bed,' Polly replied.

'Later, I promise,' Dexter said.

'Hang on, I've forgotten something.' Polly dived back down below, emerging seconds later with Nero and Fred Bear clutched tightly to her.

'Can't leave them behind,' she said. 'They'd miss me.'

It took some time to make any progress towards the clubhouse as everyone they passed wanted to congratulate Polly.

Cassie watched proudly as 'Little Polly', as everybody now

seemed determined to call her, made her second-place acceptance speech.

It was only as Nigel made his speech and laughingly warned her, 'I'll be chasing you even harder in the next leg, Little Polly,' that Cassie remembered this wasn't the end.

In ten days' time, Polly would set sail again, with over 20,000 miles to sail, and a lot of those miles would be in the inhospitable and dangerous Southern Ocean.

26

Polly glanced at Cassie as she packed. 'It's been a great four days. I'm so glad you came, Mum.'

'Thank you for making it possible,' Cassie replied. She looked at her daughter affectionately.

'It didn't bring back too many sad memories?' Polly asked quietly.

Cassie shook her head. 'It's completely different from the days when your dad was competing. There's much more razzamatazz – more fun altogether. Although I don't suppose the actual sailing has changed much. It's still pretty tough out there, isn't it?'

'I love the challenge,' Polly replied. 'And at least I didn't disgrace myself on Leg One. Even Tom admitted second place was a result!'

'The next two legs are a different prospect, though, aren't they? The Southern Ocean followed by Cape Horn,' Cassie said quietly.

'Mum, it will be fine,' Polly reassured her. 'Now, are you going to wear your new dress this evening?' she said, changing the subject.

'You don't think it's a bit over the top for me?' Cassie fingered the soft chiffon material of the dress she'd fallen for in an upmarket boutique down on the waterfront.

'Of course not,' Polly said. 'It really suits you.'

Cassie glanced at her watch.

'What time is Dexter picking us up?' she asked.

'In about half an hour. While you finish packing, I'll grab a shower.' Polly vanished into the bathroom.

Dexter was waiting for them in the hotel foyer when they went downstairs, ready to drive them out to Becky and Trev's house in the suburbs. Becky had insisted on organising a farewell evening for Cassie and had naturally included Polly and Dexter.

'It's the least I can do now we've met up again. Besides, I want you to see my home.'

Situated on the edge of a cliff overlooking the Atlantic Ocean, the house with its seven bedrooms had spectacular views and was clearly a much-loved home.

Trev had done well with his yachting and chartering business, Cassie thought.

Inevitably, the conversation was very yacht-orientated and Cassie found herself laughing as Trev told the other guests about events from their shared past.

She even found herself recalling a couple of incidents Trev had forgotten, involving herself and Miles – happy memories she hadn't thought about in years.

Looking at her old friends, Cassie felt a tinge of sadness for the lost years. She'd been silly to cut herself off from those people who'd meant so much to her.

It was Polly who brought her back into the conversation.

'Has Mum told you her plans for changing her life now that Tom's married and I'm off sailing?' she asked Becky. 'It's her way of beating the empty-nest syndrome.'

Becky glanced at Cassie. Like Polly, she knew it was more than empty-nest syndrome Cassie was attempting to fight. They'd always been able to confide in each other. The years apart hadn't changed that, and Cassie had talked to her about thinking that life was passing her by.

'She's mentioned moving into a small cottage. Doing her own thing,' Becky said. 'I think it's an excellent idea.'

'Actually,' Trev interrupted, 'I've got an even better idea.' He turned to Cassie. 'Why don't you come and live here?'

'Trev, you're brilliant,' Becky exclaimed. 'Why didn't I think of that? Cassie, why not? You say it's time to think about your life, do something different, lay all those ghosts. Well, you've started to do that, why not finish the job and move here? Come and live with us. We've plenty of room. Come for six months and see what happens.'

'There you go, Mum. What an opportunity.' Polly was full of enthusiasm for the plan, but Cassie was rendered completely speechless.

* * *

'How does it feel to finally have the brace off?' Mai asked, driving Tom home from the hospital after having the external fixation device removed.

'Strange, actually,' Tom said. 'The leg feels very weak. It's going to take a long time for me to trust either of them.'

'They've given you lots of exercises to strengthen them. Just make sure you do them,' Mai said. 'But don't try to do too much too soon. The doc said the bones will take time to heal completely.'

Tom nodded.

'I know it's early days yet, but the months are flying past at a rate of knots and I've been thinking about godparents for the baby,' Mai said, changing the subject.

'Polly for one of the godmothers,' Tom replied. 'No question.'

'How do you feel about Dexter for godfather?' Mai said, with a grin on her face. 'I doubt that Sebastian will be in Polly's life when she returns.'

Tom glanced at her. 'Are you suggesting something is going on between my kid sister and my friend?'

'Mmm, if I'm reading the signs correctly, I think there could well be.'

'Good choice for godparent, then. We'll have to choose names, too. Or should we wait and see what the baby looks like first?' Tom said a few moments later. 'I have to admit, though, I like old-fashioned names rather than trendy modern ones.'

'Good,' Mai agreed. 'I've been favouring Alice for a girl and Samuel for a boy.'

Tom nodded. 'I like those.'

'Your old room can be the nursery. We'll paint it pale yellow and light blue,' Mai continued enthusiastically. 'I've seen some lovely wallpaper.'

'We're taking Mum up on her offer, then?' Tom asked quietly.

'You have doubts?'

'I just don't want Mum feeling she's being pushed out of her own home.'

'According to Veronica, this is something she really wants to do.'

Mai drove into the boatyard and parked.

'Mum's due back in a couple of days. Before then, we must all get together and make plans for her birthday next month. She's fifty, so we'll have to organise something special,' Tom said.

Just then, Veronica appeared to give Mai a hand helping Tom out of the car and onto his new crutches for the first time.

'Is something the matter, Veronica? You seem a bit distraught,' Mai said, looking at her anxiously.

Veronica sighed.

'River View has been broken into. James says it looks as though someone was planning to squat there. Nothing seems to be missing and they've found a sleeping bag upstairs. Bill's there now, repairing the window and trying to make the place more secure.'

'When did it happen?' Tom asked.

'James noticed the broken window this morning as he was doing one of his regular river patrols. He suggested we tighten security here and in the boatyard. A couple of the boats down river have had outboard motors taken,' Veronica said.

'Does James have any idea who's responsible?' Tom asked.

Veronica shook her head. 'Apparently there's been a few strangers around recently, including the shifty man we saw on the river path, but there's nothing to link them to anything. I wish now we'd walked on to River View the other day and checked it out. I'm off to the cottage to do a spot of clearing up before Cassie gets home. Would you have time to join me, Mai?'

'Of course,' Mai agreed.

'You'd better take Solo with you,' Tom said. 'And if you see Gramps, can you ask him if he has any ideas for Mum's party?'

27

During the long flight home, Cassie's thoughts were once again about James and their friendship. She couldn't help but wonder what his reaction would be to her moving to South Africa. After the initial buzz of adrenaline the moment Trev had suggested the move, Cassie had thought about the pros and the cons of such a move. It was a lovely place, and it would certainly be a completely new beginning for her. But she would leave behind a lot of the things and people she held close to her heart. Tom, Polly, Mai and the new baby, Bill, Veronica, James – and what would she do over there? She'd need a job of some description. As she sipped a glass of chilled South African chardonnay, she decided there was no rush to make a decision, she'd mull it over for a few weeks at least.

Cassie shivered as the cold British air hit her the moment she stepped out onto Heathrow airport concourse. The all-too-familiar overcast sky after the blue of South Africa was an instant reminder of the warmer weather she'd left Polly enjoying in the countdown to the next leg of the race.

She was about to drag her suitcase along to the taxi rank when she heard her name being called.

'Cassie, wait.'

Turning, she was surprised to see Doug striding towards her.

'I'm sorry I'm late. I wanted to be in the arrivals lounge to meet you, but I was held up. Here, let me take that.' Doug grasped the handle of the suitcase from her. 'Did you have a good flight?'

Cassie nodded. 'Yes, thanks. What are you doing here anyway?' she asked.

'I was on my way back from Scotland and thought you might like company for the last part of your journey home.' Doug smiled at her. Doug's car, a seriously upmarket model with a luxurious leather interior, was soon eating up the motorway miles and Cassie began to relax when she remembered the flowers.

'I haven't thanked you for the wonderful bouquet that was waiting for me in my room when I arrived. Thank you.'

'My pleasure,' Doug said. 'Tell me about your holiday. Did you take the cable car to the top of Table Mountain? Visit Robben Island? Go whale watching?'

'Yes, yes and no. There simply wasn't time for a whale watching trip. There was so much else to do and see, the days went by far too quickly. Polly and I had a wonderful time. And I had a lovely surprise, too. I met up with some old friends.' Cassie told Doug about Becky and Trev. 'They've given me something to think about too – they've suggested I move to Cape Town.'

'That would be a big step,' said Doug. 'I hope you're not tempted.' As his words fell into silence, he gave Cassie a quick glance. 'You're not, are you?'

Cassie, stunned by his reaction, sighed. 'I'm determined to try to do something different, get out of the rut I feel I've sunk into, but like you say, it's a big step. I'll have to give it a lot of thought.'

A few miles further on, Doug pulled off the motorway for petrol.

'I thought we'd stop for lunch. There's a good restaurant where I usually call in on my way down. You don't have to be back by any particular time, do you?'

Cassie shook her head, not wanting to be rude and protest at Doug's plan, but really all she wanted to do was get home.

At the restaurant, Cassie popped into the cloakroom to freshen up. When she made her way back to the table, she found Heidi had joined Doug.

'Hi. I took a chance Dad would be here. I know it's a favourite watering hole on his drive south. There are a couple of things I need to discuss with him. Didn't expect to see you.' The emphasis on the last word was slight but Cassie heard it. Had she imagined it, or was there once again a definite edge to Heidi's voice when she spoke to Cassie?

'I didn't expect him to meet me at the airport either,' Cassie said lightly.

'You could have called me on the mobile if things were that urgent,' Doug pointed out brusquely.

'I know, Dad,' Heidi said, 'but I wanted to see you.' She threaded her arm through her father's, smiling up at him.

'You've been in Scotland for ages.'

They ate their meal, which was as delicious as Doug had promised it would be, and Cassie sat and listened as Heidi firmly kept the conversation business-orientated, despite Doug's attempts to include Cassie in a more general way.

Doug was clearly irritated.

'Right, that's enough business talk, Heidi,' he said before their desserts arrived. 'Poor Cassie must be wondering where our manners are.'

'Oh, Cassie, I'm so sorry,' Heidi cooed. 'Do tell us about your holiday. Dad and I love Cape Town, don't we? Do you remember the time...' and she launched into a rambling reminiscence of a long-ago holiday incident.

Cassie, finding herself once again excluded from the conversation between daughter and father, began to wish for the meal to be over. Why was Heidi being so rude? And why was Doug letting her get away with it?

Part of the answer came when Doug excused himself and went to pay the bill at the bar.

'Daddy has never looked at another woman since Mummy left, so don't get any ideas about bagging a rich husband,' Heidi said aggressively.

Cassie was completely taken aback. Her first instinct was to tell this disagreeable young woman to mind her own business in no uncertain terms. However, she managed to keep her temper under control, and when she spoke, her voice was calm.

'Heidi, your father and I met only recently, and he's been very kind to me and my family. I've been on my own for twenty years and I assure you I'm not desperate for a husband, rich or otherwise. The idea that Doug regards me as anything other than a friend is ludicrous.' Cassie took a breath. 'I will just say this. Don't you think your father is entitled to choose his own friends, without your interference? Maybe after all the years on his own, he's feeling lonely – especially now you and your sister live your own lives.' She paused before standing up and gathering her coat and bag together.

'I'll leave you to say goodbye to your father. Perhaps you'd be kind enough to tell him I'll see him by the car. Goodbye, Heidi.' Cassie turned away.

By the time Doug joined her ten minutes later, Cassie had recovered her composure.

'Thank you for lunch.' She greeted him with a smile.

Doug put the ignition card in place, but instead of starting the car, he sat back, hands gripping the steering wheel tightly.

'Cassie, I can only apologise for Heidi. I had no idea she would waylay me here. Or that she would behave as she did. I'd hoped she'd outgrown the antagonism she's always shown towards any of my female friends. The last thing I want is for her to frighten you away.'

'Doug, it's all right,' Cassie said, touching his arm. 'I'll survive. And we can still be friends. The only thing that bothers me is why didn't you stand up to her in the restaurant?'

Doug looked at her.

'If it had happened somewhere private, I would have. But you have no idea of the scene Heidi can throw if she wants to. I had no intention of subjecting you to that in public.'

He started the engine and slowly reversed the car out of its parking space.

'I suppose I made the classic mistake when their mother left me of overcompensating with the girls. Caroline coped really well, but Heidi has always had a possessive streak and I did nothing to curb it. I guess I was out of my depth. I should have done things differently.'

'We can only do our best in the circumstances at the time. Looking back, wanting to change things is a futile exercise.' Cassie sighed. 'Trust me, I know all about wanting to change things when Miles died.'

Doug glanced at her. 'Losing your husband so young must have been difficult for you. I admire your ability not to cave in and give up.'

'Giving up was never an option. I had Tom and Polly to consider – they were both so young. But I do admit I wouldn't have coped without my mum and dad. How old were Heidi and her sister when your divorce happened?'

'Thirteen and fifteen – right bang in the middle of teenage angst,' Doug said with a rueful laugh. 'I can promise you one thing, Cassie, the next time we have a meal together, it will be just the two of us. Now, let's get you home. It's been a long day for you.'

Cassie, happy to sit watching the countryside flash by, let her thoughts drift. She'd spent most of the flight wondering about Becky and Trev's tempting offer. Now, though, as the car crossed the familiar Somerset Devonshire border, a comfortable feeling came over her.

She was nearly home. This was where she belonged and where she'd build the new life she intended to forge for herself.

Going to South Africa to live was a tempting idea, but not one she intended to put into practice. She would return to Cape Town and have a holiday with Becky and Trev, but nothing more. She simply couldn't see herself living alone in a foreign country, even with close friends around. Devon was home. Strange how just a few hours ago she was going to take her time and mull over the idea of moving but now the decision had been made effortlessly.

28

The sun was setting, throwing Table Mountain into silhouette against the evening sky as Polly made her way towards the Yacht Club. All around, the lights of the city were beginning to twinkle with their nocturnal invitations to 'come and socialise'.

Smiling to herself, Polly remembered the evening Dexter had taken her and Cassie on a whirlwind exploration of the city's nightlife. It was two o'clock in the morning before he'd led them back to the hotel, totally exhausted.

It was Dexter who'd taken them around during the daytime too, showing them the sights. A visit out to Robben Island, a drive along the Stellenbosch Wine Route and, of course, the cable car up Table Mountain.

He'd spent as much time as he could with them during Cassie's visit. Since she'd left, Dexter had returned to his mountain of paperwork and Polly had seen little of him.

The days had passed in a blur of chores as she and the shore crew worked all hours preparing *Holdsworth Clotted Cream* for the next stage of the race. Tonight, though, just a day away from the start, she was meeting Dexter for a final mooch around Cape Town.

'Just you and me, Polly,' he'd said. 'No shore team. No other skippers.'

Dexter was waiting for her as promised outside the Yacht Club.

'I thought we'd just wander and listen to some jazz down on the waterfront,' he said, glancing at her hand as he took hold of it gently. 'Your hands look much better for the rest.'

'Mum found a tube of Scandinavian Fishermen's Hand Cream in a chemist down on the harbour and that has really helped.'

'Have you talked to Tom yet about your route?' Dexter asked.

'He emailed his recommendations this morning. You've sailed this route before too, haven't you? Do you have any advice for me?'

'Not really, and anyway I'm sure Tom has given you everything you need to know. I always think of this section as offering some seriously good sailing, although it is dangerous, no doubt about it. I was fortunate enough to have reasonable weather when I did it.'

He looked at Polly. 'If you're really lucky, you'll get to see the Southern Lights. An incredible experience.'

Further along the quay, they found a table at one of the many cafés, and Dexter ordered coffee.

'Are you flying straight to New Zealand from here or do you get time off to go home whilst we battle our way through the Southern Ocean?' Polly asked.

'I have to stay in touch 24/7 in case there are any emergencies, but thanks to the internet, I can do that from anywhere in the world. I'm going back to the UK to see my family. I'm also trying to sell my apartment in New York, so I guess I should try and get over there too.'

'Are you buying somewhere else in America?'

Dexter shrugged. 'I don't know. My contract with the race organisers finishes after this race. I have to decide whether to renew it and stay in America, or join my dad on the family farm.'

'I thought you loved being involved with boats?'

'I do, but the problem is I don't get to do much sailing these days. If I take a regular land-based job, I could at least do some pleasure sailing. What about you? Do you have any plans for when the race is over?'

'Not really. Hopefully I'll finish in a good position and somebody will offer me a boat of my own.'

She shrugged.

'If not, I'll probably do some more crewing and help Tom and Mai build up the sailing school. I know Mum favours that option,' and she smiled at Dexter.

'Are you still in touch with Sebastian?' Dexter asked unexpectedly.

'He phoned me yesterday, actually. Believe it or not, he's still trying to persuade me to give up the race.'

She took a breath.

'I'll email him again once I'm at sea and try to get him to accept the fact that my answer to everything he's asked has to be no.' She remembered the ring in the drawer at home and added, 'But I guess he won't admit it's all over between us until I tell him face to face.'

There was silence for a moment before Dexter stood up and held out his hand.

'Come on, let's walk back to *Cream*.'

Sitting out on the yacht's deck an hour later, Dexter's arm casually around her shoulders, Polly felt a moment of pure happiness sweep through her. This was an evening she would remember and relive many times as she made her way across the Southern Ocean.

She turned towards him as Dexter gently pulled her closer.

'I'll be waiting for you in New Zealand, Little Polly,' he whispered, before kissing her and holding her tight.

'Please make sure you sail safe.'

* * *

Back in Devon, Cassie was regarding her handiwork in the sitting room at River View. Empty for a couple of months since Mai and Tom had joined them in the house, the cottage had needed a bit of a spring clean and an airing. The sun was shining in through the cleaned windows of the sitting room and the tiny kitchen, where Mai had painted the walls a delicate shade of primrose yellow.

Cassie jumped as Solo barked and a loud knock on the door interrupted her thoughts.

'It's only me,' Veronica called. 'I wondered if you had the time and energy for a walk. Hey, this place looks great.'

'I can't believe I'm moving here before you move into Glebe House,' Cassie said. 'Don't forget, if you want a hand cleaning and painting, I'm your woman.'

'I'll hold you to that,' Veronica said. 'Cassie, are you sure you're happy about living here on your own – especially after the break-in?'

'I don't think I'd be happy without Solo,' Cassie said slowly. 'But I've got her and the telephone. Also, it's the first break-in in all the years Dad's owned the place, so I think it was just an isolated incident – some kid running away from home or something.'

'Have you seen James since you've been back?' Veronica asked.

Cassie shook her head. 'I've spoken to him on the phone, but things have been so hectic I don't seem to have had a moment to spare.'

Solo bounded ahead of them down the river path, leaving Cassie and Veronica to follow. One of the large tourist boats was making its way down river, loudspeaker booming information.

As the boat drew level with Holdsworth Boatyard and Marina, the loudspeaker crackled into life again.

'Here on the right is the childhood home of Polly Lewis, the yachtswoman. It was on this river that Polly learned to sail. Now she's the youngest skipper taking part in a gruelling solo race around the world.'

Cassie looked at Veronica in amazement before bursting into laughter. 'I don't believe it. Polly's a local tourist attraction. I can't wait to tell her.'

When Cassie got back to the house, Tom was waiting for her. 'Mum, can I ask you a favour? My legs are slowly getting some strength back and I reckon in a couple of weeks I won't need to rely on a crutch. The thing is, I'd like to take Mai away before she has the baby – just for a few days in a couple of weeks.'

'Good idea,' Cassie said.

'But there are a couple of problems,' Tom went on. 'One is the barge. We have bookings, so it would mean a lot of extra work for you. And you're already doing so much.'

'Don't worry about me,' Cassie said quickly. 'Besides, Veronica will come and give me a hand. She likes being here. Next problem?'

'Polly's Operational Room, it doesn't necessarily have to be manned twenty-four hours a day, Race HQ are on the ball. But you would need to switch on and update the computer a couple of times a day.'

'I'm sure I can manage that if you show me how before you leave. Where are you thinking of going?'

'I thought we might go up to London – see a show, do some shopping, be tourists for a day or two. I think Mai misses city life occasionally.'

'It sounds fun. Why don't you decide on a date and book the hotel? I'm here and happy to handle things.'

'Thanks, Mum. Keep it to yourself, please. I don't plan on telling Mai until nearer the date, okay? She'll only tell me that I'm trying to do too much too soon.'

29

Cassie finally moved into River View Cottage the day Polly set sail from Cape Town for New Zealand. Earlier, she'd been in the kitchen at Boatyard House with Mai and Tom, avidly watching the internet link-up with its minute-by-minute updates of the race.

To everyone's delight, Polly managed to cross the start line in second place, sandwiched between Colin on *Flight of the Seagull* in the lead and Nigel on *World Wanderer* in third place. The first three in from the previous leg were the first three out across the start line for the second leg.

Tom had quickly sent an email.

Congratulations on your excellent start, Polly. Good luck for the next 7,000 miles. Speak to you later. Love from everybody.

Now, as Cassie emptied the last of the boxes and put her books and photographs on the newly cleaned built-in shelves in the sitting room at the cottage, she firmly pushed worrying thoughts about Polly out of her mind. There was, after all, very little she could do if anything were to go wrong – which it wouldn't.

Going through to the tiny kitchen, Cassie made herself a cup of coffee and checked the time. Veronica had returned to Wales for a few days, organising the removal of some of her things.

Cassie had promised to collect her from the station. If she wasn't going to be late, she'd better get a move on.

* * *

'How was it?' Cassie asked as she helped Veronica put her suitcases in the car boot.

'Rained non-stop as usual.' Veronica smiled. 'It was great to see everyone. I organised transport for the few pieces of furniture that I want and packed up personal stuff in boxes. Anything that the removal firm don't bring, David has promised to bring down some-time in the next couple of weeks. I've warned him he might well end up sleeping on the floor – I haven't organised a bed for the spare room yet.'

'There's always my old room at Tom and Mai's,' Cassie said. 'Solo and I finally moved into River View Cottage today.'

'Congratulations. Are you fed up with decorating, or can you face giving me a hand at Glebe House?'

'Mornings are out this week, I'm afraid. There's a party of three on the barge who want sailing lessons. But I can definitely offer my services a couple of afternoons. When are you planning to move in?'

'Probably the day the furniture arrives. I hoped to stay on at Boatyard House few more days – if it's okay with Tom and Mai.'

'I can't see it being a problem,' Cassie said.

Declining coffee when she dropped Veronica at the house, Cassie left her car in the garage at the yard, collected Solo and walked back to Riverside Cottage.

It felt strange, closing the kitchen door behind her and leaving everyone talking away in what she still thought of as her kitchen, to go back to the empty cottage. Fleetingly, Cassie wondered if she'd done the right thing.

Was she going to be lonely living on her own? At least this evening it wouldn't be a problem. She had a guest for supper.

Music playing in the background, scented candles to keep the twilight midges at bay, table set for two on the small patio, supper sizzling in the oven, wine opened to breathe, and Cassie was ready.

She saw the launch coming upriver and she and Solo walked down to the small landing stage to meet it and help tie it up.

'I hope it's still warm enough to eat outside,' she said. 'But if you're cold, we can carry the table indoors.'

'Outside is fine,' James said, lightly brushing her cheek with his lips. 'Do I get a guided tour before we eat?'

'It won't take long,' Cassie laughed. 'What you see is all there is. Oh, before I forget, I have a present for you from South Africa. I'm sorry I'm a bit late giving it to you.'

'You've been busy getting this place ready and I've, well, I've had other things on my mind, too,' James said. Cassie looked at him questioningly, but James shrugged. 'Later.'

As Cassie had hoped, James loved the original watercolour painting of an old 'J' class yacht sailing hard, its decks awash, off the South African coast.

'I remember seeing the picture you have hanging in your sitting room of a "J" class racing off St Tropez and I thought it would go well with that.'

'It certainly will. Thank you so much, Cassie.' James gave her a grateful hug.

They'd almost finished supper when Cassie asked, 'What's been on your mind these past few weeks, then?'

James gave a big sigh. 'The powers that be are trying to rearrange the management of all the harbours along this part of the coast. Their aim is to cut expenses – and reduce manpower.' James looked at Cassie.

'Their latest proposal is to combine my job with that of Harbour Master for the Old Port.'

'But the Old Port is fifteen miles down the coast. You can't be in two places at once. And think of the waste of time commuting between the two. It's just silly.'

'I know. You know. But the committee is determined. The question now is, which Harbour Master's job is going to disappear?'

Cassie looked at him as he absently rearranged the salt and pepper pots on the table.

'Perhaps more to the point is the question, do I want the combined job enough to apply for it and then wait to see if they even offer it to me?' James glanced up at her. 'I've had enough stress with just one harbour to look after. The thought of being responsible for two...' He shrugged before giving Cassie a serious look. 'If they offer me redundancy, I think I'm going to take it.'

'Do you have any idea what you'd do afterwards?'

James shook his head.

'Depending on the pay-out, I could look around for some part-time work. Or move somewhere else. There is a rumour about a vacancy happening soon in one of the harbours up on the east coast.'

Move away? Cassie was surprised at how desolate she felt at the thought of James moving out of her life. But his next words allayed her fears temporarily.

'I'll certainly be free to do more sailing, which will be a bonus. Incidentally, are you free to crew for me in a race this Saturday? It's the course out in the bay just past the Mew Stone.'

'As long as we're back by about six o'clock. It's my birthday next week, and I gather Tom and Dad are organising a dinner with family and friends at the Seafarers for me on Saturday evening. I hope you've been invited. You're not on call, are you?'

'I wouldn't miss it. In fact, I've promised Bill that I will be your chauffeur for the evening.'

'Thanks,' Cassie smiled.

'Saturday isn't your actual birthday, is it?'

'No, that's on Wednesday. But partying is always better at the weekends. Most people can stay in bed on Sunday morning.'

Cassie shivered suddenly.

'Come on, let's take our coffee indoors. I'm sure you're feeling cold by now. I know I am.'

She stood up and led the way into the sitting room.

* * *

Extract from Polly's private journal

Wednesday, 21 July

Well, at least I made a good start again. It was a shame I couldn't get across the line in front of *Flight of the Seagull* – but I've got the next 7,000 miles to catch Colin up and pass him.

I've settled back into my daily routine and I've even emailed my latest piece to the newspaper a day early. They've asked if I'd be prepared to visit some schools during the stopover in Brazil and give talks to the children.

I'll have to think about that. I've got to reach New Zealand first and then make my way around Cape Horn. Everybody says the leg from New Zealand to Brazil is the toughest of the race.

Six days after rounding Cape Point, Africa is behind me and the fleet is well spread out. I can't even see another sail in the distance and I'm getting used to being alone again.

The sailing, as Dexter predicted it could be, has been fantastic, but I'm beginning to worry about icebergs.

Having Mum around in Cape Town was great. I hope she enjoyed it as much as I did. Pity she's not joining me in New Zealand too. Good to hear too, that Tom is not only out of plaster but also the fixation brace has been removed.

Dexter has been either emailing or telephoning me every day. He's still in the UK with his family and it sounds as if he's coming round to the idea of joining his father on the family farm in Somerset. I can see Dexter as a farmer. He'd enjoy the life, I'm sure.

According to HQ, we're in for some stormy weather. I'm as well prepared as I can be. The guys back in Cape Town did a brilliant job on *Cream*, getting her ready for this leg. I've battened everything down that I can and keeping my fingers crossed that the winds don't blow too strong.

Two emails just came in. One from Sebastian, telling me his exercise is over and he's back in the UK. He hopes I'm OK and he's looking forward to seeing me when the race is over to sort things out. Mmm. Wish I could say the same.

I hate the thought of hurting him, but since I've been at sea, I've had time to really think and I know I don't want to spend the rest of my life with Sebastian. Somehow I have to tell him and make the break.

The other email was from Dexter, adding his personal warning about gale force winds.

* * *

Wednesday, 28th July

I've just lived through the most amazing week of my life. The storm was unbelievably violent. For three days, *Cream* took a tremendous pasting. I was so lucky that nothing major broke. I took the mainsail down and just put the pocket handkerchief-size jib up so we could keep steerage and direction as the storm raged.

I've managed to clear up some of the mess in the cabin but my main concern has been the sails. As soon as the winds drop a bit, I'll get the sewing stuff out and have a major maintenance session on them.

Yesterday the sun forced its way through the grey clouds and the change in the sea colour was incredible.

And last night the Southern Lights were all around me – flashes of green and yellow exploding in the sky. It was an incredible performance that I wanted to share with someone, so I rang Dexter on the satellite phone. I think I got him out of bed – I'd completely forgotten the time difference.

He was incredibly sweet about it and stayed chatting for ages. He flies out to New Zealand tomorrow to start organising things for us all there.

With luck, fourteen days should see me sailing into Tauranga. *Flight of the Seagull* is still ahead of me, so I know I've got some hard sailing ahead of me if I want to catch Colin.

30

Cassie woke the morning of her birthday to hear the rain still drumming onto the cottage patio. It had been pouring non-stop now for four or five days. Summer seemed to have forgotten to arrive this year.

Glancing out of the window, Cassie could see that the river had risen several inches overnight. The landing stage was submerged, and with mounting horror, she realised the water was now over the bottom two steps of the flight leading up to the cottage.

Bill had sent up some sandbags the day before and she'd dutifully placed them around the front door of the cottage, never believing that it would be necessary. This morning, with the water only a foot away, it looked as if they might be needed after all.

She picked up the phone.

'Tom, is everything all right down there? The river seems to have burst its banks up here.'

'It's very swollen and running a lot faster than normal, but so far we're okay,' Tom said. 'I think you should make your way down here, though. Shall I get Gramps to come up in the launch for you?'

'No. I reckon Solo and I can come round the back way. I'll just pile things on top of each other first and hope for the best. I'll see you within the next hour.'

'Okay. And, Mum, happy birthday!'

In the kitchen, Cassie unplugged the fridge and the oven and pulled the mat up in front of the back door. In the sitting room, she piled as many of her electrical things as she could on top of the table.

Finally, she unplugged the phone charger and put it and the phone itself in her pocket.

'Come on, Solo, let's make for dry ground,' and she slammed and locked the door behind her before placing the sandbags firmly in place against it. The water was still a foot away from the top step and Cassie could only hope that it would stop raining soon.

By the time she made it into the kitchen at Boatyard House, she was exhausted and soaked through. Gratefully she cradled the mug of hot coffee that Mai handed her.

'D'you think it's ever going to stop raining?' she said.

'According to the Met Office, it should ease off this afternoon, but they are forecasting more for the weekend,' Tom replied.

'How are the people out on the barge?' Cassie asked.

'Quite safe. Gramps has been out to check the mooring and it's holding fast in the swell. He's told them not to attempt to leave the barge until the tide turns later. He's offered to ferry them to and from shore in the launch.'

Cassie's phone rang at that moment. James.

'Happy birthday, Cassie. Have a lovely day. I'm sorry I won't be seeing you today but I'm looking forward to Saturday.'

'Thank you, James. You take care out and about on the river today, won't you? It's running very fast at the moment.' James promised he would before ringing off.

Mai put some cards and packages on the table. 'Happy birthday, Cassie,' Mai said. 'I hope you're planning to spend the day here.'

'Thank you, Mai. I'm supposed to be having lunch with Doug on *Megabyte* and this evening I'm having supper with Veronica in town. Other than that, I'd love to spend the day here.'

'Birthday lunch with Doug? Is there something you should tell us, Mum?' Tom teased.

'Certainly not,' Cassie laughed. 'Today just happens to be the only day Doug has free from business commitments. I don't think he even knows it's my birthday.'

She could feel the colour rising in her cheeks and hoped Tom would change the subject.

She liked Doug and enjoyed his company, but she didn't want anybody reading things into their relationship that simply weren't there.

* * *

Doug, however, did know it was her birthday, as was evident by the bottle of champagne in the ice bucket and the gift-wrapped package waiting for her in *Megabyte*'s dining saloon that lunchtime.

'Happy birthday and many more of them.'

'Oh, Doug. I didn't think you knew.'

Doug poured her a glass of champagne, before handing her a small box. 'I hope you like this, Cassie. I can change it if it's not to your taste.'

Cassie smothered a gasp as she took the delicate gold necklace with its inlaid aquamarine stones out of the box. It was exquisite.

'I wanted to give you something to remember such a momentous occasion,' Doug said quietly, taking her hand in his. 'And to mark what I hope is the beginning of more than friendship between us.'

His words hung in the air as he looked at her, waiting for her reaction.

Cassie took a deep breath and withdrew her hand.

'The necklace is beautiful, Doug, but I can't accept it. It's far too early in our friendship for you to be buying me such an expensive birthday present. What happens if our friendship doesn't last? I'd feel guilty every time I wore the necklace, and you'd regret having spent such a lot of money on someone who didn't return your feelings.'

It was several seconds before Doug spoke.

'Cassie, I'm sorry, I didn't mean to embarrass you. I merely wanted to give you a nice present. It's been a long time since I've met a woman I like as much as you. I'm clearly out of practice with the social niceties and have jumped in too quickly.' He paused. 'Please accept the necklace as a special present for a significant birthday from a new friend with no other motive. Next time, I'll ask your permission before I buy you anything.'

This last was said with such a twinkle in his eyes that Cassie laughed in spite of herself.

'It's been a long time for me, too, since anybody wanted to buy me expensive presents and it *is* beautiful,' she confessed. 'As a special birthday present for the big five-O then. Thank you very much.' Shyly, she stood on her tiptoes and kissed his cheek.

Doug sighed with relief.

'Good. Now that's sorted, let's have lunch.'

* * *

Walking back through the boatyard mid-afternoon, thinking about the expensive present and the way that Doug was so attentive to her every need, Cassie answered a call on her mobile. James. He'd been on the river earlier to check how the various moorings were coping with the swollen and fast-running river and wanted to update her.

'The water is still lapping the cottage steps and the patio but hasn't covered the top step and reached the sandbags. The rain has stopped, so hopefully everything will start to calm down. Are you staying with Tom and Mai again this evening?'

'After I get back from supper with Veronica, yes,' Cassie said.

'Good. Somebody seems to have taken advantage of the bad weather and broken into several boats.'

'I did lock the cottage up securely before I left it,' Cassie said.

'I've got to do another patrol tonight, so I'll make sure to check on the cottage, just in case.'

'Thanks. James?'

'Yes?'

'You will take care, won't you? No heroics?'

There was a chuckle at the end of the line before James replied, 'I promise, no heroics. Enjoy your supper with Veronica and I will see you on Saturday morning.'

As Cassie went to put the phone in her pocket, a text pinged in from Polly.

Happy, happy birthday, Mum. We'll celebrate when I'm home. Lots of love. Polly. xxx

Quickly Cassie typed a 'thank you' reply and tried not to think about Polly and *Cream*, thousands of miles away in the Southern Ocean.

31

Veronica had moved into Glebe House when her furniture from Wales had arrived two days earlier and was keen to show Cassie how the house looked when she arrived for supper.

'There's still a lot to do, of course, and not every room is furnished yet, but it's coming together,' Veronica said. Back down in the kitchen after a quick tour of the bedrooms, she offered Cassie a glass of rosé while they waited for the lasagne to finish cooking in the Aga.

'I'd better not. I'm driving and the road was still flooded in places as I drove in tonight. I'll stick with coffee, you have a glass, though.' Cassie reached into her tote and handed Veronica a package.

'Housewarming present. It's just a bit of fun I couldn't resist when I saw it.'

Veronica undid the wrapping and opened the box before bursting into laughter.

'Oh, my God, it's a Dartmouth Pottery gurgling jug. Where did you find it?'

'On eBay. They are quite sought after these days, now they're no longer made.'

Carefully Veronica lifted the water jug, made in the shape of a fish, out of the box. 'I remember when we were kids, we were both fascinated by the glug glug noise it made when you lifted it to pour.'

'They were eventually made in all sorts of colours, but that copper green is the original colour the pottery used,' Cassie said.

'I love it. Pride of place on the dresser,' Veronica said, placing it on the middle shelf. 'Thank you so much.'

The buzzer on the cooker sounded then and, within minutes, the two of them were tucking into plates of lasagne. While they ate, Cassie brought Veronica up to date on the news from the boatyard, Tom learning to trust his legs again, how Polly was doing and also about the Harbour Commission wanting to combine the two harbours.

'James is thinking about applying for another job on the east coast rather than trying for the new combined position,' she said as she finished her meal.

'How do you feel about that?' Veronica gave her friend a quizzical look. 'Would you miss him if he left?'

'Of course,' Cassie answered instantly. 'He's been Harbour Master for years now, he does a brilliant job.'

'Never mind the river and his job. Would you miss him personally?'

'Yes, he's a good friend,' Cassie said, not admitting to Veronica how her heart had plummeted at the news James was thinking about leaving. She knew she'd miss him terribly. 'He also says if he's offered the option of early retirement, he'd take that in preference.' She shrugged. 'So we'll have to wait and see what he decides to do.'

Veronica got up and cleared the plates. 'Local strawberries and clotted cream for dessert?'

'Sounds good.' Cassie smiled at her friend. 'Doug gave me a

birthday present at lunch today. I brought it to show you.' She reached for her bag and placed the box containing the necklace on the table and watched to see Veronica's reaction when she saw it.

Veronica's eyes were wide as she glanced from the necklace to Cassie. 'Very nice.'

'It's a lovely present, but I did try to refuse it, saying it was too expensive for someone he barely knows. He did listen to what I was saying and apologised if he'd embarrassed me but insisted I kept it. From a friend for a significant birthday.'

Veronica handed the box back. 'He's obviously hoping you will get to know each other as really good friends.'

'But I feel as if he's bribing me to like him,' Cassie admitted. 'Do you think that's what he's doing – or am I being silly?'

Veronica shook her head. 'No, you're not being silly. Maybe that is what he's doing, who knows? But he clearly likes you.'

Cassie sighed. 'And now I feel guilty because he's not invited to my birthday dinner on Saturday – even though he did say he was away again at the weekend, which was why he invited me for lunch today. Incidentally, do you know who exactly is coming? Tom and Dad haven't said. And the Seafarers is a bit on the expensive side for too many people.'

'I shouldn't worry,' Veronica said. 'I think your dad is more than willing to push the boat out for you. Just enjoy it.'

32

By Saturday, the rain had eased, and the fears of flooding had receded. Cassie and James, making their way out to the bay in James's dinghy, found there was a strong enough wind to make for exciting sailing. Although they finished the race in ninth place, they both agreed it had been a good day.

'I'll be back to pick you up at eight o'clock,' James said. 'Cottage or Boatyard House?'

'Boatyard House, please. It's still very muddy at the cottage.'

Tom and Mai had already left for the Seafarers by the time James arrived that evening. Cassie was wearing the dress she'd bought in Cape Town, which drew an appreciative whistle from James.

'You look beautiful, Cassie. These are for you. If you don't like them, please say so. We can take them back and you can choose something else.'

He watched anxiously as Cassie undid her present to reveal a pair of topaz drop earrings.

'James, they're lovely. I'm going to wear them tonight. They're a perfect match for my dress.' Cassie fixed them into her ears, banishing a fleeting pang of guilt for loving them more than the gold and aqua-marine necklace she'd left lying upstairs in its box. James clearly knew the kind of jewellery she favoured. Turning to give James a thank you kiss, she found herself enveloped unexpectedly in a tight hug.

'Happy birthday, Cassie,' James whispered before he kissed her. Seconds later, when he released her, she was surprised to find how much she had enjoyed the kiss and found herself disappointed that it had been so short.

'Come on, let's party,' James said, holding her hand and taking her to the car.

Once they'd parked at the country club, he took her hand again and they made their way through the foyer. At the foot of the stairs, she automatically turned for the Seafarers Restaurant.

'No, this way, Cassie,' James said and walked towards the function room.

Cassie pointed at the sign. 'It's closed for a special...' Her voice trailed away as James opened the door and she was greeted by a large crowd, all shouting 'Surprise!' at the tops of their voices.

Turning to James, she laughed. 'You could have warned me,' she said, before walking into the room to be surrounded by her family and friends.

Cassie was dancing an energetic Charleston with James later in the evening, when she saw Tom answer his mobile phone and glance across at her. His expression was serious, and she was already moving towards him as he beckoned her over.

'Mum. It's Polly.' He handed the phone to her.

'Hi, Mum. Sorry to interrupt the party. I hope you're having fun.'

'Yes, thanks. Are you all right?'

'I need to tell you something before you hear it on the news.'

Cassie waited, her heart in her mouth.

'One of the other skippers has had an accident. As I'm the

nearest boat, I've been asked to alter course and give assistance. Dexter will ring you later and tell you all the details. I just wanted to tell you not to worry.'

'I'll try not to, so long as you're okay,' Cassie said. 'Take care and stay safe.'

Cassie put the phone down and turned to Tom.

'Polly said Dexter will ring with more details. I suppose she means in the morning.' Cassie's lips quivered.

'Try not to worry, Mum.' Tom's tone was reassuring. 'It's not Polly who's in trouble, remember.'

In the background, Cassie heard the band start to play another tune.

'James is waiting for another dance,' Tom pointed out.

'Oh, I couldn't,' Cassie began.

'Yes, you can,' James interrupted and led her back onto the dance floor. 'It's still your birthday party, so try and enjoy the rest of it.'

And Cassie found herself doing just that. Maybe the extra glass of champagne James gave her had something to do with it, but she did manage to put all worries about Polly to the back of her mind and enjoy the rest of the evening.

It was after midnight before the last of her friends said good-night and James drove her home.

'They say fifty is the new forty, these days, so how does it feel to be forty?'

Cassie smothered a yawn. 'I'm looking forward to my bed tonight more than I did after my real fortieth. I definitely haven't got the stamina for late nights any more.'

'I know what you mean,' James agreed. 'I'm good on early mornings, though.'

'I can't help worrying about Polly, too,' Cassie said quietly. 'I wonder what kind of accident the other skipper has had? What Polly will have to face when she gets to him?'

'Dexter will tell you more in the morning,' James said.

'It's a bit on the misty side tonight, isn't it?' Cassie peered out of the windscreen.

'Actually, I think it looks more like smoke. There's probably a chimney fire somewhere,' James answered.

'Now, are you spending what's left of the night at Boatyard House or am I parking and walking you back to the cottage?' he asked as they approached the crossroads.

'Boatyard House, please. I haven't got the cottage to rights yet since the river burst its banks. Besides, I left Solo at the house.'

Just then, James pulled over to the verge and stopped. Cassie looked at him in surprise.

'Is something the matter? Have we broken down or something?'

'No. There's a flashing blue light behind.'

They both watched the police car drive straight past with a grateful toot of its horn.

Cassie looked at James in dismay.

'Apart from the Henshawes' place that we've just passed, this road only goes to the boatyard.'

James nodded as he began to follow the police car as it made its way quickly down to the boatyard. As they drove, the atmosphere outside became steadily thicker and there was a definite smell of pungent smoke. Cassie took a deep breath.

'James, I think Boatyard House is on fire.'

'I can't see any flames,' he answered shortly, but as they drove into the yard, it became evident that there had been flames – lots of them. Not in the house itself, but in the workshops.

Bill, Tom and Joshua were talking to the police as the firemen began to tidy up their equipment.

'Where's Solo? What's happened?' Cassie asked anxiously.

'Mai is in the house with her and she's fine,' Bill assured her. 'Everything is under control.'

'By the look of the front door, somebody tried to break into the house and your dog went potty. The front door is scratched to bits inside,' one of the policemen said.

'I'm afraid they had better luck with the workshops,' said Bill. 'They got away with a lot of tools and things before setting fire to the place.'

'Oh, Dad, I'm so sorry. If it hadn't been for my birthday party, someone would have been here and it wouldn't have happened.'

'That's silly talk, Cassie. I reckon they were just biding their time.'

'Any ideas yet who's responsible?' Cassie asked the policeman.

He shook his head. 'It's too soon to say. All we know so far is they came and left by boat. There were two or three of them, judging by the number of new muddy footprints we've found. We'll need to get forensics out here first thing in the morning. The brigade will be doing their own tests too.' He nodded in the direction of the firemen.

'I'm afraid I have to ask you not to touch anything before forensic have been.'

'I reckon we all want our beds anyway,' Bill said. 'We're all too tired to start clearing up now.'

'By the way, who called the fire brigade?' Cassie asked.

'The couple on the barge. Used their mobile,' a fireman said.

One of the policemen glanced at James. 'Could I have an official word, Captain White, before we go?'

'Of course.' James nodded.

Tom had gone to join Mai in the house, and Bill and Joshua gave Cassie a hand taking her presents indoors whilst James talked to the policeman. Finally, Cassie touched James on the arm.

'I'm sorry to interrupt, James, but I'm off to bed. I just wanted to say goodnight – and thank you.'

'Goodnight, Cassie. I'll ring you tomorrow,'

As she went indoors, Cassie heard the policeman speak quietly to James.

'If it could be a joint operation, I feel we'd have a better chance of catching them.'

* * *

Extract from Polly's private journal

Monday, 1 August

It's thirty-six hours now since I altered course and effectively took myself out of the race for this leg. I can't help feeling disappointed, but I know if I'd run into trouble, one of the guys would be doing the same for me.

The weather isn't too bad – no storms are forecast in the immediate future, anyway.

I've been reading up on my first aid in case Jean-Paul is in a worse state than he says.

We've been emailing each other and I've spoken to him on the phone, so he knows I should be with him in the next twelve hours.

The plan is for me to get alongside and get him on board *Cream*. Then we wait for an Australian frigate that's been asked to divert and assist.

They'll take Jean-Paul on board and I'll sail back to my last official position and head for New Zealand again.

I've re-angled the video camera on the mast so I should have a record of what happens when I reach Jean-Paul. We're so far from land I know there won't be any TV crews around to film any drama.

Dexter has warned me, though, that they'll be waiting for me in their hordes when I finally get to New Zealand. He's also promised to try and sort out something re time penalties for me.

I'm going to have a bowl of pasta and a quick sleep before I have a mammoth session on the satellite phone. I know Mum and Tom will be anxious for news and Dexter always rings to wish me goodnight.

33

It was a question of all hands to the mop and broom in the boatyard over the next few days, once the forensic teams had given them the all-clear and the insurance assessor had been.

Cassie and Tom were throwing pieces of charred wood into the rubbish skip Bill had organised. Cassie was trying to keep her mind away from thoughts of Polly and what she was currently facing when her mobile rang.

It was Dexter.

'What's happening?' Cassie asked anxiously.

'Polly's due to reach Jean-Paul in a few hours and everything is looking good. She was fine when I spoke to her this morning. She's a bit apprehensive as to what she's going to find, but Jean-Paul says the yacht is in a worse state than he is.'

Although Dexter spoke confidently, there was a certain edge to his voice and Cassie knew he would be worried about Jean-Paul as well as Polly. She'd noticed how close he and Polly were becoming when she'd flown out to South Africa for the end of the first leg of the race.

'She's going to ring you later.'

'Thanks, Dexter. I'll speak to you again soon.'

Cassie quickly relayed the conversation to Tom, who gave a sigh.

'You do realise this rescue has scuppered any chance she might have had of a place not only in this leg but probably also in the race result as a whole?' he said. 'Hopefully the committee will be able to work out and adjust her times.' Tom smiled at Cassie. 'Her name will be on everyone's lips now,' he said philosophically. 'Win or lose.'

Cassie nodded. 'Where's Mai this morning?'

'She's gone out to the barge with a large box of chocolates and a bottle of wine to say thank you for raising the alarm so quickly.' Tom glanced around.

'Bad as it is, it could have been a lot worse. Do the police reckon they'll catch whoever did it?'

'It's too soon to say.'

Just then, Cassie's phone rang again.

'I'll see you later, Mum, I promised Gramps I'd give him a hand in the yard when we'd filled the skip,' Tom said as she answered.

'Cassie, I've just heard about the fire.' Doug's voice made Cassie jump. She'd been expecting James. 'Is there anything I can do? I could send some of the crew over to help clear up.'

'Thanks for the offer, Doug, but we're fine,' Cassie said. 'Where are you?'

Doug spent so much time travelling on business that she was never quite sure where he was.

'Brittany, waiting for the ferry home. I wanted to ask you to pencil a date in your diary.'

Cassie waited.

'Normally all my business dinners are in London and Heidi acts as my hostess.' There was a hesitant pause before Doug continued. 'I've got an important awards dinner coming up in Cornwall and I know Heidi is unavailable. Cassie, would you consider being my partner for the evening?'

'Oh, Doug, I don't know if I'm up to business dinners.'

'I have no doubt you are more than up to it.'

'Where's it being held? And what's the date?'

'Royal Carlton.' Doug named the most prestigious hotel and conference centre in the region. 'First Saturday in September.'

Cassie gulped. The Royal Carlton? 'May I think about it, Doug? It's not really my scene…'

'Cassie, I need a partner for the evening and I would love it to be you. And, of course, as this is a business dinner, all expenses will be on me. I'll even treat you to a new frock, if you like. I'm back on *Megabyte* at the end of the week, so come for supper one evening and let me know then.' And the call ended.

Thoughtfully, Cassie turned off her phone. Had she imagined it, or was Doug applying gentle pressure for her to agree immediately to being his partner for the evening? The Royal Carlton was a real upmarket hotel – the kind of place Cassie always preferred to avoid if she could. Doug's high-flying social life took her way out of her comfort zone but she couldn't help feeling that maybe she owed him for the expensive necklace.

* * *

Twelve thousand miles away in the Southern Ocean, Polly was struggling to bring *Cream* within range of Jean-Paul's stricken yacht.

A change of wind direction had delayed her original estimated time of arrival by a couple of hours and now the same wind was hampering the rescue operation itself.

With the yacht hoved to, she struggled in the large swell that was rocking both yachts. She was very aware of how ill Jean-Paul looked. He was clearly in no fit state to give her much assistance.

Although, judging by his greeting, he still had his sense of humour.

'Hi, Little Polly. What kept you?'

Standing on *Cream*'s deck, trying to judge the right moment for throwing a line across to the other yacht, she could hear the ominous sound of the damaged keel banging. That could mean only one thing.

Water would be seeping slowly into the hull and it could only be a matter of time before the yacht sank. They needed to work fast.

Somehow, she was going to have to haul Jean-Paul aboard *Cream* despite his obvious injuries.

Several waterproof bags were lying on the floor of the stricken yacht's cockpit. Jean-Paul had stowed as much of his gear as possible, including his laptop and yacht's log. Now, as Polly threw him the line, he clumsily tied bags onto it, ready to be hauled across the heaving gap between the two boats.

At last Jean-Paul gave her a thumbs up sign.

'Winch away!' he yelled.

Several minutes later, his dripping possessions were on the floor of *Cream*'s cockpit, having safely survived being dragged through the water. Polly looked across at Jean-Paul.

'You're next. Unless, of course, you fancy swimming across? No, thought not.'

His reply was blown away in a gust of wind, but he began the difficult task of hooking his safety harness onto the line, before slipping into the sea.

The heavy swell was lifting both yachts, not in unison but alternately. Polly wished the gap between the yachts was smaller, but it was impossible in these huge seas. For a heart-stopping moment, as she slowly winched him across, Jean-Paul disappeared when a huge swell engulfed him.

Forcing herself to keep on turning the winch, Polly willed him to reappear and allowed herself a small sigh of relief when she saw the orange flash of his lifejacket. Winching a heavy man across was a far harder task than rescuing his possessions had been.

Turning the winch as quickly as she could, she watched as the line pulled Jean-Paul closer and closer to *Cream* and the point where she would finally be able to haul him on board.

Half an hour later, they both collapsed on the deck of *Cream* – Polly from sheer exhaustion and Jean-Paul from exhaustion and the huge amount of pain he was in.

Polly roused herself to try to assess his injuries and handed him some painkillers.

'Here, take these and let me see if I can do something about that gash on your leg. Not to mention your hand.'

'Thanks, I took the last of my painkillers a few hours ago,' and Jean-Paul gratefully swallowed the tablets.

'I'm eternally grateful,' he said quietly. 'Thanks, Polly.'

'Hey, they're only tablets,' Polly was about to say, when she realised that he was thanking her for rescuing him. Embarrassed, she patted him on the shoulder instead.

He flinched in pain.

'I think I've fractured my shoulder, too.'

'I'll let Race HQ know you're on board and see if they know when the frigate is likely to arrive. Their doctor will soon sort you out. But first I'll put the coffee on,' Polly said. 'I think we both deserve a cup and some food. I might just put a splash of my emergency brandy in the coffee.'

As they sat there with their hot drinks, Jean-Paul started to tell Polly what had happened. 'It was all going so well, good wind and I was making good time. I'd set the self-steering and gone down below to make some food when the boat hit something and the force of the impact threw me all over the place. Think I bashed every bit of me into everything before I ended up on the floor right down by the bow. Hearing the sound of the keel banging,' Jean-Paul shrugged, 'I knew I was in deep trouble.'

'Any idea what you hit?'

'I reckon it was a submerged container because there had been no sign of anything untoward on the surface.'

As Jean-Paul finished speaking, the satellite phone pinged with a call from Dexter.

'The frigate will be with you in about eight hours. You'll have to sit tight until then. Jean-Paul, there is a doc on board who'll check you out before the helicopter takes you on to New Zealand. Polly, once Jean-Paul is on board the frigate, you're free to set sail.'

Polly closed her eyes as her body tensed at his words. All she could think was, where was that damned container now?

34

Driving into town to have a coffee with Veronica, Cassie tried to do
the impossible and push all worrying thoughts about Polly and the
rescue mission out of her mind. There was no way she could relax
until she knew everyone was safe and the rescue mission was over.

Veronica greeted her with a hug. 'I've put a couple of chairs in
the summerhouse. I thought we'd have our coffee down there.
How's the cleaning up after the fire going?'

'We're nearly finished. Dad's a bit depressed. The thieves got
away with more than he'd originally reckoned, and the insurance
company are querying everything. But things should be back to
normal soon. I just hope they catch the culprits.'

'Any developments on that front?'

Cassie shook her head.

'No. They're working on the theory the thieves used a small boat
that they keep hidden somewhere. James has been doing a detailed
inventory of all the small boats he sees on the river and inspecting
the smaller creeks for any hidden craft.'

'How is James?'

'Fine, I think. Polly agreed to me using her yacht, *It's Mine!*, while she's away and I've entered a race in the Dartmouth Regatta at the end of the month. James is crewing for me. That is if he's calmed down and forgiven me. I haven't plucked up the courage yet to phone him.'

Veronica raised her eyebrows enquiringly.

'Last time I saw him, we had a bit of a disagreement,' Cassie explained.

'What about?'

Cassie looked at her friend wryly.

'Doug wants me to attend an important business dinner with him next month, all expenses paid, including a new evening dress if I would like one. James is not happy.'

'I suspect he's jealous.' Veronica smiled gently.

'Yes, possibly, but he has no reason to be,' Cassie said. 'What he mainly hates is the thought of Doug buying me an expensive outfit. In his world, men don't buy single women clothes without an ulterior motive.' She sighed. 'But he also thinks Doug is using me. I got cross and ended up telling him it was none of his business what I do, or who I do it with.'

'Which it isn't, is it?' Veronica said.

Cassie shook her head. She took a sip of her coffee before replying. 'No, but I can see his point because actually, I'm not comfortable with accepting the new outfit offer, either. Hotel and travel expenses are one thing, but clothes...' She shook her head doubtfully. 'Anyway, I've given Doug a tentative yes. But the whole thing has upset James and I'm really sorry about that. Honestly, life was a lot simpler when I stayed at home.'

'Maybe. But you weren't really living then, were you?' Veronica pointed out quietly.

Cassie smiled. 'True. It's taken me a long time to realise it, though.' She stood up and put her cup on the tray.

'Thanks for the coffee. I'd better be getting back. Now, are you sure about coming up to the boatyard to help me while Tom and Mai are in London?'

'Positive. How's Tom coping now the hospital has more or less signed him off?'

'Fine. Both his legs are weak, of course, particularly his right one, but he's doing his exercises religiously. The biggest problem is making him take things slowly. He's desperate to get back into the swing of things. And both he and Mai are looking forward to their break.'

'I'll see you bright and early next Tuesday morning then,' Veronica said. 'And Cassie, phone James and clear the air.'

* * *

Days later, however, Cassie still hadn't contacted James. She was feeling very guilty and knew that her apology was overdue.

Having taken Tom and Mai to Totnes station to catch the ten o'clock London train, she decided to drive into Dartmouth and call in at his office.

James greeted her with a big smile and a kiss on each cheek.

'Cassie, I was going to ring you. Come in and have a coffee.'

'James, I wanted to apologise,' Cassie began, but he interrupted.

'I'm the one who should be apologising. I overreacted,' he said. 'Much as I would like it to be my business, as you pointed out, who you see has nothing to do with me.'

'I'm really sorry I've upset you,' Cassie said. 'I know it's because you care and are concerned for me.'

James brushed her words aside.

'Do you still want me to crew for your regatta on Saturday?' he asked instead.

'Please. I can't possibly manage without you.'

The look of longing in James's eyes at her words brought a flush to Cassie's cheeks. What on earth was she thinking of, upsetting such a lovely man?

Impulsively, she went across and gave him a gentle kiss.

'James, you are very special to me.'

'You know I want more than that, Cassie,' James said quietly and drew her towards him in a tight hug. 'This is not the place to tell you again how I feel, but you know I'm always here for you.'

The unexpected kiss he gave her was not as gentle as the one she'd given him, but Cassie found herself relaxing into his embrace.

As James reluctantly let her go, Cassie changed the subject.

'Any news on the job front?'

'I should hear this week about the redundancy package they're prepared to offer me. Then it's decision time.'

A buzz and flashing light on the office intercom caught his attention.

'Excuse me, Cassie.' James picked up his internal phone.

He listened intently.

'I'll be with you in about fifteen minutes,' he said, then turned to Cassie. 'I'm sorry, I'll have to go. There's been an incident upriver. Your burglars are possibly involved.'

Cassie opened his office door.

'Take care, James. I'll see you on board *It's Mine!* on Saturday morning. Eight o'clock okay?'

'Oh, I'll be in touch before then. And I'll let you know if there are any developments as far as your burglary is concerned.' Another quick peck on her cheek and he was running downstairs towards the quay and his launch.

Watching James go, Cassie felt a strong surge of affection for him. She really regretted hurting him over Doug and this business dinner that she didn't want to go to anyway.

Fleetingly, she considered telling Doug she'd changed her mind, but decided against it. She'd agreed to go and didn't like the thought of letting him, or anyone for that matter, down at the last minute.

The misunderstanding and harsh words between herself and James had been cleared up and they were friends again, which was all that mattered. So she'd tell Doug she'd definitely go with him. And then afterwards she'd step back and make sure Doug understood it was only friendship on offer.

35

'Will you cope all right with these steps?' Mai looked anxiously at Tom.

'I think so. I'm getting used to trusting my legs again and not relying totally on a crutch,' Tom grinned at her. Mai had insisted he brought one of his crutches, not wanting him to overdo things.

'Anyway, there's a handrail. So long as it doesn't break, I'm good.' Tom gave Mai a wry smile before he carefully hauled himself up towards the theatre restaurant where he and Mai had plans to enjoy a leisurely meal before the play's evening performance began.

It was the last day of their break and Tom knew that Mai had enjoyed the bright lights and town life.

When they'd met and fallen in love eighteen months ago, he'd told her about the sleepy corner of the West Country he came from. She'd laughed and confessed to being an out-and-out townie.

Once they were seated at a table and had ordered a meal, Tom looked at his wife. 'Mai, you don't have any regrets, do you?'

'Regrets? What sort?' Mai sounded surprised.

'Marrying me. Live in the country. Giving up all this. It's not exactly been a bundle of fun the past few months, what with my accident and everything. And the lack of social life.'

'Tom, I love you. Where you are is where I want to be. Sure, I did miss the social life initially. But I've made lots of friends back home now, and I feel really settled at the boatyard, especially since we moved into the house.' She paused and looked at him.

'It's the first time I've ever had much of a home life. That more than compensates for any lack of shops or entertainment.'

She reached out and held his hand across the table.

'My life has never been this good. Your family have welcomed me with open arms, which is wonderful. And now you're well on the road to recovery from your accident, the baby is due to put in an appearance soon, it can only get better. I truly can't wait to get home tomorrow.'

'You know...' but whatever else Tom was about to say was lost as Mai's attention was caught by somebody at the bar and she interrupted him.

'Tom, turn round slowly, isn't that Sebastian over there?'

Tom looked around.

'Yes, it is. Mum said he was back in the UK now his exercise is over. I'm surprised he hasn't been in touch. Shall I ask him to join us?'

Mai shook her head. 'No. Best not. I think he's got company.'

Tom shifted slightly in his chair to get a better view and they both watched as Sebastian affectionately kissed a tall brunette and put a proprietary arm around her shoulders.

Moments later, the couple left the bar and vanished into the theatre auditorium.

Mai looked at Tom.

'Mmm. What d'you make of that, then?'

Tom was speechless – only his clenched fist gave Mai a clue as to how he felt about witnessing the actions of the man who was supposedly in love with his sister and wanted to marry her.

'Cassie, quick! Polly's on the news! They're carrying a report of her arrival in New Zealand. They're going to show her rescue video, too,' James called out as he turned up the volume on the TV.

It was Saturday evening and Cassie and James had finished supper, having returned to the cottage after competing with *It's Mine!* in the local regatta. They were very pleased with themselves, having come in third in their class.

Now, they watched the TV footage of the harbourside crowded with people waving flags and cheering to welcome Polly. Then the cameras swung across to the official launch for a close-up of Jean-Paul. One shoulder was heavily strapped, and his right wrist was in plaster, but there was a broad smile on his face.

'This is a man who is determined to welcome Little Polly to New Zealand and to say thank you publicly,' the commentator's voice continued.

'Rescued by Polly and then flown here to New Zealand by the Australian Navy for urgent medical treatment, Jean-Paul has spent the last few days anticipating his saviour's arrival. He's had time to relive these scenes and to reflect on how lucky he is to be alive.'

The pictures of cheering crowds faded into Polly's video.

Cassie watched in silence. Looking at the huge seas and the way the two yachts were rolling violently at the mercy of the elements, she realised Polly had played down the whole incident when she'd spoken to her. The rescue had been a lot more dangerous than she'd let on.

Cassie swallowed hard, but the lump in her throat refused to go away and the tears started to trickle down her cheeks.

James moved across and took her in his arms.

'It's over, Cassie. She did it and she did it well. You have a daughter to be extremely proud of and now she's safe in New Zealand. Look at the crowds. They love her. She's the heroine of the day.'

As the rescue video finished, the cameras went back to witness live the emotional reunion between Jean-Paul and Polly.

'Thanks, Little Polly. I owe you,' and Jean-Paul held her tight.

'*Holdsworth Clotted Cream* and Polly now have to spend a minimum of three days here in port before leaving to try and catch up with the rest of the fleet. During this time, Polly will sleep as much as she can, and her shore crew will be preparing the yacht for not only the Southern Ocean but also the notorious Cape Horn.'

The commentator went on to discuss how Polly's final position would be affected by the time spent rescuing Jean-Paul.

'Because of the handicapping system, Polly will have to finish the next two legs in higher than seventh place to achieve a podium position. We wish her well.'

As the report finished and the programme reverted to domestic news, Cassie's mobile on the coffee table rang.

'Can you answer that, please?' Cassie called from the kitchen. 'It's probably only Tom.'

James smiled at the note of surprise he detected in the caller's voice when he answered.

'James? It's Tom. Have you got the TV on? Polly seems to be on every channel! We've recorded one report just in case Mum missed it.'

'I'm sure she'll be pleased about that. We've just seen the rescue video on the news,' James said. 'Do you want a word with Cassie?'

'No, don't worry. I'll catch up with her tomorrow. Sorry for interrupting your evening.' Tom hung up quickly, leaving James amused.

'I think Tom was surprised to hear my voice,' he said to Cassie. 'You didn't tell him I was coming to supper after the race?'

Cassie shook her head.

'No. I didn't feel the need. Besides, I've barely seen him since he and Mai got back yesterday. I haven't even had the chance to tell him about the lead on the burglars.'

'We're not too sure about that yet,' James warned. 'It isn't enough simply to be convinced that the men who were arrested last week are also responsible for the break-in and fire at the boatyard. We need hard evidence before we can charge them. I know the police are hopeful that forensics will be able to come up with matching finger and footprints.'

'When will they have the results?' Cassie asked.

'Sometime this week. Then the police will decide whether to press charges or not.' James sighed. 'Crime on the river is becoming a real problem – and the merging of the two Harbour Masters' jobs isn't going to help.'

He looked at her.

'I shall be glad to hand over the responsibility to someone else.'

'When are the changes likely to come into effect?' Cassie asked.

'Some time after the end of the season if I accept early retirement. They want me to stay on for a month to hand things over to the new chap. And that will be the end of my official working life,' he said pensively.

'Look on it as an adventure.' Cassie smiled. 'It could be exciting.'

'Perhaps you're right. Maybe I should think about moving to another area, but I really like it around here. I definitely like the company.'

The look in his eyes made Cassie blush. Before he could say more, Cassie spoke quickly.

'Finish your coffee, James. I'm going to turn you out in about five minutes. I'm whacked after all that fresh air and exercise. I need an early night.' She deliberately kept her tone light.

James sighed as he watched her carry his empty coffee cup through to the kitchen. He picked up his jacket, and then kissed her lightly on the cheek.

'Thanks for a good day. I'll give you a ring in the morning.'

Without another word, he was gone, the door closing behind him with a sharp click.

* * *

Extract from Polly's private journal

Thursday, 1 September

The rest of the fleet are now well ahead of me. Colin on *Flight of the Seagull* is currently in the lead – again – and the others are well spread out behind him. The race committee are working on time adjustments that will take into account my diversion, so fingers crossed.

This leg has already given me some difficult sailing. I know there is still more to come if I'm to finish in a decent position in Brazil.

It's raining hard at the moment with some tremendous seas out there and I'm very tired.

Getting only three days' rest in New Zealand instead of the ten days everybody else got didn't give me enough time to regain all my strength.

I'd hoped by sailing a slightly northern course I'd find some better weather, but so far that hasn't worked.

Everyone warned me this would be the toughest leg of the race and the closer I get to Cape Horn, the more I realise how right they were.

Two days ago, I sailed through an iceberg field.

Seeing those huge, huge, towering lumps of ice gave real meaning to me of the word awesome. They were truly magnificent. Considering the consequences of *Cream* connecting with one of them, however, was a sobering thought and truly didn't bear thinking about.

I have never felt so alone and so vulnerable in my life.

It took me hours to get through the ice field and away from all the dangerous loose floating growlers that had broken off. Finally, I passed my last berg – the largest of them all. Its menacing beauty was breathtaking.

I feel absolutely drained now. All that concentration and lack of proper sleep has taken its toll.

Dexter phoned before I started to write this and he insisted that I get some sleep.

'You have the Cape to face in a few days. You're going to need all your strength for that. And remember, Polly, I'm rooting for you. Please take care.'

36

Cassie stood in front of the mirror in her hotel room and surveyed her appearance. For a woman who had recently passed a milestone birthday, she didn't think she looked too bad.

Veronica had been right about the dress. It was perfect.

Cassie had felt distinctly guilty about spending such a large amount of money on one dress but having refused to allow Doug to buy her an outfit for the occasion, the bill was all hers. She could only hope she'd have a special occasion to wear it again in the future.

She smoothed a stray piece of hair back into place, pleased with the new highlights.

Cassie had just pinned the second one of her favourite pearl stud earrings when there was a quiet knock on the door.

'Cassie, it's time we went downstairs,' Doug called from outside.

'Come in. I'm ready. Will I do?'

Doug, looking debonair in his tuxedo, smiled at her before taking her in his arms and gently kissing her.

'You look beautiful. The guys are going to be so jealous of me this evening.'

'I hope I don't let you down. I'm not used to businessmen en masse.' Cassie moved out of his arms and picked up her bag.

'Cassie, they'll love you. Don't worry.'

He glanced at her neck and sounded disappointed as he said, 'You're not wearing my necklace?'

'I didn't think a necklace would go with the neckline of this dress,' Cassie explained quietly. 'It really needs silver and I didn't bring anything silver with me. But the necklace is in my case if you'd like me to wear it.'

Doug shook his head. 'No, you're right. It doesn't go. Oh, Cassie, I'm just so pleased you agreed to come this evening.' He caught hold of her hand in his and raised it to his lips.

Downstairs, they crossed the foyer and joined the throng making their way slowly into the large ballroom. There was a couple already seated at their table. With his arm possessively around Cassie's waist, Doug made the introductions.

'Josie, Ben, this is Cassie, a very special friend of mine. I'd be grateful if you'd look after her for me while I make a quick phone call.'

He turned to Cassie. 'Ben and I go way back – all the way to university – so he knows my darkest secrets. Josie is also an old friend and I'm sure the two of you will get on. I won't be long. Please tell Cassie only nice things about me, guys.'

Cassie hid her annoyance at Doug deserting her so early in the evening and smiled at his friends. Josie and Ben, Cassie decided, were as nice as Doug had indicated they were, but the three of them weren't alone for long. It was only a matter of minutes before the rest of their party joined them and Cassie found her head swimming with the effort of trying to remember which name went with which face.

A man who introduced himself as 'Edwin' sat in the empty seat on her right. Apparently he was Doug's technical right-hand man.

He and his wife also seemed to regard themselves as having some sort of proprietary right over Doug, and when Josie introduced Cassie as a special friend of Doug's, both sets of eyebrows went up and the inquisition began.

'How long have you known Dougie, then?' Edwin asked.

'Where did you meet?' his wife wanted to know.

Cassie took a breath before replying, keeping her answers brief. Then she smiled at Edwin.

'And you, how long have you known Doug?' she countered.

'Forever. I was best man at his wedding. My wife's godmother to both the girls. Heidi's usually with Doug at these functions.'

Josie, who clearly thought Edwin was out of order, tried to stem the flow of questions, but Edwin simply ignored her and carried on cross-examining Cassie.

'How long have you been a widow?'

'Twenty years. How long have you been married?'

'It's our pearl anniversary this year,' Edwin said smugly, looking at his wife.

'Congratulations,' Cassie said, wondering why any woman would stay married that long to such an objectionable man. She'd braced herself for the next personal question when she was relieved to see Doug making his way back towards them and she pointedly turned away from Edwin.

If Doug noticed the strained atmosphere between Cassie and his 'right-hand man', he made no comment.

Inevitably there was a lot of business talk around the table as they ate, but Doug made a point of including Cassie.

When dinner and the short awards ceremony were over, the tables were cleared away and disco music began to fill the air. The doors leading out onto the terrace were opened and people began to circulate. Doug's business, although shortlisted for an award, didn't win, a fact which he accepted with a philosophical shrug.

Unlike his 'right-hand man' Edwin, who was furious that they'd been beaten by a rival he didn't rate.

Doug stood up and held his hand out to Cassie.

'I need some fresh air. Will you join me on the terrace?' Once outside, Doug turned to Cassie. 'I always seem to be apologising to you,' he said. 'Josie tells me Edwin gave you the third degree.'

'Your family and friends are obviously very protective of you,' Cassie said diplomatically.

Doug sighed.

'What none of them seems to realise is the amount of time I spend on my own these days. Edwin goes home to his family. Heidi – well, Heidi is a popular girl and leads a busy social life. For me, after work it's invariably either a TV dinner or a hotel meal, alone.' He looked at Cassie.

'I realise we haven't known each long, but I'm already really fond of you. I want you to know I'm offering more than friendship.'

Cassie felt herself blush under the intensity of his look.

'Doug, I...' She took a deep breath before continuing. 'I've been on my own for so long, it's difficult for me too. I've only just started to step outside of the world I'd hidden in for so long. I need time to sort things out before I make any commitments to anyone.'

'So long as you're not frightened away even before we begin.' He leant forward and gently brushed her forehead with his lips. 'I have a small thank you present for you.' Doug reached into the inside pocket of his dinner jacket.

The twisted bands of silver made an unusual bracelet.

Cassie looked at him in surprise. 'Where and when did you get this?'

'The hotel shop was still open. I couldn't resist it. I hope you like it. Certainly goes with your dress.'

'Doug, I wasn't hinting.'

'Shh. I know. No protests. Like I said, it's a thank you present.' This time, he pulled her into his arms and kissed her properly.

He smiled as he released her.

'Cassie, we are going to make a great couple.'

Cassie stiffened at his words. Had Doug even listened to her? Taken her feelings into account? Or was he the sort of man who prided himself on knowing what, or who, he wanted and ploughed ahead regardless?

James, she knew instinctively, would never ride roughshod over her feelings in the way Doug just had.

37

Doug dropped Cassie back at the boatyard at midday on Sunday. He'd wanted to stop in Plymouth for lunch on their return journey from Cornwall, but Cassie had said a firm no. She needed to get home. 'Busy week coming up, need to get myself organised,' she'd said. 'And I need to catch up with Polly's progress. Tom will have lots to tell me.'

None of the reasons she gave Doug were lies, but they weren't the whole truth either. Last night, when Doug had presented her with the silver bracelet, followed by those self-assured words about them making a great couple, Cassie knew she was in danger of finding herself slip-sliding under pressure into a relationship that she wasn't sure she wanted. Doug had already made plans for the two of them to have dinner in the week and had mentioned a charity golf tournament he was involved with at the Devon Country Club. It was all too much, too soon. She desperately needed some space, time to herself to think.

She was out on the decking in front of the cottage, now recovered from the flooding and filled with potted geraniums, drinking a cup of tea in the late afternoon and watching the activity on the river, when Dexter rang.

'Polly is probably going to ring you soon,' he said. 'She sounds a bit low. I know she's tired and there's probably a bit of a kick-back reaction from the rescue she did. I'm sure talking to you will help. Once she arrives in Brazil, I can give her all the TLC she needs, but right now she seems very vulnerable.'

After Dexter had rung off, Cassie sat there, trying unsuccessfully to put worrying thoughts about Polly out of her mind and wondering what on earth she could say to her daughter.

When her telephone rang, Cassie answered quickly.

'Polly. What a lovely surprise.' She'd decided she wasn't going to mention Dexter had phoned her in case Polly thought they were discussing her behind her back.

'Hi, Mum. Got time to talk?' The tension in Polly's voice was obvious.

'Always. Are you all right, love?' Cassie asked, forcing herself to keep calm. 'Has something happened?'

'No. Nothing's happened. I just need to talk to you. Mum, I think I'm cracking up,' Polly wailed.

Cassie felt herself stiffen when she heard the desperation in Polly's tone.

'I'm not cut out to be a solo sailor. I'm exhausted, fed up with my own company and I'm going to let everyone down. There's no way I'm going to win the race even if I do manage to sail round Cape Horn and get to Brazil. The whole thing has been a pointless exercise. All I want is to come home.'

Her sobs travelled down the line in great gulps.

Cassie took a deep breath.

'Now, you listen to me, Polly Lewis. You're the one who was determined to do this race. You're the one who badgered everyone into agreeing to give you the chance. And you're the one who *will* see it through. Do you understand?'

Cassie sensed rather than heard Polly swallowing her sobs, trying to regulate her breathing.

'The fact you won't win the race has nothing to do with anything. What is important is that you've tried, you've done your best. And more. Polly, you saved a man's life. Winning any race has to take second place to that. Now, how much sleep have you had recently?'

'Catnaps.'

Cassie was silent. With Cape Horn looming, it was extremely unlikely that Polly would get more than catnaps for the foreseeable future. If she could only hove to and get a couple of hours' decent sleep, she might see things in a better perspective.

'How far are you from Cape Horn?'

'About two hundred miles.'

'Well, I suggest you back your jib and hove to, increase both your catnaps and your food intake. Try to get some strength back that way. Have you spoken to Dexter or Tom recently? They've both done a lot of single-handed sailing. They'll know much better than me what you're going through. Keep talking to them.'

Cassie paused.

'And Polly, remember we all love you. We are all proud of your achievements so far and we know you *can* do it. Get to Brazil and see how you feel then.'

The delayed action of the satellite phone seemed to accentuate the tension. The sigh that travelled down the line was as deep as ever. Cassie held her breath. Had her pep talk worked?

'Mum, I'm sorry, but I really don't think I can carry on.'

The connection died.

Cassie covered her face with her trembling hands. The call had left her in limbo, knowing that there was absolutely nothing she could do to pull her daughter out of the depths of despair she had clearly sunk into. The only person who could do that was Polly herself. Cassie sat there, praying that her daughter could dig deep enough to find the hidden strengths that she was going to need to survive.

* * *

When her phone rang at five o'clock the next morning, Cassie's first frightened thought was of Polly, but it was Tom.

'Tom? Is everything all right? Where are you?'

'At the hospital. Mai's contractions started a couple of hours ago. I just wanted you to know things are happening. I'll ring you again when there's more news.'

'Give Mai my love,' Cassie said.

Half an hour later, having been unable to get back to sleep, Cassie got up.

Waiting for the kettle to boil, she absently stroked Solo. Sighing contentedly, the dog leaned against her legs.

Taking her mug of coffee outside, Cassie sat on the patio and thoughtfully watched the breaking dawn, worrying and wondering if her pep talk had been enough to convince Polly that she simply had to keep on trying and not give up.

She sipped her coffee. She had to stop worrying. There was nothing she could do to help Polly from this distance, she could only pray that her daughter's fighting spirit would see her through.

Tom's accident had kick-started so many changes this year already – more changes than there had been in all the years since Miles had died. Cassie gave a deep sigh. She knew as well as anyone that the future was never certain. That all one could do was to hope that everything would work out for the best.

But today was a new day with the promise of a brand-new life about to start. A new life that would bring yet another dimension to the dynamics of their small family. She'd cling on to that positive, happy thought.

It was another four hours before a tired but happy Tom phoned again.

'You'll be pleased to know both mother and baby are doing well, Grandma.'

Cassie breathed a huge sigh of relief.

'The Wriggler weighed in at five pounds, twelve ounces. And she's beautiful.'

Cassie smiled at the pride in her son's voice.

'Can I visit later?'

'Anytime this afternoon. Mai needs to get some rest now.'

Later that morning, Cassie drove into town to have lunch with James before going to the hospital.

James was as thrilled as she was and gave her a huge pink teddy for the baby.

'I wish I could come this afternoon, but I've got a meeting I can't get out of. Give Mai and Tom my love.'

A stubble-chinned but bright-eyed and smiling Tom was waiting for her at the ward entrance when she arrived at the hospital.

'Hi, Mum. Come and meet Alice, your granddaughter.'

38

Cassie and James were enjoying an after-supper coffee, sitting on the decking in front of River View Cottage. A lingering smell of sweet honeysuckle filled the air and in the quiet of the evening, all they could hear was the gentle lapping of the river and the occasional call of a homeward-bound curlew.

James, sitting there with Solo's head resting on his knees, was absently fondling the dog's ears as Cassie glanced at him, thinking how much a part of her life he was now and how much she enjoyed his quiet uncomplicated company and the things they did together – sailing, theatre visits and simple suppers together like this evening.

During the last few weeks, their relationship had slipped effortlessly onto a new level. Last weekend, when she'd been so worried about Polly, his support, over the phone when he couldn't be with her, in person when he could, had been tireless. He'd had a lot to do with her coping with the stress and worry. His delight at Alice's arrival had been lovely too.

James caught her glance.

'You okay?'

Cassie nodded. 'What with Polly messaging to say she is well on her way to Brazil, and Alice arriving, I'm fine. If I'm honest, I haven't been this good in years.'

Sitting companionably there together, Cassie was suddenly overwhelmed with the desire to tell him how much he meant to her. But before she could say a word, James spoke.

'You've turned this place into a real home, Cassie. I love coming here.' He looked around appreciatively. 'Mind you, I love the company too.'

Cassie knew that he spoke the simple truth. She could see it in his eyes. He did love her.

He raised his hands in resignation. 'Sorry, Cassie. I promised myself I wouldn't push you.'

'James, I...'

He shook his head.

'You like living on your own then? You're not lonely?' Even to his own ears, James sounded wistful.

Cassie smiled.

'I've really enjoyed setting up home here and I don't have time to be lonely. What with work at the boatyard, sailing with you, helping Tom and Mai out, seeing Veronica, walking Solo, not to mention all the suppers we have together,' she teased, 'time flies by. And now there's Alice too.' She leant across to stroke Solo's head. 'My life has turned into something of a social whirl.'

There was a short silence before James spoke. 'Cassie, I'm leaving at the weekend for a few days' holiday in Wales.'

'That's a sudden decision, isn't it?' Cassie looked at him, surprised.

James shrugged. 'I thought I might as well take the last of my holiday entitlement. I need to think about my future too. I don't suppose there's any chance of you coming with me, is there?'

Cassie shook her head. 'Oh, James, I can't. You know I've got that golf charity tournament with Doug at the end of the week. I'm sorry.'

'Will you come up afterwards? No, of course not,' James tersely answered his own question.

There was a strained silence for several seconds.

'James, I'm sorry but both Veronica and I did promise Doug that we'd go when he mentioned it,' Cassie said eventually. 'If it's any consolation, I don't really want to go. Golf is a pretty boring game, I think.'

'You seem to do a lot of things you don't really want to do when Doug asks you to.'

It was unlike James to make bitter comments. And Cassie realised that once again, she'd upset him.

'I've got an early start in the office tomorrow. I'm trying to tie up as many loose ends as I can. Walk to the launch with me?' James stood up.

'Of course. James, I'll miss you while you're away,' she said, trying to make amends with the truth. 'Will you phone me from Wales? Let me know you've arrived safely in that sports car of yours.'

'If you want me to,' James answered, but there was a resigned note to his voice.

The evening air was cooler down by the river, with a breeze coming up off the water, and Cassie shivered involuntarily.

James hesitantly turned towards Cassie before taking her in his arms.

'Don't get cold.' He held her tightly for a moment or two.

'While I'm away, will you please think about us, Cassie? About our relationship and where it's going? I'd like to plan a future that includes you and me together. I can't wait much longer. You are going to have to decide what you want.'

He drew her towards him again and kissed her gently. 'I love you, Cassie. I had hoped you felt the same and would do me the honour of being my wife.'

39

Cassie was spending the night with Veronica at Glebe House, ready for an early start the next day. Doug was collecting them both at 7 a.m. to drive them up to the Devon Country Club for the golf tournament. When Doug had heard that Veronica had been a keen golfer with her late husband, often joining him in tournaments, he immediately roped her in for the charity golf match. Both he and Veronica had drawn early places in the competition and Cassie was simply going along as moral support for the two of them.

'Doug is very attentive these days,' Veronica observed as she filled the kettle.

'He's good fun and we enjoy each other's company.' Cassie sighed. 'But that's still as far as it goes – on my side, anyway – and I am trying to ease back. At least you and he can talk golf together, whereas he and I have nothing in common, really. All I know about golf, for instance, is that it is extremely lucky to get a hole in one and I have no desire to take up the sport.'

Veronica raised her eyebrows, but Cassie refused to be drawn further, so Veronica changed the subject.

'Have you told Polly yet about Tom seeing Sebastian in London?'

'Yes. She just said it was one less thing for her to worry about. It will stop her feeling guilty about breaking things off with him when she gets back. I must say, I'm relieved. I never could quite see Polly as a naval wife.'

Veronica handed Cassie a mug of hot chocolate.

'Have you heard from James?'

'He rang to say he'd arrived in Wales safely. I thought he'd ring this evening too but...' Cassie shrugged her shoulders philosophically. 'I guess he's enjoying himself.'

'There's still time,' Veronica said, glancing at the clock. 'Has he decided what he's going to do when he finishes at the Harbour Commission?'

'No, not yet. He's got several options but can't decide which one to take. That's what this holiday is about – in part. He needs time to do some serious thinking without any distractions – including me.'

Veronica looked questioningly at her.

'You?'

'James wants to marry me.'

'And you said?' prompted Veronica.

'I'm thinking about it. He wants my answer when he gets back.'

Cassie sighed.

'I know he loves me. And I think I love him. He makes me laugh and we're... we're comfortable together. I can certainly see us together more than I can ever see myself with Doug.'

She paused.

'It's just my heart doesn't miss a beat the way it used to whenever I saw Miles. And I can't help wondering whether I love him enough.'

'Miles was a long time ago,' Veronica said quietly. 'You were both young. Second time around is bound to be different, but that doesn't make it any less real. James adores you. Anybody can see that from the way he looks at you when he thinks no one else is watching.'

'The problem is I've been on my own for so long and what I had with Miles was so good, I dread making a mistake.'

'Are you sure Doug and the kind of life he could offer isn't clouding your judgement?' Veronica asked hesitantly.

Cassie shook her head.

'Definitely not. I like Doug a lot and the social whirl of the last few months has been fun. But you know me, I'm a home bird at heart and I'm not really interested in the social scene that Doug seems to inhabit on a daily basis. I've enjoyed getting a glimpse of how the other half live, but I much prefer something more low-key.'

She looked at Veronica. 'I've already decided that after tomorrow's tournament, I'm going to do a bit of back-pedalling as far as invitations from Doug are concerned.'

'Talking of tomorrow, I think it's time we went to bed. We've got an early start.'

* * *

Within hours of the early start the following day, it was clear that the charity golf tournament was going to be a success. Good weather and an enthusiastic turn-out of Devonshire business people ensured that the local charities would all benefit from large donations.

Cassie watched Doug and then Veronica tee off before making for the club's health and beauty rooms. As she'd told James, she'd never been a golfer and to pass the time today she was treating herself to a massage and a facial in the club's spa facilities. Afterwards, she planned to return to the club room to wait for Doug and

Veronica to finish their rounds and make for the nineteenth hole – the name the golfers tended to call the bar.

An hour or so later, she accepted the offer of a glass of orange juice from one of the waiters as she wandered into the club room. A radio somewhere in the background was tuned in to a local station and Cassie could hear the DJ urging everyone to 'Get yourself over to the country club and play a round for charity.'

Lunch was a lavish buffet and as Doug, Veronica and Cassie began to help themselves, the radio switched into a news bulletin.

'And now for news of a local hero,' Cassie heard the newsreader say. 'Whilst on holiday in Wales, Captain James White, a Harbour Master at one of our ports down here, has been injured while saving the life of a three-year-old toddler.'

As her plate silently hit the carpeted floor, Cassie fought the nausea that threatened to overwhelm her, and she struggled to remain upright. Veronica was at her side in an instant.

'Cassie, are you all right?'

Cassie nodded. 'Listen.'

'The three-year-old ran into a busy road and the captain followed, scooping her out of the way of oncoming traffic. Captain White took the brunt of the impact from a speeding van and is now in hospital.'

As music signalled the end of the bulletin, Cassie turned to Doug.

'I must go to him. I'm sorry to leave, Doug, but—'

'Cassie, I understand,' he interrupted. 'I'll get someone to take you home to collect some things first and then drive you to the station.'

Doug's matter-of-fact way of handling the situation was his way of coping. He did understand. He understood she was sorry to leave, and that perhaps their relationship had also unexpectedly undergone a significant change.

'I'm sorry, Doug,' she said again.

'I know, Cassie. We'll talk later. Go and see how James is. And remember, if there is anything I can do, ask me.'

* * *

Extract from Polly's private journal

Undated

The idea of this journal was to keep a truthful record of my private thoughts and fears during the race. So with that in mind, I'm going to try and write as rationally and as honestly as I can about the events of the past few weeks. The weeks I couldn't face writing in this journal.

Cape Horn is behind me. Two days on from that grey outcrop with its fearsome reputation, and I was in a different world. The days were beautiful – blue sky, sunshine and a real 'great to be alive' feeling in the air.

I think *Cream* sensed we'd literally turned a corner because she started to skim across the water as though she, too, was happy to be back in the Atlantic Ocean. And now, in a week or two, Brazil beckons.

I hope, when I think about this adventure of mine in years to come, I can re-capture not only the memory of the good days but also the sheer terror of the time I spent in the South Pacific Ocean. Because, if nothing else, it will serve to remind me that having survived that, I should be able to survive anything life can throw at me.

I definitely owe Mum a BIG hug and the biggest box of chocolates I can buy when I get back. I was way out of order, ringing her like that. I feel so guilty for hanging up on her, just because I didn't want to acknowledge the truth of what she was saying.

It's no excuse, I know, but at the time I wasn't thinking straight, I was so exhausted. Being so tired was terrifying in itself, without the tumultuous weather conditions I had to contend with. Talking to Mum may have been upsetting for her, but it was the best thing possible for me.

Dexter rang me a few minutes after my outburst with Mum. He, too, was quite brutal and matter of fact.

'Polly, you have no choice. Just get on with it and stop moaning. Many solo yacht racers get really low, especially in the non-stop races. You are not unique feeling the way you do.'

I'd never heard such a steely edge to his voice before. He's always encouraged me, but in a much gentler way. This time, he definitely sounded cross and upset with me. But then he went on to say, 'By the way, I have some news for you about future sponsorship which I'll tell you about in Brazil. That is, if you haven't lost your bottle for yacht racing. I know it's tough out there, Polly, but you can cope. And don't forget, I'm here willing you on and waiting for you.'

I guess I owe Dexter as much as Mum because it was their united onslaught that made me pull myself together.

It was forty-eight hours before I felt in control again and just three hours later, I was on course for rounding Cape Horn. The sea was rough and I was approximately two miles from the rock as I passed it. The light was spectacular. The waves, frighteningly huge, sent tingles of adrenaline down my spine as *Cream* and I made our way.

I remember breathing a huge sigh of relief and feeling a wave of euphoria sweep over me after passing safely through one of the world's most dangerous sea areas and I'd made it to the South Atlantic Ocean. With several thousand nautical miles still to go before I'm home, I'm trying to hang on to that euphoric feeling.

According to Race HQ this morning, I am currently in ninth position, which puts me way down in the points, but at least I'm still in there fighting. I shall be on the start line too with the others for the last leg, not pushing to try and catch up.

I messaged Tom and Mai my congratulations on the birth of Alice – love the name. I'm going home as an auntie and I can't wait to meet my niece.

40

Tom took the call from the police in the boatyard office. Fully mobile again, he was spending a lot of time with Bill, becoming increasingly involved in the family business.

'Sergeant Winston here. We've got the results from the forensic department and there's enough evidence to charge the three suspects with burglary and arson.'

'That's great news. Thanks for letting us know, sergeant.'

Bill looked at him as he replaced the receiver.

'Finally doing something, are they? Good. Don't suppose the courts will give 'em more than community service, but there you are. Won't bring back what the fire damaged either.'

'No,' Tom agreed, 'but it could have been a lot worse. At least the insurance have finally agreed a figure so we can start replacing tools, get back into the boat maintenance business and try to recoup the business we've lost over the last few weeks.'

He glanced at his grandfather.

'I've had an idea about that too.'

Bill held up his hands in mock horror.

'Here we go again. You and your modern ideas. What now?' he asked good-naturedly.

'We need to set up a website to attract more business into the yard,' Tom said.

'Beats me how a website can attract new business. In my day, it was a question of building up a reputation for good work,' Bill grumbled. 'But you go ahead if you think it's what's needed. Watch the expense side of it, mind. Need to talk to your mother about available funds when she gets back from Wales.'

Tom glanced at his grandfather.

'Gramps, what d'you make of Mum rushing off like that?'

'I reckon it's a good sign.'

'Sign of what?'

'That your mum is finally getting a life of her own,' Bill said, looking at Tom.

'I thought she had a life of her own. She always seems happy, and she's got a busy social life, too, these days. And I know she's looking forward to being a grandmother.'

Bill nodded.

'All that's true. But it's been a long time since there was anyone special in her life. Now it looks as though James might be about to fill the void.'

'Things change,' he added, giving his grandson a sympathetic look. 'Your dad will always be her first love, but your gran and I had always hoped he wouldn't be her last.'

* * *

Walking down the hospital corridor, Cassie felt unsure of herself and full of fear, despite the reassurances the ward sister had given her over the telephone.

'Captain White doesn't have any life-threatening injuries. He's very bruised, he's sprained an ankle and a couple of his ribs are broken. We kept him in overnight for observation and he'll be discharged sometime today. It was a brave thing he did. He's lucky to have got off so lightly.'

As she pushed open the swing door of the hospital ward, Cassie prepared herself for an emotional meeting.

At first, she couldn't see James. Then her heart skipped a beat when she finally spotted him sitting talking to an elderly man.

It was his companion who nudged him and pointed Cassie out to James.

'Looks like you've got a visitor.'

As James turned, a smile of sheer delight crossed his face and he struggled to stand up.

'No, no, James, be careful,' Cassie said, kissing him gently. 'What am I going to do with you? I let you out of my sight for a day and you play Superman.'

'He's a real hero,' James's companion said, standing up to shake Cassie's hand. 'I'm Ivor, grandfather of the toddler he saved. I can't tell you how grateful the family are. We'll always be in the captain's debt.'

James looked embarrassed.

'Well, now that your wife's here, I'll say goodbye. Thank you once again,' Ivor said.

James looked at Cassie apologetically.

'Oh, Cassie's not...' he started to explain. Then he saw the look on her face and stopped mid-sentence. 'Goodbye, Ivor. Take care of that granddaughter of yours. She's very precious,' James said, still looking at Cassie in amazement.

Before either of them could say anything, the ward sister bustled up.

'How are you feeling? The doctor's on his way to discharge you, Captain White.'

'I've never felt better,' James said reaching out for Cassie's hand and holding it tightly. 'Never, ever better.'

* * *

It was nine o'clock that evening before Cassie rang Boatyard House.

Mai had gone up for an early night and it was Tom who answered. 'Hi, Mum. How are things? Is James going to be okay?'

'He's bruised and battered, but otherwise fine. How's my favourite granddaughter? And Mai?'

'Alice is great. Currently asleep. Mai is good too. Tired but happy.'

'Give her my love.'

'I will.'

'Listen, Tom, we're going to stay up here for a couple of days James has still got his hotel booking and they've found a room for me. The idea is for James to have a bit of a rest, give the bruises time to fade, and then I'll drive him home.'

'Sounds like a good idea. Solo's fine, by the way. Taken to sleeping on the floor of the nursery. And Mum,' Tom hesitated before adding, 'You know we all like James, don't you?'

Cassie tried to keep the laughter from her voice as she said. 'Good, I'm glad you told me that, Tom. I like him too.'

She was still laughing when she rejoined James in the hotel lounge.

'For some reason, completely out of the blue, my son has just told me that they all like you.'

'That's a relief,' James said. 'I shan't have any troubles with the in-laws, then.'

'Do you think they've guessed about us?'

'I would think your mercy dash to my side gave them a fair indication of the way things are,' James smiled at her. 'I still can't quite believe you're here,' he added, catching hold of her hand. 'I was sure I was going to lose you to Doug. He has so much more to offer you – a lifestyle that I couldn't possibly begin to compete with.'

Cassie leaned forward and placed a finger against his lips.

'Shh. You're the one I want to be with. Now, I think, considering your condition, you should be tucked up in bed recuperating. We'll talk tomorrow.'

41

The customary fireworks and bottles of champagne were popping as Polly arrived in Brazil. The official boat took her in tow, and they headed towards a berth in the marina, where Polly looked out for Dexter. For a heart-stopping moment, she couldn't find him in the crowd, but at last she saw him standing on the quay waiting for her, just as he'd promised.

Once *Holdsworth Clotted Cream* was moored in her berth, he leaped on board and hugged her to him, the tension visibly leaving his body.

'Well done, Little Polly,' he exclaimed, and she could clearly hear the relief in his voice.

Once the official side of things was over, Dexter walked Polly to her hotel, his arm protectively around her shoulders.

'It's so good to have you here safe and sound. You had me really worried for a while.'

'I'm sorry,' Polly said quietly. 'Forgive me?'

'Of course. I'll see you for supper. I have some news for you, but first you need to rest.'

Three hours later, Polly was sitting next to Dexter in a small café on the waterfront.

'Come on, Dexter, you said you had some news,' Polly said impatiently.

Dexter looked at her thoughtfully as he crumbled his bread roll.

'The first thing is, I've heard unofficially you are about to be offered a sponsorship package in your own name – not as Tom's little sister, or as a stand-in skipper. This deal is for you, Polly Lewis. You've impressed a lot of people during this race.'

When he told her the name of the sponsor and the huge amount of money they were proposing, Polly was stunned. Her dream of being a professional yacht skipper was about to come true.

'Secondly, the finish of this race in Plymouth will also signal the end of my involvement with the organisation of yacht races. I've decided I want to do more sailing and take part in some of the smaller competitions myself again.' He took a breath. 'I've also decided to join Dad on the farm.'

'That's great, Dexter. You'll have the best of both worlds – sailing for pleasure and building up a business you enjoy.'

'There is a third thing,' Dexter said, looking at her. 'I had hoped you and I could get together. But the timing is all wrong, isn't it? You're about to get your big chance and set the yachting world alight, racing around the globe for the next few years. I'm going to be working equally hard in the heart of the English countryside with the occasional Round Britain yacht race to look forward to.'

'We can still see each other, though, can't we? Your family farm in Somerset isn't that far from Devon and I won't be on the high seas all the time,' Polly said fearfully.

Dexter took her hand in his.

'Sure, we can try, Little Polly, but I have a feeling it isn't going to be that easy. I don't believe absence always makes the heart grow fonder.' He paused before continuing. 'Sometimes, people get so busy with their individual lives they just drift apart, with regrets on both sides for what might have been. I can only hope and pray that doesn't happen to us.'

42

Cassie knew that if it hadn't been for his sprained ankle, James would have insisted on driving. As it was, he'd no option but to let her get behind the wheel of his precious Alpine sports car to drive them home.

It was the first time Cassie had ever driven such a fun car and she found herself making the most of it.

'I thought we'd stop for lunch in Bath?' said James. 'I know it's a bit of a detour, but there's a nice convenient restaurant in the city centre. And a good friend of mine I'd like you to meet also lives nearby.' He smiled enigmatically, refusing to be drawn further.

Traffic was heavy and it was well after midday before Cassie pulled into a car park.

'There's somewhere we have to go before we eat,' James said.

Holding Cassie's hand tightly and leaning on the walking stick the hospital had loaned him, he led her towards a small shop with a discreet green and gold blind above its window display of jewellery.

'Come and choose your engagement ring,' James said. 'And meet the friend who I hope will be my best man.'

Charlie George was delighted to see James and gave Cassie a congratulatory hug when he heard their news.

'Now, what sort of rings would you like me to show you? Modern? Traditional? Or perhaps you've already seen something you like?'

A square sapphire in an old-fashioned flat gold setting had caught Cassie's eye and hesitantly she pointed it out. James had given her no idea of how much he wanted to spend, and she didn't want to choose a ring he couldn't afford.

'Try it on. I can always alter the size,' Charlie said.

It was then Cassie realised she was still wearing Miles's wedding ring. She'd never taken it off. It had been a constant reminder of him over the years.

Disconcerted, she unobtrusively slipped off the gold band, replacing it with the sapphire ring, then held out her hand for James to see.

'It's beautiful,' she said. 'Do you like it?' she asked anxiously. 'You must say if it's too expensive.'

James interrupted her. 'It's perfect. It looks as if it was made for your hand. We need to choose wedding rings now.'

Some time later, they headed off, with Cassie's engagement ring safe in a box in James's pocket, and leaving the two gold wedding bands in Charlie's safekeeping, having failed to persuade him to join them for a meal.

'It'll be a privilege to be your best man, James. I'll try not to forget to bring these along on the day!'

'You'll be in real trouble if you do,' James said.

It was mid-evening before they got back to Devon. Cassie left James in his apartment, promising to see him early the next day.

'I love you very much, Cassie.' He kissed her tenderly. 'Can we please get married as soon as possible?'

Cassie smiled.

'Polly will be home in a couple of weeks. I want her to be my bridesmaid, so we'll have to wait for her.'

Once back at River View Cottage, Cassie unpacked her suitcase, before getting ready for bed.

She took off her watch and placed it on the bedside table, glancing at the silver-framed photograph that had stood beside her bed for over twenty years.

She slowly reached out and picked it up. Carefully she opened the back and slid out the black and white photo.

It was time to say goodbye. Her finger traced the blurred outline of Miles's face. While photos still brought instant memories, these days she had difficulty in recalling the timbre of his voice. This evening, though, she could definitely hear Miles's soft West Country accent.

'Bon voyage, Cassie. Be happy.'

* * *

Extract from Polly's private journal

Wednesday, 12 October

This is turning out to be the best leg so far. I think I'm getting the hang of this solo yacht racing.

Not only did I manage to cross the start line in Brazil first, ahead of Colin on *Flight of the Seagull*, I've held on to the lead for the last fourteen days. Just to think I might be in with a chance of winning this leg makes me want to hoist all the sails I've got.

It won't make any difference to my overall position as I haven't accumulated enough points in the other legs to put me in the top three. That means no podium place, but at least I'll have shown those new sponsors what I'm capable of.

All these weeks at sea have given me lots of time to do some serious thinking about my life. One of my first decisions was not to marry Sebastian.

I think, deep down, I knew when he asked me that it wasn't what I really wanted. Telling him I'd think about it was the coward's way out, but I just didn't have the courage to say 'No' straight off.

When Mum told me Tom and Mai had seen him in London with someone else, all my guilty feelings of not wanting to hurt him vanished.

I rang him from Brazil and told him I'd decided against accepting his proposal. I am very proud of myself for not mentioning 'the other woman'. Mind you, he didn't say a word about her, either.

We had a very civilised conversation and he even told me I could keep the ring if I wanted to. Of course I won't. At least we've parted on friendly terms.

A few more days and I should have Land's End in my sights and then home to Plymouth. The weather systems have been so different from the ones on the way out. Tom helped me plot a different course to pass the Azores and I've made good time.

Dexter has been negotiating with lots of people on my behalf and says I'll have some important decisions to make when I get back.

I've always dreamed about competing in the Vendée Globe and it is still sinking in that the essential sponsorship is finally within my grasp.

However, although this race has been a brilliant experience, if I'm totally honest, which is what this journal is all about, I found the weeks of isolation very hard to cope with at times.

The compulsory stopovers at the finish of each leg of this race saved my sanity. Taking part in the non-stop Vendée Globe means being at sea from start to finish – with no outside help of any kind.

Ellen MacArthur took ninety-four days to complete her record voyage, so realistically I'd be looking at nearly three and a half months. I'm not sure I can handle that amount of time continuously on my own at sea.

But it is such a great opportunity. If I turn it down, I know it will never be offered again.

Another thing worries me. I know Dexter and I haven't seen a lot of each other, but I know I've fallen in love with him and I think he feels the same about me.

If I carry on with a solo sailing career, I'm afraid I'll lose any chance of that love growing and I sense he feels that too. I guess I have some big decisions to make in the near future.

43

One evening, soon after their return from Wales, James insisted he and Cassie went for a meal at the manor house restaurant where, on that long ago evening before she left for South Africa, he'd first told her that he'd fallen in love with her. There was no outdoor concert on this occasion and a different trio were up in the minstrel gallery playing modern music quietly, as James and Cassie were shown to their table.

The bottle of champagne in the ice bucket on their table confirmed what Cassie had suspected when James had told her about this evening. He'd refused to give her the engagement ring she'd chosen until 'I've actually asked you to marry me and we've made a proper memory for us to look back on.' She smiled as James waited until they were both seated and the waiter had poured them each a glass of champagne before discreetly leaving them.

'Cassie Lewis, will you please marry me?' James said, taking hold of her hand as he reached into his pocket with his free hand.

'Yes, please,' Cassie answered instantly, and James slipped the sapphire ring they'd chosen together onto her finger, before leaning in to give her a lingering kiss. As they drew apart and James picked up the two champagne glasses and handed Cassie hers, the trio in the gallery burst into an exuberant rendition of 'Congratulations' and everyone around them clapped.

'Shall we get married here?' James asked after they'd decided on their main course – crispy roast duck with sauté potatoes and glazed carrots. 'The private chapel out in the grounds is licensed for weddings now.'

'That would be lovely,' Cassie said. 'But please can we have a quiet wedding? Family and close friends?'

James nodded. 'We could have the reception here as well. Or we could have a party in the evening at the country club if you'd prefer that?' James said.

Cassie shook her head. 'Let's keep it small and intimate and have both here. Will we have a honeymoon?'

'Of course. And before you ask, I'm not telling you. Just make sure your passport is valid.'

'We'll also have to decide where we are going to live afterwards,' Cassie said.

'The lease on my apartment finishes with my job,' James pointed out. 'I know you love River View Cottage. D'you think it's big enough for both of us? Would Bill sell it to us?'

'Dad has talked in the past about selling the place, so I'm sure that's an option.'

James sighed happily.

'Good. Now all we have to do is decide upon the date. You reckon Polly should be back within the next seven or eight days, so how about two weeks this Saturday?'

'Two weeks this Saturday will be wonderful, James.'

* * *

Life from that evening on became dominated by wedding preparations. The chapel in the grounds of the manor house was booked for the next three weekends, so Cassie and James decided on a weekday wedding, which simplified organising everything else. Flowers, photographer, cake, reception, all were easier to arrange for a wedding outside of the more usual weekend. Although Cassie dearly wanted to wait until Polly was home so they could shop together for a dress, she didn't dare risk leaving it so late.

Instead, she and Veronica spent a delightful day in town, eventually tracking down the perfect wedding dress in an individual shop in one of the small shopping lanes away from the busy town centre. They even found a dress that Cassie knew would be just right for Polly.

To Cassie's embarrassment, as they made their way back to the car park, they bumped into Doug. She'd wanted to tell Doug about her and James before he heard it on the local grapevine but had failed to get hold of him.

'Doug. I've tried to ring you several times,' Cassie began. 'But you were away on business. I need to tell you something.'

'I've just got back from a business trip. How's James? Last I heard he was recovering in hospital.'

He clearly didn't know about their engagement and Cassie felt bad about breaking her news in such a public place.

'He's home and well on the way to recovery. Doug, I have something to tell you,' Cassie said again, dimly aware that Veronica was tactfully moving away.

'Cassie, I know. The lovely ring on your finger gives the game away and anyway, I sort of guessed he'd won your heart when you ran off from the golf tournament. I wish it were me.' Doug's voice was soft before he kissed her gently on the cheek. 'Congratulations

Cassie. James is a very lucky man. I'm sure you'll be very happy. Don't forget to send me a wedding invitation.'

As she watched him walk away, Cassie hoped she was imagining the droop in his shoulders.

She sighed. There was nothing she could do. She loved James, not Doug, but she would always remember him and their times together with fondness.

44

With Polly leading the fleet home, it was decided that Cassie would drive Bill, Tom and herself down to Plymouth to surprise Polly and welcome her home. The morning Polly turned *Cream* into the English Channel, the three of them set off.

The joy of sailing up the English Channel towards Plymouth Sound at the head of the returning fleet was to be an enduring memory for Polly.

She couldn't believe she'd won the last leg. It was an incredible feeling to know that Little Polly had outsailed some of the best yachtsmen in the world. Her sailing and Tom's invaluable tactical advice had won out.

Once into Plymouth Sound, a stiff breeze had *Cream* speeding towards the line. Within minutes of the finish gun ringing out, the official support boat with Cassie, Bill and Tom on board was alongside the yacht. Polly let out a scream of delight when she saw the three of them and could barely contain herself as they clambered aboard.

Tom was the first to climb on board *Cream* and Polly sensed the emotion he was feeling as he stepped into the cockpit of his beloved yacht for the first time in months.

'Well done, sis. I'm so proud of you!' he said, giving her a hug.

'Thanks.' Polly hugged him back. 'I couldn't have done it without your advice and back-up support. Family effort all round. Congratulations to you too – Daddy. How are Mai and my new niece?'

'Brilliant. Waiting for you back at the house.'

Cassie was next on board and gave Polly a tight hug, relieved beyond words to finally have her home safe and sound. Bill hugged his granddaughter tight. 'Well done, Polly,' he said gruffly. 'Knew you'd do it.'

The celebratory cheering that welcomed her into harbour increased the nearer *Cream* got to her berth. To Polly's amazement, there were hundreds of people chanting her name and shouting their good wishes as the yacht was tied into her berth and Polly prepared to go ashore.

The next time she came on board, it would be to clear things away, sail the yacht back to the yard and hand her over to Tom. After all they'd been through together, it would be like saying goodbye to an old friend.

Once on the quay, the crowds of people swarmed around her. Even though she was exhausted, she smiled and waved and tried to sign everything that was thrust at her – pieces of paper, sailing caps, yachting programmes. The world, it seemed, wanted her autograph.

Dexter was waiting for her by the prize-giving table. Oblivious to everybody, he took her in his arms and held her tightly.

'Welcome home, Little Polly. Well done. This is the moment that makes it all worthwhile,' he whispered. 'Enjoy your success.'

There was a discreet cough from the Chairman of the Race Committee. Smiling, Dexter released her to receive her prize and make her acceptance speech.

The winning trophy for this, the last leg, was a glass model of an Open 60s yacht mounted on a polished wooden base. As Polly stood there, clutching it tightly, she prayed it wouldn't slip through her shaking hands.

She took a deep breath.

'I can't believe I'm standing here holding this trophy. I have lots of people to thank and believe me, I do from the bottom of my heart.'

She paused and looked directly at Cassie, Tom and Bill.

'There are so many people to thank for their love and support. Tom, my big brother, who barely flinched when it was decided I could replace him as skipper, my mum, my grandad, Dexter, they've all been with me mentally and sometimes physically. I love you all.' Polly paused for a second before holding her trophy aloft. 'I dedicate this trophy to the memory of Miles Lewis, my father. I never had the chance to know him properly and I've always missed his presence in my life. But today I truly feel like his daughter and hope he would have been proud of me following in his footsteps. To my dad.'

In the silence that followed her moving speech, and before the cheering started again, Polly turned away from the microphone and stumbled to Dexter's side. Wordlessly he placed his arm around her shoulder and handed her a handkerchief to wipe away the tears that were flowing freely down her cheeks.

45

The sun was streaming in through the window when Cassie awoke on the morning of her wedding day. Tom and Mai had persuaded her to move back to Boatyard House for a couple of days before the wedding and she was glad she'd taken them up on their offer.

She glanced across the room and smiled happily as she saw her outfit hanging on the wardrobe door – a pale cream silk full-length shift dress with a lace overcoat in a slightly darker shade with a hood that delicately covered Cassie's hair.

The coat was long enough to gently fold into a small rounded train at the back. It was the most romantic dress Cassie had ever owned.

There was a quiet knock on the door and Polly entered carrying a tray carefully.

'Morning, Mum. Coffee and toast. I thought I'd join you.'

Cassie poured them both a cup of coffee and helped herself to a slice of buttered toast.

'How are all your sponsorship deals working out?' she asked casually.

In the days since she'd been home, Polly had been busy sorting out her schedule for the coming months, trying to fit together talk and visits all over the country in a logical sequence so she wouldn't have to repeat journeys too often.

She'd also been trying to fit in meetings with Dexter at least every ten days in between things. It was proving almost impossible.

Polly looked at Cassie. 'Mum, do you think I should give up my solo sailing career before it really begins?'

Cassie saw the anguish on her daughter's face.

'Polly, love, only you can decide that. But why would you want to? When Sebastian demanded you gave up the race, you wouldn't consider it for a minute.'

Polly stared at the bottom of her coffee cup and was silent for several minutes.

'It was different then. I had something to prove. Now...' She shrugged. 'I still love sailing. But there are two problems. One, I'm not sure I'm cut out to be a long-distance solo sailor. And two, I think I'll lose any chance of a relationship with Dexter if I start spending week after week at sea.'

'How important is Dexter to you?'

'Very – I think!' Polly smiled. 'No, scrap that. Definitely very important.'

Cassie took a sip of her coffee.

'Life is never simple, is it?' she said. 'You think you're getting exactly what you want and then something unexpected happens and everything changes. All I can say is, there are always compromises available if you search hard enough. But I do think you will eventually have to decide who or what you cannot live without.'

Polly took a bite of toast and chewed thoughtfully before looking at her mum.

'Is that what you did when you met Dad?'

Cassie nodded.

'Can I ask you something, Mum?' Polly hesitated before going on.

'Do you love James as much as you loved Dad?'

Cassie looked at her daughter, not wanting to hurt her, but she had to tell her the truth.

'Yes. I finally realised I do. But your dad will always have a special place in my heart.'

Cassie went across to the dressing table and opened her jewellery box. Taking out her old wedding ring, she held it out to Polly.

'Polly, would you like this? I know one day you'll have a wedding ring of your own, but maybe you'd like to wear this on your right hand? After your little speech last week, I thought you might appreciate a tangible heirloom from your dad and me. And never doubt that he would be as proud of you as I am.'

Polly slipped the ring onto her finger and Cassie took a deep breath.

'I think we'd better start getting ready. Otherwise I'm going to be late for my wedding.'

'Bride's prerogative!' Polly laughed and took the breakfast tray away.

Two hours later, Polly looked at Cassie.

'Mum, you're beautiful. And your outfit is perfect. Right, the cars are here. I'm off to church with Tom and Mai and Alice. Gramps is waiting for you downstairs.'

Half an hour later, standing in the church porch as Polly handed her the bouquet, Cassie glanced into the chapel. James was waiting by the altar, his back towards her.

As though he sensed her watching, he slowly turned and smiled at her. Cassie felt the now familiar lurch of her heart as she smiled back.

As Polly took her place behind her, Bill took her arm. 'Ready,

Cassie? As your father, I have to say there's still time to change your mind if you're having second thoughts, but I don't think you are, are you?'

'No second thoughts,' Cassie said firmly. She was finally ready to make her way down the aisle towards the man she loved.

* * *

Their reception was an informal affair, at Cassie's request. No top table, no speeches and no set up 'first dance', although James and Cassie did take to the floor for the opening waltz and dancing continued until late in the evening.

Watching Polly dancing with Dexter, Cassie couldn't help wondering, in the midst of her own happiness, which path her daughter was going to choose – career woman, wife or try for a mix of the two? Cassie hadn't been going to throw her bouquet like tradition demanded, but in that split second, she decided she would. And she'd try to throw it in such a way that would ensure only Polly caught it.

46

A day after Cassie and James left on their honeymoon, Veronica drove Polly to Plymouth to collect *Cream*. Polly had been hoping that Dexter would be able to join her, but the night before, he'd phoned to tell her he couldn't make it.

Veronica turned the car onto the main road.

'Do you have any idea where James has taken Cassie?'

'A place called Udaipur in north-west India. Mum rang to let us know they'd arrived safely and said it's the most amazing place. They're staying in a marble palace built so close to the edge of a huge lake it's like being on board a boat when you look out of a window. It's apparently incredibly romantic.'

'It sounds the perfect place for a honeymoon. How long will they be away?'

'A week. They're due back on Sunday,' Polly said.

Veronica glanced at her goddaughter.

'And what about you and Dexter? You seemed very happy together at the wedding. And you did catch the bouquet.'

'You mean Mum thrust it into my arms when nobody else was expecting it,' Polly replied, laughing. 'As for Dexter and me, well, we're certainly trying to make a go of things but even now I'm back on dry land, we're still miles apart most of the time.'

She sighed, remembering the last time she and Dexter had seen each other. They'd wandered off together into the secluded rose garden of the manor house during James and Cassie's wedding.

She'd gone willingly into Dexter's arms and returned his kisses with a fervour that surprised both of them.

'Oh, Polly, what are we going to do?' Dexter had murmured, holding her close.

Standing in the circle of his arms, Polly had looked up at him.

'We simply won't let life drive us apart.' Her tone was defiant.

Now, though, she wasn't so confident. She glanced at Veronica.

'Do you believe that absence makes the heart grow fonder? Or do you agree with Dexter it can sound the death knell for relationships?'

Veronica took a few moments before answering.

'I think it depends on how strong the relationship is in the first place – and whether not being together all the time suits both parties. It's when resentment creeps in that trouble starts. Things have a way of working themselves out,' she added comfortably. 'You just have to decide on your priorities.'

An hour later, Veronica dropped Polly on the quay alongside *Cream*. Climbing back on board the yacht was like returning home.

Everything was so reassuringly familiar. Polly took a deep breath. Oh, it was good to be back on board.

Motoring out of the Sound into the Channel, Polly took an easterly bearing before cutting the engine and starting to hoist the mainsail. Tom had hinted he'd be up to collecting *Cream* with her, but she'd gently turned him down. She wanted to enjoy a final solo sail before handing the boat back to Tom.

Standing at the tiller, holding the yacht on her course up the

Channel towards Dartmouth, Polly tried again to think coherently about her future.

Everybody, including Dexter, kept telling her to do what she wanted. The trouble was she no longer knew what that was.

But as she enjoyed the familiar sensation of *Cream* riding the waves, Polly realised she couldn't give up her involvement in the yachting world any more than she could give up Dexter.

What was it that Veronica had said about priorities and Cassie about compromise?

It was the final evening of their honeymoon and Cassie and James were enjoying a romantic moonlit dinner on a raft moored several metres out into the lake.

On shore, the floodlit marble palace was reflected in the quietly lapping waters and there was the gentle sound of a sitar drifting out on the breeze towards them.

'Cassie, we have to talk about the future,' James said, filling her glass with champagne.

Cassie looked at him and waited.

'This letter arrived the morning of our wedding as I left for the church. I shoved it into my case to look at later and promptly forgot about it. Until this evening.' James handed Cassie an envelope.

'It's from an old naval friend congratulating me and... well, read it for yourself.'

Cassie quickly scanned the short note.

'It's a year's contract to help run...' she glanced back down at the letter, 'La Marina des Oiseaux.'

James was watching her anxiously.

'It's right down on the Med. Close to the French-Spanish border.

I haven't been there for years, but it's a very beautiful part of the world.'

'Do you want this job?' Cassie asked quietly.

'Well, it's the only firm offer I've had since my redundancy. And yes, I do quite like the idea of a year down south, but it's no longer a decision I can take alone. The new Mrs White has a major say now.'

He reached across the table and took hold of her hand.

'Cassie, I only opened the letter two hours ago, so I haven't had much time to think about it either. But it did cross my mind that maybe we could sell my boat, buy a bigger one, sail down there and live on board for a year. Then, when the contract ends, we'd sail back to England. It would be an adventure for our middle years.'

'I thought you'd virtually decided to take early retirement,' Cassie said slowly.

'I still can, but I do feel as though I've been thrown on the scrap heap too soon at the moment,' James said, his tone thoughtful. 'But how would you feel, leaving the family business?'

'Tom's playing a much bigger part now, so it's probably a good time to let the new generation take the helm,' Cassie said.

There was a short silence during which James regarded her anxiously before she spoke again.

'Well, it would certainly be a completely new start to our married life together. It's a long time since I lived on board a boat but, like you say, it would be an adventure to remember together.'

She picked up her wine glass and took a sip, hoping James wouldn't notice her shaking hand. Sailing down to the Mediterranean and living down there was something that had been planned once before in her life. It wasn't something that she'd expected to ever be offered again. She reread the letter.

'Your friend says the contract would start in a couple of months. That doesn't give us much time to organise everything.'

She did a quick calculation of dates. 'It would mean leaving immediately after Alice's christening.'

Cassie took a deep breath. 'Okay. You'd better tell your friend you'd like the job. Tell him too, Mr and Mrs White would like a berth reserved in the marina for their as yet un-purchased floating home.'

47

Now she was back on dry land, Polly was inundated with requests for interviews. The latest one, for a local radio station near Bristol, meant that afterwards she could visit Dexter and see his family farm for the first time.

Once her initial nervousness disappeared, she found she thoroughly enjoyed talking about her round-the-world experiences.

Suzie, the producer, switched her microphone off at the end.

'Thanks, Polly. That was great. You're a natural. Will you come back at the end of the month and take part in a discussion with some teenagers? The schools around here followed your trip and I know some of the girls look on you as a role model.'

'Gosh, that's scary,' Polly said. 'I'd love to, if I can fit it in. Let's take a look in the diary.'

Half an hour later, having agreed to do another two programmes, Polly set off for Dexter's family farm.

Not far from the north Somerset coast, the farm sat at the end of a long track with woods behind it. In the distance, across the fields, the occasional glint of the Bristol Channel could be seen.

After coffee in the farmhouse kitchen with his parents, Dexter found her a pair of wellingtons and took her on a tour of the farm.

When they returned, he stopped in front of some outbuildings on the edge of the farmyard.

'Well, apart from my surprise in here, I think you've seen everything Home Farm has to offer.'

The building Dexter had stopped in front of had large double doors. He lifted the closing bar up and swung the doors open.

Inside, shored up with lengths of timber, was a forty-foot fibreglass sailing boat.

'I bought it with the proceeds from my flat in the States. I thought in the dim and distant future you and I would enjoy sailing her together,' Dexter said. 'She only arrived two days ago. The hull is basically okay but the interior needs a lot of work.'

He looked at Polly.

'It's my project to keep me out of mischief and occupied while you're busy sailing the seven seas. Hopefully it will stop me missing you too much.'

Polly was quiet for a moment as she walked the length of the hull.

'Lovely lines. She should be quite fast. Can we go on board?'

'There's a ladder around the other side. I'll give you a hand up.'

Sitting next to Dexter on one of the bunks in the cabin, Polly spoke.

'I've been thinking about missing you, too. And I've decided to do something about it. But first I need to ask you something.'

'Ask away,' he said, giving her a hug.

'You know how you helped me with taking over *Cream* after Tom's accident, sorting out the media business and recently drumming up sponsors for me? I was going to ask if you'd continue to do that, be my manager, if you like. But now you've got the boat as a project, you're going to be even busier...' Her voice trailed away.

Dexter pulled her closer. 'Polly, I'd love to be your manager. The farm has to be my main priority for the next few months, but I'll definitely be able to help you. There's no time limit on restoring the boat.'

'Thank you.' Polly smiled happily. 'Now, the other thing is, I've got to find somewhere to live. I know I can still stay at Boatyard House, but Tom and Mai would probably appreciate having the place to themselves. I was thinking I might move nearer here – Bath or Bristol, maybe.'

'We'll have a look in the local paper later. See what's available for rent. You really have been thinking about things, haven't you?'

'Yep. There's something else too, but until it's finalised, I'm not telling you what it is. By the way, I'm going up to London next week to see the sponsors.'

'Do you want your new manager to come with you?' Dexter asked.

Polly shook her head.

'Not on this occasion, thanks.'

'Now, tell me your plans for the yacht.' She deliberately changed the topic of conversation before Dexter could ask for details about her planned meeting with the sponsors. She was going to sort her future out by herself.

* * *

The weeks leading up to the weekend of the christening passed in a blur of activity for everyone.

The whole family greeted the news that Cassie and James were to live in France for a year with enthusiasm.

'Good for James,' Tom said. 'We'll definitely be down to see you both.'

Polly had hugged her. 'It'll be great, Mum – all that sunshine. I'll be visiting too.'

Bill too was pleased for her, even though he knew he'd miss her. 'The year will fly past,' he said.

Only for a year or not, there was a lot of organising to do. One of the first things Cassie and James talked about was what to do with Solo.

'There's no problem with the quarantine laws these days, so she can always come with us,' James said. 'She'd soon get used to the boat.'

But Cassie was doubtful. She felt Solo would be happier staying on land. Bill said he'd be happy to keep her down in the yard.

'She's a good guard dog, that one.'

But Cassie couldn't bear the thought of Solo being in a kennel on cold winter nights.

Solo solved the problem herself by disappearing from River View Cottage one afternoon while Cassie and James were busy packing things away. When a distraught Cassie finally tracked her down, she was asleep in the small garden of Boatyard House.

Mai had put Alice outside in her pram for a sleep and Solo had taken up position alongside.

'She really took to Alice while you were away. She's very protective towards her. We'd love to have her – not just while you're away but permanently,' Mai said. 'If that's possible?'

'That would be wonderful,' Cassie said. 'I was worried about leaving her, but I know she'll be happy with you.'

Then there was a question of finding a suitable boat for the trip down to the Mediterranean. Days were spent looking through sales brochures and scouring the yachting press.

Finally, two weeks before they were due to leave, they found the perfect vessel.

Moored in Fowey, it was a forty-two foot motorsailer, more than capable of coping with the trip down south. The good news, as far as James and Cassie were concerned, was that she was in a totally seaworthy condition.

When they looked her over, they couldn't believe how lucky they'd been to find her. Cassie had smiled when she'd first seen the name *My Dream*. It couldn't have been more appropriate.

She and James motored her back and moored her on one of the boatyard pontoons where Bill had checked her over and serviced the engine. Now the boat was anchored outside River View Cottage and Cassie and James were busy loading her up for the voyage to the south of France.

* * *

With just a week to go before the christening, Polly was on her way to see Dexter. She'd had news about her sponsorship and wanted to tell him face to face.

She phoned from a service station on the outskirts of Weston-super-Mare to let him know she was coming.

'Is something wrong?' he asked worriedly. 'You're all right?'

'I'm fine. I'll see you soon.'

Dexter was waiting for her at the top of the farm drive. As she stopped the car, he looked anxiously through the window.

'Shall we go for a walk?' she suggested as she got out.

Taking her hand, he led her in the direction of a small wood in the distance.

'Right, Polly, what's this all about?'

'I've had a phone call from the sponsors. There's a new contract for me in the post. Actually, it's on its way to you for checking and final approval.'

Dexter waited.

'You'll notice a few adjustments when it gets here, and I wanted to tell you about them myself.' Polly took a deep breath. 'The last few weeks have been really difficult, trying to decide what to do. I love you. I love sailing. I couldn't bear the thought of not being with you, but I also couldn't bear the thought of not sailing competitively any more. So, I've taken Mum's advice and compromised. I've decided not to do any more races like the Eco Challenge or the next Vendée Globe.'

She glanced at Dexter, trying to judge his reaction, but his face was expressionless as he waited for her to continue.

'Instead, I'm going to concentrate on shorter races like the Route de Rhum and the Mini Transat. I'll still be away at times, but it won't be for months on end. I'm also going to try and increase my media work. Suzie at the local radio station up here is keen for me to present a sporting quiz programme. I've been approached to write a book about the race and there are lots of talks lined up for the next few months.'

'Those are still big races. Why didn't you tell me what you were trying to do?' Dexter asked.

'I thought you might say I was silly not accepting such a fantastic offer. Besides, I wasn't sure whether the sponsors would agree to altering the contract.'

Dexter was silent for a moment or two. 'It's wonderful news, Polly, I'm really pleased it's all working out,' he said eventually.

'But what?' Polly said. 'I can definitely sense a "but".'

'I just wish you hadn't made these decisions behind my back. I know you meant well, Polly, but if we're going to have any sort of future together, we must talk to each other. No secrets about anything. Promise?'

'I promise. Am I forgiven?' she asked quietly.

By way of an answer, Dexter pulled her into his arms. 'It's going

to be wonderful to have the time to get to know each other properly,' he said.

'And we have a goddaughter to look after together,' Polly said.
'We can work on your new boat together too – as a team, there will
be no stopping us.'

48

The day of the christening dawned bright and clear. Cassie gazed out of the window of River View Cottage at *My Dream*, gently bobbing up and down on her anchor. Tonight, she and James planned to sleep on board, ready for a dawn start the next morning.

Cassie suppressed a sigh. James was so enthusiastic about his new job that most of the time, he carried her along with him. It was only when she was on her own that she grew apprehensive.

Although she was looking forward to the year ahead, a tiny part of her was afraid they were doing the wrong thing.

As though sensing her thoughts, a sleep-tousled James appeared in the kitchen and put his arms around her.

'Morning, wife. Penny for them?'

Cassie shook her head. She couldn't bring herself to voice her worries, but of course James realised she was concerned about their decision.

'Cassie, my love,' James began, holding her close. 'I know it's a big step we're taking but it will be all right, you'll see. It's only natural for you to miss the family, but you and I will be together.

This is our time. I promise you, Cassie, come what may, I'll always be there for you. And we can always come back if you're unhappy.'

Cassie smiled at him. What he said was true. Her life was with James now. She had to learn to let go.

She stood on tiptoe and kissed him.

'I know, James. Once we've set sail tomorrow morning, everything will fall in place and I'll be fine.'

Later that afternoon, standing in St Petrox, the ancient church out on the Dartmouth headland where Tom and Mai had decided to have Alice christened, Cassie looked around at her family gathered together in front of the font.

Polly was carefully holding Alice, who looked beautiful in the antique christening gown that generations of Lewises had been christened in. Dexter, at her side, looked nervous. Would their wedding be the next time the whole family were together again in church? Cassie could only hope.

Tom and Mai, the proud parents, stood alongside, listening as the godparents made their promises. Bill, a proud great-grandfather, was standing alongside them with a happy smile on his face. Veronica and Doug, standing together, were also part of the small group and Cassie smiled at her friend as she caught her glance. They'd been invited separately but had arrived together in Doug's car. Veronica had told Cassie that since the golf tournament, she and Doug had spent time together as friends who liked golf. Cassie couldn't help but hope that maybe, just maybe, their friendship would turn into something more.

The vicar had given permission for James to take photographs of the ceremony. Now, as he raised his camera, he smiled at Cassie before he pressed the button and took a photograph of the whole Lewis family that was to become one of Cassie's most treasured possessions over the months to come.

Back at Boatyard House, the champagne was poured and slices

f christening cake eaten, while baby Alice snoozed happily in her rib.

Cassie, standing hand in hand with James, tried to implant the amily scene in her mind so that she could recall every detail when hey were far away in France. As if he knew what she was thinking, ames leant in close, squeezing her hand as he did so.

'Tom told me earlier that he plans on flying down with Mai and Alice as soon as we drop anchor in La Marina des Oiseaux. So don't vorry, you'll scarcely have time to miss them before you see them again in just a few weeks.'

* * *

At 5.30 the next morning, *My Dream* slipped her anchor and on an ebbing tide slowly began to make her way down river to the Channel and then on to the open sea.

As they motored past the boatyard, Cassie saw a light on in the vorkshop and knew that her father was watching them leave. She raised her arm in acknowledgement, hoping that Bill could see her final goodbye in the breaking dawn.

Bill, drinking his early-morning tea in his customary place in he workshop, saw the wave and raised his own hand in farewell as he boat motored past.

'Bon voyage, Cassie and James. Stay safe.'

ACKNOWLEDGMENTS

Once again, big thanks to all the Boldwood Books team, especially to my editor, Caroline Ridding, the woman with infinite patience. The re-writing, lengthening and editing of this, my very first book, originally published as *Call of the Sea*, was hard, mainly due to the way technology has developed in the fifteen years since it was originally published. As always, any mistakes are mine.

Thanks to all the bloggers out there who support and promote not only me but so many grateful authors.

Big thanks to my husband, Richard, for being his usual sounding board for me and calming me down whenever I got stressed with a technical detail or a storyline that wasn't working.

And lastly, but definitely not least, thanks to all my readers who make it worthwhile. Thank you, one and all. I hope you enjoy this one.

Love,

Jennie

xx

MORE FROM JENNIFER BOHNET

We hope you enjoyed reading *Making Waves at River View Cottage*. If you did, please leave a review.

If you'd like to gift a copy, this book is also available as an ebook, digital audio download and audiobook CD.

Sign up to Jennifer Bohnet's mailing list for news, competitions and updates on future books.

http://bit.ly/JenniferBohnetNewsletter

Explore more gloriously escapist reads from Jennifer Bohnet.

  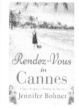  

ABOUT THE AUTHOR

Jennifer Bohnet is the bestselling author of over 10 women's fiction novels, including *Villa of Sun and Secrets* and *The Little Kiosk By The Sea*. She is originally from the West Country but now lives in the wilds of rural Brittany, France.

Visit Jennifer's website: http://www.jenniferbohnet.com/

Follow Jennifer on social media:

 facebook.com/Jennifer-Bohnet-170217789709356

 twitter.com/jenniewriter

 instagram.com/jenniebohnet

 bookbub.com/authors/jennifer-bohnet

Boldw**oo**d

Boldwood Books is an award-winning fiction publishing company seeking out the best stories from around the world.

Find out more at www.boldwoodbooks.com

Join our reader community for brilliant books, competitions and offers!

Follow us
@BoldwoodBooks
@BookandTonic

Sign up to our weekly deals newsletter

https://bit.ly/BoldwoodBNewsletter

Lightning Source UK Ltd.
Milton Keynes UK
UKHW040259261022
411093UK00004B/308